Firefly Beach

Meira Pentermann

Cover Design by Amy Feiman

Duck in a Bubble by Nikonite

ISBN: 1470180642

ISBN-13: 978-1-470-18064-5

Second Edition 2012

Originally Published 2009

1. Mystery 2. Paranormal

3. Firefly Beach

To Carrie
For believing in me
even when I didn't believe in myself

Prologue

In a clearing, somewhere between the edge of the forest and a jagged cliff, a lone firefly danced in graceful circles. It was beautiful, stealing attention away from the moonlight shimmering on Penobscot Bay. For a brief moment, the captivating creature was more hypnotic than the wispy clouds that brushed the face of the moon.

There was something highly unusual about that firefly. Beth couldn't quite put her finger on it. She had only seen fireflies once before, when she went camping with the Girl Scouts. She vaguely recalled their random flashing in the woods and how magical they seemed to her as a ten-year-old. She remembered dozens of fireflies, blinking sporadically, flittering about as if they were at a cocktail party, all vying for center stage, and all talking at once.

She looked out at the peculiar glowing insect and realized that there was *definitely* something different about that firefly.

It did not blink. . . and it was all alone.

Chapter 1
A New Canvas

Beth LaMonte hated moving boxes. They represented change, chaos and uncertainty. Anyone in their right mind would avoid them, but it was too late to reconsider. Drowning in a sea of cardboard and packing materials, she shook her head in frustration.

What happened to the days when I could load everything I owned into a station wagon?

She sighed, made a space for herself on the couch, and slumped down in defeat. The couch faced a bay window, which overlooked the backyard of a cozy, two-bedroom cottage. About twenty feet from the window, the unfenced yard met up with a small forest dominated by white pines and birches. Several American beech trees and a lush undergrowth including ferns, moss and saplings enriched the woodland. A fifteen-foot clearing allowed a view of the Penobscot Bay opening into the Atlantic. Sixty yards from the back of the house a twenty-foot jagged cliff dropped straight down to meet the bay. The insurmountable shoreline gave the cottage a sense of

3

protective seclusion.

Beth leaned back and took a deep breath. The fragrance of seawater and evergreens drifted faintly through the open kitchen window. She closed her eyes and let the scent wash over her tired spirit, as she sought a renewal that was beyond her reach.

The anticipation of warm summer months was of little comfort. Beth's fortieth birthday loomed less than two weeks away. Her mother, Sophia, had died unexpectedly of a heart attack the previous December, only days before Christmas. Her husband, Bill, asked for a divorce in January, having the courtesy to allow her a couple of weeks to grieve before unleashing the bomb he had been planning to drop since Thanksgiving. After sixteen years of marriage, Bill had fallen in love with a thirty-year-old associate at his Albuquerque-based software company.

The affair should have come as no surprise to Beth, as the marriage had been passionless for years. Both partners were workaholics, and they seemed to pass one another in the hallway, occupying the same space, yet living separate lives. They no longer shared special moments of the day during their evening meal. Eating together was merely convenient when neither of them happened to be working late. They had not gone on a date or a weekend retreat since their tenth wedding anniversary, and they rarely shared the same bed. This arrangement was deemed sensible since they often kept different hours. As the years accumulated, along with a thick layer of indifference, was it any wonder that Bill sought comfort in the arms of a young woman who looked upon him with great admiration and affection?

Beth was more troubled by the numbness she felt when Bill left than she was by the divorce itself. She questioned her capacity for human emotion. She never desired children, having neither the patience nor the compassion for nurturing. She allowed her marriage to crumble like a dead piece of wood eaten away at its core. She found her only comfort in crunching numbers and obsessively going over the books to find errors made by members of her staff. Accounts payable, accounts receivable, and bank reconciliation reports were more satisfying to her than a warm embrace. She had been the controller for a small firm that manufactured plastics, and she justified her long hours by continuously nitpicking at small mistakes. In reality, she longed to linger at her computer, and she dreaded going home.

Now she missed home – the stable, the familiar. The move to Maine was supposed to be her fresh start, but after a day of unpacking she felt drained and dispirited.

Beth wandered into the backyard and sat on a large, smooth boulder near the edge of the forest. She rested for nearly an hour, staring at the islands in the distance as the sun set behind her. An orange-pink hue engulfed the horizon, reflecting off the water in shimmering pale and dark patches. Something stirred inside of her, a warmth with which she had been out of touch for years. She smiled optimistically, recognizing the courage in her decision to make such dramatic changes in her life. She felt an ounce of hope that she might actually find a human being under the layers of meticulous accountant and passionless wife.

It was a capricious moment, entirely out of character, that fateful day she made her decision. The divorce had become final in May. Bill had moved out months before. As Beth boxed up her things, intending to move to a small, luxury apartment in the city, she came across several paintings that she created when she was a junior in high school in Minneapolis. She sat on the floor remembering her romantic dreams of going to an art college in Boston, moving to a small town in the northeast, and enjoying rocky coastlines with sparsely populated beaches. She planned to make her way by painting shorelines and lighthouses to sell on consignment. Sometime during her senior year, the dreamer took a backseat to the realist, and she secured a scholarship at the University of New Mexico, where she studied economics and earned her CPA. She met Bill and started working for Nilson Plastics as an administrative assistant. Then she married Bill, went on to get her MBA, and moved up the ladder at Nilson's until she secured the position of controller. At the time, she believed she had realized her true ambitions. The paintings were forgotten and stowed away in the attic, not even earning a place on one of the many walls of her spacious home.

But on that cloudy day in May, as she sat cross-legged remembering a dream she'd buried in her youth, the disorientation of the divorce overcame her sensible nature. She pulled a tattered atlas off the bookshelf, took a pencil in her hand, and closed her eyes. She took one quick peek to locate Boston on the map and then plunged the pencil down. . . Virginia Point, Maine, a small town on the mid-coast with a population of just over fifteen hundred.

She spent the following couple of days surfing the Internet and making phone calls. The number for the Chamber of Commerce rang through to Mary Schmidt, the owner of Virginia Point's most popular bed and breakfast. Mary gave Beth the number for Bobby Downy, the proprietor of a tourist shop that sold several craft items on consignment. Beth sent digital photos of two of her paintings to Bobby. One was a crisp oil painting of a lighthouse on a cliff, the other, an impressionist-style rendition of a vase of flowers. Bobby said he would be happy to display Beth's artwork, but he emphasized that paintings of lighthouses and the coast of Maine were more likely to sell in his store.

Beth found a cottage for rent on the coast. From the description and the photos, the place seemed perfect. Although the yard left something to be desired – weed infested gardens and untamed bushes – the house was freshly painted and the landlord promised it was in good working order. Beautiful, hardwood floors covered the first level of the two-story home. It had two bedrooms, one bath, and a view of the Penobscot Bay – an artist's dream.

The landlord, Rod Thompson, mailed her a key after she sent him a hefty security deposit. He didn't want to be bothered with trying to meet her when she got into town. Mr. Thompson did agree to open the house for the moving company drivers who delivered their precious cargo two days before Beth's arrival. The movers had unloaded the boxes, designated by color-coded stickers, into the specified rooms. Beth spent the day setting up the kitchen and making the bed before tackling the rest of the boxes. She was unable to accomplish even half of her goal to be eighty percent unpacked by nightfall.

After twilight settled in, an evening chill crawled across Beth's skin, driving her back inside. She glanced around at the disorder and decided to let it go, take a shower, and get a decent night's sleep. The stairs creaked beneath her feet as she climbed to the bathroom on the second level. She caught her reflection in the mirror and paused to take a long look at herself. She was a moderately attractive woman – slender, of medium height, and fair skinned. Silver streaks graced her dark, shoulder length hair. Although very few lines gathered around her soft brown eyes, her forehead was beset with creases, the identifying marks of a woman who fretted more often than she smiled.

By the time Beth stepped into the shower she was exhausted. Long, deep breaths calmed her mind and allowed her to make peace with the fact that the house was not going to be in full working order for at least a week. The hot water melted away her anxiety and she emerged refreshed and ready for bed.

She towel dried her hair as she wandered down the hall. The corner room would be the studio. Two windows overlooked the bay, giving it a panoramic view. The lighthouse, which had been out of operation for nearly a decade, was not visible from the cottage. Nevertheless, the windows provided a clear view of the water and the diverse forest as it wandered up the curving coastline toward a point where the land became rocky and devoid of vegetation.

Beth's bedroom was at the top of the stairs. An oak

dresser stood on one side of the room next to a make-do computer desk. Both were empty; their contents remained in boxes stacked in the far corner.

Just before retiring, Beth looked out the window toward the coast. The moon cast eerie shadows in the woodland. The large rock gleamed, and the islands were silhouettes in a shimmering sea.

Beth saw the firefly for the first time that night. It turned gently, making carefree circles, like a child pretending to fly. "I didn't know they had fireflies on the coast," Beth mused sleepily as she crossed the room and slipped into bed, mildly puzzled by the insect's behavior. "The firefly is a good sign," she whispered to herself before sleep eased her tired mind into its much-needed state of rest.

The firefly danced in the moonlight, as if welcoming its new neighbor.

Chapter 2
Burst of Light

Beth awoke under a cloud of dark emotions stemming from a series of unsettling dreams, the details of which blurred and then evaporated altogether in the time it took her to pull her head from the pillow and search for the clock. 8:39 a.m. She sat up and shivered, attempting to shake the gloomy sensation. When her head cleared, she pulled on her clothing, tied back her hair, and set her mind on the tasks of unpacking and organizing. The former CPA relished order, so she began to look forward to the promise of a satisfying day.

By late afternoon, she had cleared out the entire first floor, stacking empty boxes and packing materials on the windowless side of the house. The kitchen, living room, and entryway were tidied and decorated. Books sat neatly on the bookshelves. Dust-free knickknacks settled on the mantel, along with a photo of Beth's mother, the only picture of a person on the entire property.

Later that evening, Beth toured the house, evaluating her progress. The studio was a disaster, but the main floor felt like home. She made a cup of herbal tea and sat on the couch, looking out the bay window into a clear evening sky.

She noticed the firefly swirling and swooping near the cliff. A sweet sadness resonated in its graceful movements. Beth decided that the firefly was, like herself, a loner, mourning for what had slipped from her hands – or wings, in the case of the firefly – yet filled with hope for what lay ahead. "What are you hoping for, firefly?" she whispered. Then she laughed. "Have I become so pathetic I'm talking to insects?" She stood, collected the mug and coaster from the coffee table, and turned toward the kitchen.

Out of the corner of her eye, Beth saw the firefly zoom at what seemed like a hundred miles an hour, covering the distance in a fraction of a second, flying straight up to the window and then disappearing, dropping out of sight. Slowly Beth turned to face the window, her heart pounding in her ears. She no longer saw the firefly circling near the coast. Except for the waxing moon, it was dark behind the cottage, all the way to the horizon.

Beth shuddered, staring out the window for several minutes. Her face had grown ashen, and her heart continued to pound mercilessly. When she was able to pull herself away, she dashed upstairs, turning on lights as she ran. The creaking of the stairs frightened her so she doubled her speed taking them two at a time. When she reached the bathroom, she shuffled through her cosmetic bag looking for her emergency stash of anti-anxiety medicine.

This is ridiculous. She gazed in the mirror after downing two pills and splashing her face with water.

You are a grown woman afraid of the dark. . . or afraid of a dancing speck of light. Your imagination is playing tricks on you, she thought with some uncertainty. *It was a metaphor. Think about it; something about being a lonely firefly going up in a burst of flames. It's just a bunch of nonsense.* After giving herself a good scolding, or more likely, after the anxiety medication began to take effect, Beth tiptoed through the house turning off lights before she cozied up under the covers. *It was nothing,* she reminded herself before drifting off into a drug-induced sleep.

* * * *

The next morning, Beth awoke with a slight headache. She chided herself again for her ridiculous behavior the evening before. *All over an optical illusion,* she thought scornfully. After enjoying a simple breakfast and a pot of coffee, her brain began to clear. *Today is the day to unpack and set up the studio.* Focusing on the important project at hand, she forgot all about the firefly.

By mid-afternoon, she had made significant progress. One-third of the floor was bare, with boxes stacked along the wall next to the door. Two easels stood near the windows, and art supplies rested tidily in a variety of matching plastic containers. The sections of a set of long, flat drawers, intended for storing various types of paper, awaited assembly. Beth rubbed her neck as she tried to read the Chinese translated instruction sheet to no avail.

She looked at her watch. It was 3:07 p.m. She

realized that she needed to go into town for groceries before nightfall, so she laid the instruction sheet down next to the piles of screws and plasterboard, and headed for the bathroom to take a much deserved shower. She undressed, wrapped a towel around her chest, and turned the faucet handle. A loud blast bellowed from the spout. Then the water gurgled, spat, hissed, and refused to make another appearance.

"Damn!" shouted Beth, who disliked surprises more than moving boxes. She turned the faucet to the off position and tried again. Nothing. She crossed to the bathroom sink. Nothing. She ran to the kitchen sink, where she was greeted with another belch and hiss and then nothing. She threw up her hands and groaned.

"Good working order, my ass," she grumbled, as she grabbed her cell phone and shuffled through her purse for Rod Thompson's number. She tightened the bath towel securely before she dialed.

"Hello," a deep, unpleasant voice answered.

"Mr. Thompson," she began, holding her temper in check. "This is Beth LaMonte."

"Yeah?" Mr. Thompson said impatiently. "Didn't you get the key?"

"Oh, I've got the key all right, sir. I've been here for a day and a half." *Thanks for the heartfelt welcome,* she thought. "But the water just cut out on me."

"What did you do?"

Beth's jaw dropped and she looked at her cell phone in disbelief. "What did I do?" she asked, raising her voice a little. "I turned on the faucet, that's what I did. And then, *bang*, a big splat of water followed by nothing. No water, Mr. Thompson." She took a deep breath before continuing. "I need you to get someone here to fix it."

A long silence followed, then a heavy sigh. Beth gritted her teeth, hoping to quell the slew of obscenities on the verge of pouring from her mouth. "I'll call Lou," he murmured, his gruff voice melting into annoyance. And before Beth could respond, he hung up the phone.

Beth sat down on the couch for a moment, a little dazed. She gingerly placed her phone on the coffee table as if it were a diseased handkerchief unfit for handling. She stared out the window at the bay, reminding herself that it was still a beautiful place with an amazing view, and that wonderful opportunities awaited her; new beginnings for which her grieving spirit yearned. . . a fresh start.

At this point, I'd settle for a fresh shower. But I'd better put my clothes on in case this Lou happens to be a plumber. She headed for the stairway. *And, hopefully he or she actually plans on coming over today.*

Beth decided to put her energy into setting up the bedroom. She needed to take a break from the studio, so she filled and organized her dresser drawers and arranged the bedside table. She figured she would be lucky if Mr. Thompson sent a plumber out before morning.

The doorbell rang an hour and a half later. Beth was pleasantly surprised. She raced down the stairs and pulled open the door.

"Lou Schmidt, ma'am. Plumber." He nodded

politely. He was a broad shouldered man in his early sixties, with gray hair swept away from his face, a moustache, and kind blue eyes. He wore a blue and green flannel shirt and a faded pair of jeans. He extended his right hand in greeting, and in his left hand he carried a red toolbox.

Beth shook his hand enthusiastically. "I'm so glad you could come. Thank you. Thank you," she responded opening the door and ushering him in. "Whew. You are a godsend."

"I'm a Rodsend, really, ma'am," Lou said, attempting to be humorous. Instead it sounded dreadfully goofy and the poor man blushed.

But Beth grinned. "A Rodsend indeed."

"So you're getting no water. Is that my understanding?"

"Yes, nothing. Nothing in the bathroom and nothing in the kitchen. The spouts sputtered, rather loudly," she said, grimacing, "and then they stopped flowing."

"Uh huh," Lou said, already distracted, looking around the kitchen. "Did you shut off the main valve?"

Beth looked flustered. "Uh. . . I don't even know where that is, I'm afraid."

"It's okay, ma'am. I'll find it." Lou headed toward the laundry room attached to the kitchen. "Go ahead and continue whatever it was you were doing and I'll check it out."

"I *was* going to take a shower." Beth laughed nervously, smoothing down her tangled hair. "But I'll settle for unpacking."

Lou crouched in the space where a washer would

eventually be installed, already absorbed in his work. Beth slipped upstairs and resumed tackling the boxes in her bedroom.

Thirty minutes later, she heard Lou calling from the base of the stairs.

"Ma'am?"

She hurried down to meet him. "Stop with all the *ma'am* stuff, please. I feel old enough as it is."

"Fourteen years in the Navy, ma'am. . . uh, Miss. . . uh, LaMonte," he said, shrugging. "It's a hard habit to break."

Beth crossed her arms and scowled at him playfully. "Well, *sir*," she teased. "This *ma'am* respectfully requests that you knock it off. Call me Beth, please."

Lou glanced at his feet. "I have some bad news," he blurted out. "I'm going to need to order some parts from Portland. I should get them the day after tomorrow. In the meantime. . ." His voice trailed away as Beth's face grew red with anger.

"Two days without water?" she yelled, not so much at him as at the circumstances. "In all this packing dust?" She swept her arms dramatically in an arc.

"Listen," Lou began. "My wife runs a bed and breakfast, *The Virginia Point Cove*. We don't have any guests scheduled to arrive until Friday. You could stay with us for a couple of nights," he offered. "On the house, so to speak." He chuckled, making another failed attempt to be humorous.

"Lou *Schmidt*," Beth exclaimed, realizing why the name sounded familiar. "Your wife is Mary?"

"Yes, ma'—" He caught himself just in time, but

she glared at him anyway.

"I. . . I can't ask you to take me in."

"Beth, it's what we do. Mary would be delighted. You already know her?"

"We've spoken on the phone." Beth fidgeted with her hands. She wanted to take him up on his offer. A hot shower and a moving-box-free environment sounded very inviting. "It would be nice to get tidied up. I need to take my paintings to Mr. Downy's shop tomorrow."

"Oh, you're the painter. Mary told me all about you. In that case, it's settled. You must come."

Beth cast him a wary look. How could Mary possibly tell him *all about* her? Mary knew next to nothing about her. Beth frowned and continued to fidget nervously.

"In all honesty," Lou continued. "Just between you and me. You'd be doing me a favor. The Mrs. drives me crazy when we have no guests, chattering on about nothing. A man needs a little quiet now and again, if you understand me."

Beth pursed her lips to one side. She was not very interested in chatty women herself, but she hoped to rejoin the land of the living, so on an impulse she said, "Lou, I would be honored to accept your offer."

"Perfect. The truck is a bit cluttered. If you're bringing your paintings, you may want to take your own car."

"No problem."

"I'll wait. You can follow me. Do you need time to get ready?"

"I'll just grab a suitcase," she hollered as she raced up the stairs.

"Take your time. I'll call Mary and let her know we're on our way."

A few minutes later Beth returned with a small, flowered valise in tow. She set it by the hall closet and went back upstairs to retrieve three paintings wrapped in brown paper. Lou helped her put everything neatly into her Honda.

"All right then," Lou declared. "Let's go."

Chapter 3
The Cove

The Virginia Point Cove was a beautiful, two-story Colonial home built in the 1850s. White with midnight blue trim, it sat a couple of blocks away from Main Street on Spruce Road and Knox Lane. Six steps led to the small, covered front porch located precisely in the middle of the house. Around it, eight symmetrically placed, shuttered windows reflected the afternoon sun. An American flag jutted out at a forty-five degree angle, centered above the door. Two-foot high shrubs ran along the sides of the house marking the property, and a pair of pots filled with pink petunias hung from the porch roof. On either side of the stairs, flowerbeds graced the entire front of the house. Rose bushes flourished near the porch. Freshly turned dirt around the annuals indicated recent planting, while several perennials were already in full bloom. An assorted mixture of dahlias, bleeding hearts, oriental poppies, zinnias, and a variety of wildflowers greeted Beth as she ascended the stairs.

A slightly plump woman in her early sixties burst

out the door, bubbling with hospitality. Her wiry gray hair hung past her shoulders, a bit Bohemian for Beth's taste. But Mary had warm, hazel eyes and an accepting smile, and she swiftly drew Beth in, washing away her negative first impression. Mary wore a blue cardigan sweater with a dark blue cotton t-shirt and black jeans. "Beth LaMonte," she cried with open arms, crossing the distance between them to offer Beth an embrace.

A startled Beth returned the embrace listlessly. "Mary, it's good to meet you. And it is so generous of you to take me in on such short notice."

"Nonsense." Mary waved her hands dismissing Beth's needless concern. "What are we here for? We're prepared for guests night and day. Come along then. Lou, please grab her suitcase," she hollered after him. "In," she said to Beth, pointing inside. "I've got dinner on the table."

Beth shrank and took a step back. "You didn't have to—"

"Stop, for goodness sakes," Mary scolded. "Or I'll have to slap you right here on this porch. I'm dying to learn all about our new resident artist."

Beth smiled shyly and relaxed her shoulders. She allowed Lou to relieve her of her suitcase, and she followed Mary across the threshold.

An antique writing desk stood near the door and a faux quill pen rested on its surface next to a leather guestbook. The guestbook, open to the most recent page, awaited the next visitor's signature. A creeping plant sat in one corner of the desk. Its vines wound around the back right leg, almost reaching the ground. To the right of the desk a narrow stairway,

20

padded with an auburn antique rug runner, led to the second floor. Beyond the stairs, visitors were welcomed by a sitting room complete with a sofa, two chairs, a glass coffee table and several large windows. Along the windows two small, narrow tables accommodated numerous houseplants. To the left of the entrance, a hallway disappeared into the back of the house. Beyond that there was a library with five full bookshelves, three cushy maroon recliners, and one dark, antique armchair. The foyer glowed in a warm, pinkish shade of off-white and a floral print border ran along the edge where the walls met the ceiling.

Lou passed the ladies and began to ascend the stairs with Beth's suitcase in tow.

"Put her in Mother's room," Mary called up to Lou. "She won't be needing it."

Beth cringed.

Mary's face lit up in amusement. "Oh, dear, this isn't the psycho mansion. My mother lives in Palm Beach. She won't be visiting until later this month."

Blushing, Beth followed Mary down the hallway. Several generations of family photos arranged in small groups decorated the walls. Pictures of the Schmidts' three children – school photos, vacation photos and senior portraits – surrounded Lou and Mary's wedding photo. Another cluster of photos celebrated their parents at various stages of life. There were other wedding photos, presumably those of Lou and Mary's children, and a number of photos of toddlers, most likely grandchildren. Although she passed by the photos only briefly, Beth felt a momentary pang of regret for her solitary lifestyle, but Mary's ceaseless chatter drowned out wistful thoughts.

"Anyway," Mary pointed to a door. "You can wash up in here. The dining room is down the hall to your right."

Beth stepped into the bathroom, splashed a little water on her face, smoothed back her hair, and washed her hands. She dried her face and hands with one of the four small hand towels arranged neatly in a small basket next to a dish of miniature soaps. She would have preferred to apply a little make-up and use a hairbrush, but the Schmidts' hospitality made her feel at home. As she emerged from the bathroom, the smell of roasted chicken and potatoes made her realize how hungry she was.

She found the dining room and nearly gasped when she saw the table decorated and loaded as if it were Thanksgiving. "I hope you didn't do all of this on my account."

Mary laughed joyously. "Oh, just a flower arrangement and the cloth napkins on your behalf. The chicken's been roasting since this afternoon."

"We always eat like royalty," Lou said, as he entered the room patting his protruding stomach.

"Sit, sit," Mary said, gesturing to the chair next to the head of the table. Beth settled in next to Lou and across from Mary.

Dishes were passed back and forth, plates were loaded, and the glasses were tinkling with ice water. All the while Mary chatted boisterously, asking Beth dozens of questions about the drive, the house, and the weather. Beth answered as politely as she could. She was not comfortable sharing stories in vivid detail, and she had barely spoken at a dinner table setting for years.

"Anyway," Mary said at one point, interrupting Beth's hesitant response to a simple question. "If anyone gives you trouble about being *from away* and all, you just let me deal with them."

Beth looked confused. "From away?" She suddenly felt self-conscious about her nonresident status. It hadn't occurred to her to be concerned until that moment. "People don't want me here? Will they threaten me?"

"Oh, no, no, no. Goodness, no. Lou, how do I describe it?" she asked, turning to her husband.

He shrugged.

Mary looked up at the ceiling. "It is just a feeling hanging in the air, you know, like a cloud of cigar smoke. . . a little stifling. We encountered it when we returned in 1992. Lou was in the Navy, you know. We lived all over. When we moved back, I had to put a couple of people in their place. Then the air cleared and things have been normal ever since." She took a sip of water. "Remember Betsy Mallard, Lou?"

Lou groaned. "She was a piece of work."

Mary turned to Beth and explained. "She was the town manager for a number of years. She was so full of herself. Unbelievable. Eventually the townspeople got sick of her. She didn't last past 1995, I believe. But, anyway, at one town meeting, shortly after Lou and I were settling in, she started going on about 'people from away,' looking straight in my direction, you know, and I gave her a piece of my mind. 'I'm a true Mainer, Mizz Mallard,' I told her, drawing out the Ms. for dramatic effect. 'It's just that in all my *extensive* travels I've picked up a few ideas here and there that might be useful in Virginia Point.' Ooh, that really got to her because, of course, she's never been out of Maine in her life. And several of the selectmen were interested in what I had to say. It was a golden moment, I tell you. Pure gold."

Beth feigned a smile. Town managers. Selectmen. She had no idea what Mary was talking about. Confused, she looked down at her plate and felt a bit out of place.

"Oh, don't worry, you'll win 'em over," Mary said enthusiastically. She took a large bite of chicken, paused for a moment, and changed the subject. "Anyway, so old man Rod let the plumbing go, huh?"

"Uh, yes, I guess so," Beth replied.

"You can't leave a house empty for six months and expect it to manage itself," Mary said with disdain. "I don't know what goes through that old geezer's head sometimes."

"Mary!" Lou scolded. "Mind your tongue. He's our neighbor and a client."

"Pfft," Mary replied. "A fine client he is. He may be prompt with the check, but he needs a kick in the pants in the manners department."

Beth listened with interest, delicately balancing peas on her spoon.

Mary took a sip of water and leaned toward Beth almost whispering, even though she knew perfectly well that Lou could hear her. "We have to mail him Lou's invoices. Heaven forbid we drop by in person. He won't even answer the door. I know when he's there, the old coot. He just won't answer the bell."

Mary enjoyed a bite of potato and a big gulp of water

before resuming her character analysis. "It's like he has no need to interact with other human beings."

Beth looked down at her chicken and cut off a small bite. She took a brief inventory of the last ten years of her life and wondered if her acquaintances and co-workers would say the same things about her.

Mary prattled on, oblivious to Beth's internal dialogue. "If it weren't for people's boats breaking down—" She interrupted herself, turned to Beth, and explained, "He fixes boats at the marina, but he spends most of his time on his own boat, tinkering and sailing. *The Bottomless Blue,* he calls it. . . the boat that is. A rather sad name if you ask me." Mary took a sip of water and continued. "Anyway, if it weren't for people's boats breaking down, I don't think he would talk to anyone, period. I don't know what happened in his life to make him so cross. He's got a few gears loose in his head if you ask me."

"He's just a lost soul," Lou said.

Mary glared with little compassion. "You mean he's lost his soul." She took a bite of chicken and allowed a rare moment of silence. "My mother will tell you otherwise, dear," she said to Beth. "Mother says he used to be quite a gentleman and a decent neighbor. I rather have my doubts. I vaguely remember him. I grew up here before I became a military wife and moved all over kingdom come." She flashed an impish grin in Lou's direction. "I believe he had a daughter in elementary school when Lou and I were in high school. Obviously she hightailed it out of here as soon as she could, the poor dear." Mary sighed. "The man has no one, but it's his own damn fault. He drives people away."

Lou cleared his throat.

Mary ignored him. "It's just as well he's a hermit. I'd rather not have a conversation with the man, anyway. He gives me the willies, sucks all the good energy out of the room when he walks into it." She toyed with her potatoes. "What do you think, Beth?"

Beth fidgeted in her chair. "I've never met him, actually," she admitted.

Mary's eyes flew wide open. "Heavens! You rented the cottage without meeting the man? That's a whole new way of doing business."

"We do it all the time, Mary," Lou reminded his wife. He had a wry smile on his face.

"At least we meet them, eventually."

"Yes. And we let them run all over our house." He wiggled his fingers in Mary's direction as if casting a spell.

Beth stifled a laugh. Mary scowled.

"Never mind her, Beth," Lou said in response to Beth's apprehensive expression. "He's a good landlord. When things need fixing, he gets them done. He's not very cordial about it, but he gets them done." Lou scraped the last bite of potatoes and gravy onto his fork. "I'm sorry about the delay in getting your water back to running. The plumbing was last updated in the seventies. Old man Rod should have had me go over the house before you moved in. Houses that sit tend to develop kinks."

"Old man Rod, indeed," Mary snorted. "Old men that sit *also* develop kinks."

"He hardly sits." Lou corrected her. "The man's not idle, just quiet that's all."

Mary glared at Lou and harrumphed under her

26

breath.

Beth looked at the quarreling couple with some amusement. She broke the silence. "I'm surprised the cottage sat idle for so long. I mean it is an amazing location at a great price."

Mary and Lou exchanged a look. "You may change your mind after you've dealt with Rod for a few months."

"What were the last tenants like?" Beth ventured, trying to change the subject.

"The last ones were an odd bunch, a little family from New Jersey. They left after eight months or so. I think we were a bit too provincial for them," Mary concluded. "The couple before them lived there almost eight years. They were such a nice family. But the kids moved out, they divorced. A sad story, really."

Beth sighed quietly, feeling some empathy for the unknown woman with an empty nest and no companion. But that woman had more to show for her life than Beth did – grown children, a life of memories and scrapbooks. Beth's only achievements were years of balanced books and tidy accounts.

"But we've never had ourselves a famous artiste," Mary declared, raising her glass in Beth's direction, as the three of them finished their meals.

"I'm not exactly—"

"Nonsense," Mary interrupted. "Everybody else has one. It's high time we had one of our own."

Lou rolled his eyes.

"Where are the paintings, dear? Lou said you were bringing your paintings."

Beth blushed. "Oh, I left them in the car," she

explained.

"For goodness sakes, go on and get them. I'll put on some coffee and we'll look over them in the parlor."

Beth's face turned bright red. She was anxious to get her artistic career off the ground but suddenly embarrassed at the thought of actually showing her paintings to strangers. "I... well—"

"Go along," Mary commanded. "You can't become famous if you're going to be shy."

Beth sighed and reluctantly retrieved the paintings from her car. When she returned, Mary was fussing over a tray of coffee and cookies on the glass table in the sitting room. Beth entered the room cautiously, toting her paintings. She slowly unwrapped them. First came the flowers, which did not seem to impress Mary, then the lighthouse. Mary's eyes brightened.

"Oh, that's lovely. How could you capture such a realistic portrait of a lighthouse while living in New Mexico?"

"Actually, I lived in Minnesota at the time. Lake Superior has some stunning lighthouses. We vacationed near the lake every summer. This is the Split Rock Lighthouse," she said, pointing at the painting.

When she unwrapped the third painting, a soft oil image of her grandmother's house with the afternoon sun brightly lighting up the flowers in the front garden, Mary gasped. "For the love of God, would you look at that. You absolutely must paint *The Cove*. I insist. I'll pay top dollar. I want to be your first Virginia Point customer." She gestured toward the antique desk in the foyer. "I could hang it right there over the guest sign-in table and get rid of that drab painting of the starfish."

Beth was confused. Her eyes slowly followed the direction of Mary's outstretched hand to the earth-toned painting of starfish on a beach that hung in the entryway. She tried to unscramble what had been said. It finally dawned on her that Mary must be referring to the inn as *The Cove* and that Beth was about to secure her very first commission as a professional artist. A huge smile formed on her face.

"I would love nothing more," she replied, feeling that, finally, she had arrived.

* * * *

The following morning Beth awoke before dawn and welcomed the day with anticipation. She drove back to the house to retrieve her sketchpad and charcoal pencils and returned eager to draft *The Virginia Point Cove*. She grabbed a plastic lawn chair from the Schmidts' backyard and sat across the street, her mind lost in her work until she saw Mary's friendly face waving to her from the front porch.

"You can't start the day on an empty stomach," she scolded. "Come on in for breakfast, dear."

Beth obeyed, bundling her art supplies in one hand and dragging the lawn chair in the other.

"Oh, leave it. No one on this block is going to steal that old thing."

Beth smiled as she climbed the steps. She held out her preliminary sketch for Mary to review. An impulsive move, hardly characteristic of Beth; she was willing to expose herself and allow her unperfected work to be examined by a woman she barely knew. She made a mental note of that development, hoping it was a sign of growth, a testament to change.

"Oh my," Mary cooed. "Here you are creating beautiful things before I've even finished drinking a cup of coffee. Come on in. I'm sure you're famished by now."

Beth enjoyed a delicious breakfast on the patio with the Schmidts before heading into town. She drove through the neighborhood, which consisted of an eclectic collection of homes from a variety of periods. Many included barn-shaped structures that had been converted into garages or guest quarters. Most of the houses were white with dark shutters. She also passed a bright blue colonial, several late twentieth century models in earth tones, and a dingy trailer with an unkempt yard.

Virginia Point was tucked in a sheltered cove to the north-northeast of the lighthouse. A breaker rock wall further protected the boats at the marina. Main Street modestly sloped toward the docks, and small stores and restaurants lined both sides. Every store had its own awning and at least one window box, yet none of them matched. Buildings from the mid to late nineteenth century blended from one to the next – a rebellious group of structures forced to connect, but each determined to retain its own unique style. Most of the buildings, whether constructed out of brick or wood, were painted white, while others used natural brick. Several buildings needed repairs or a fresh coat of paint.

The bank had a bright red awning positioned at about nine feet, covering only the door. A brick window box with red and blue petunias beamed proudly under a freshly washed pane of glass. Adjacent to the bank was a seafood restaurant, shaded by a slightly faded, orange awning decorated with a smiling lobster. The lemon gem marigolds in the window box gave the restaurant a cheerful air, even though its paint was faded and its windows dirty. The children's clothing store sported a curved blue and white striped awning and a pale blue window box overflowing with marguerite daisies. Continuing on toward the marina, on her left, Beth saw a real estate office, a fish market, and a small coffee shop. On her right at the top of the hill, she found a shoe store with an overstated, bright blue awning and two meticulously manicured window boxes filled with fuchsias. Next, a hardware store with a worn exterior and a pale gray awning sat adjacent to a drug store and a woman's clothing store. Near the end of the row, a jewelry store painted bright white included a pale green awning and a window box blooming with a variety of wildflowers. Finally, at the bottom of the hill, she saw *Kelp Corner,* the gift shop owned by Bobby Downy. It had a tattered slate blue awning and a worn window box containing deep purple petunias.

No art gallery, Beth observed, her eyes twinkling.

She parked her car in front of the jewelry store and took a deep breath before emerging.

With her paintings clutched protectively in her arms and a spring in her step, Beth entered *Kelp Corner.* The small shop offered a variety of souvenirs and jewelry. Hand embroidered t-shirts and sweatshirts with pictures of lighthouses, nautical symbols, and the words "Virginia Point" hung on small racks. Beth walked tentatively to the back of the store. Next to the counter stood a multileveled display of handcrafted pieces of art made out of stones or small chunks of wood.

The man behind the counter looked up from the *Bangor Daily News*. He was a tall, lean man in his mid-forties. He wore a lightweight, red sweatshirt and a pair of faded blue jeans. His sandy blond hair showed signs of gray and a slightly receding hairline. He had a day-old beard and a warm smile.

"May I help you?" He stood to greet her. His six-foot-two frame made the tiny shop look even smaller.

"I'm Beth LaMonte." She held out her hand enthusiastically.

Mr. Downy took her hand in his, briefly covered it with his other hand, and smiled joyfully. "My southwestern artist, she arrives at last." He glanced down at her bundle of brown-paper-wrapped treasures. "Let's see them." He pointed to a tattered map of coastal Maine on the wall, which hung by itself in the middle of the store. "I'm anxious to recycle that old thing and hang your paintings."

Beth unwrapped each one. "Delightful," he exclaimed, especially pleased with the lighthouse. When she showed him the painting of her grandmother's house, he exclaimed, "Oh the ladies will love this one." And finally, she brought out the flower painting. His response was tepid like Mary's. "This one may not appeal to my clientele, but you never know. I will hang it until you bring me something new."

Beth was disappointed that no one appreciated the flower painting. It was the one piece she felt had captured a little bit of her own spirit. But she did not let his response deflate her overall good mood.

He tapped his pencil on the counter, making some calculations in his mind. "I am thinking I will try to sell them for three-twenty-five and pass two-fifty on to you."

The lines on Beth's forehead creased slightly. She had hoped for more. She was a little angry with herself for not discussing the matter before packing up and moving twenty-four hundred miles. How could such a detail-oriented woman forget that one, not-so-insignificant detail? She ran a rough estimate in her head – rent, utilities, groceries, art supplies. "How many do you think I can sell?"

"Oh, that all depends upon the season," Bobby replied. "You will do very well June through September, but things get rather slow in the winter."

Beth sighed subtly. She had a nest egg, which gave her some financial freedom. Upon her mother's death, she had inherited over five hundred thousand dollars after taxes. The amount took her totally by surprise. Sophia had lived a frugal life. *Poor Mom,* Beth lamented. *She never did anything for herself. She could have remodeled her bathroom, bought new appliances, and taken nice vacations.* A sense of guilt overwhelmed Beth on the day the funds were transferred into her name. Still, the money was hers. But it would only go so far if she could not make a steady living. The idea of eating away at the inheritance without producing something made her sick to her stomach. Should she attempt a part-time accounting job in Portland or Bangor? Or maybe she could provide an auditing service, dialing in to businesses and going over their books to find areas in need of improvement. With her credentials, she could probably build a stable clientele for such an entrepreneurial endeavor, but was that what she really came to Maine to accomplish?

Bobby looked down and shuffled his feet. "You know," he began. "You could try setting up a website. People love the coast of Maine. Paint a dozen or so pictures and post photos on the Internet. That way, you are more likely to maintain a steady income. I know a young man going to college in the fall who is a computer wiz. I'll bet he could help you set up a site."

Beth looked up at Bobby and smiled. "That is an *excellent* idea, Mr. Downy."

"Please. Call me Bobby. I'm an old salty dog. I don't be going by the name of Mistah," he mocked in a playful, fake accent Beth couldn't place.

She left *Kelp Corner* relieved of her awkward, brown paper wrapped bundles, and she decided to take a walk along Main Street. She peeked in the jewelry store. It seemed stark white and devoid of color, and no jewelry adorned the window. The clothing store's door was shaded by a ruffled, pink awning. Magenta-toned scarlet flax filled the window box. A mannequin dressed in a sporty blue jumpsuit stared impassively at the sidewalk. She stood on a blue-checkered blanket and around her feet were the makings of a picnic – a basket, blue plastic dinnerware, artificial grapes, and pathetically obvious fake sandwiches. The drug store had a more

34

utilitarian presence – a green striped awning, non-flowering plants in desperate need of water, and a simple arrangement of summer necessities in the display case. The hardware store had a small window with no display, but the shoe store sported an elaborate, almost gaudy presentation in each of its windows. A woman waved from inside. Beth grimaced faintly and returned the gesture.

Beth crossed the street. The restaurant had an arrangement of plastic chairs and tables dressed with ketchup, napkin containers, and salt and pepper shakers. Several patrons with hearty appetites enjoyed lobster as well as fried haddock and clams. A few lobster traps and about twenty lobster buoys hung from the ceiling in a colorful, chaotic pattern. The children's clothing store featured several child mannequins in bright summer clothing, along with a kite and a stuffed dog jumping in the air. The real estate office windows were covered with photos and descriptions of property for sale. The fish market was white and brightly lit. Along the back wall, a glass counter displayed fresh fish and lobster as well as a few steaks and pork chops. A woman with long, gray hair spoke with a tall, dark-haired young man who stood behind the counter. The café's yellow awning and window box, filled with a rainbow assortment of petunias, welcomed townsfolk and visitors. A small counter near the back displayed muffins and pastries. A family sat in one corner eating sandwiches and their toddler laughed as his mother tried to wipe applesauce off his face. Beth smiled, crossed to her car, and drove back to the cottage for a brief nap.

That afternoon, she returned to *The Virginia*

Point Cove eager to share her ideas with Mary. Mary poured two glasses of red wine. Then she placed a plate of crackers and small cheese squares on a round, wrought iron garden table on the back patio. The Schmidts' backyard bloomed with even more flowers than the front. A small bean-shaped patch of grass took a backseat to lush gardens, blueberry bushes, and a bubbling stone fountain of an angel. The neighboring houses were not visible from any direction due to a large cluster of trees that encircled the property.

As the ladies sipped wine and discussed the day's events, Beth noticed Mary fiddling with her wedding ring. Beth looked down at her own bare left hand and realized how empty it felt. *I should buy myself something,* she mused, *an independence ring.* Then she remembered her mother's sapphire anniversary ring, a stunning deep blue jewel set in gold and surrounded by tiny diamonds.

Her father had given the ring to Sophia on their tenth wedding anniversary, a year before he died in an auto accident. Beth was ten years old at the time of his death. She never truly allowed herself to grieve the loss of her father. Sophia put away her wedding ring and wore the sapphire ring in its place. Throughout Beth's turbulent teenage years, she sneered at her mother whenever she wore the ring. Beth believed that removing the wedding ring was a betrayal. In addition, and true to teenage inconsistency, the sapphire angered her because it was a constant reminder of her father. As Beth matured, her hostile tantrums were forgotten, and her mother continued to wear the ring until her death. In a small, handwritten will, found in her lingerie drawer, Sophia had requested that Beth keep the sapphire ring and bury her in her wedding band. She wrote, in her usual matter-of-fact fashion, that she would *hate to see this beautiful ring buried six feet below ground on the boney finger of an old woman's skeleton.* Beth shuddered and looked out over the garden.

Poor Mom, Beth thought, remembering the third anniversary of her father's death. She wished the memory had faded over time, but it always seemed to overwhelm her in vivid detail at a moment's notice.

They sat in the kitchen at a round Formica table with wobbly silver legs, the one that drove her mother crazy. Nevertheless, she did not replace it for years. It was one of the first pieces of furniture the newlyweds purchased a year before Beth was born. The kitchen radiated canary yellow, a yellow that seemed to grow brighter and deeper over the years each time Beth recalled the day. Her mother made spaghetti and meatballs that afternoon. Beth swirled the noodles around on her fork but refused to take a bite.

"It's your favorite," her mother gently reminded her.

Beth glared judgmentally at the blue sapphire. "So we just forget now?"

Sophia sighed and looked down. "We don't forget. We move on."

"We move on? You didn't love him, really, did you?"

Sophia's eyes met Beth's and held them in a gaze that betrayed a complicated mixture of feelings so intense Beth had to look away.

Beth stabbed her fork into a meatball repeatedly. In a wave of unanticipated cruelty, she retorted, "Maybe he just didn't want to come home." It was beyond out of line, what she said; it was despicable. Beth knew very well that her father had been commuting home at his usual time, taking his customary route. He must have briefly passed through the blind spot of a large Sears delivery truck. In an instant that changed Beth's and Sophia's life in the most terrible way, the truck driver changed lanes, sending Mr. LaMonte's car down the embankment. It flipped several times before hitting a tree. Her father was pronounced dead at the scene.

Beth picked up her knife and flipped it around. She smashed her meatballs, randomly and with vigor, until they were reduced to mush. Then she pushed her plate away and stormed to her bedroom.

Sophia quietly removed the plates and silverware from the table and scraped away food remnants before placing the dishes in the sink. She turned on the water and added a drop of soap. Her movements were slow and methodical. She stared blankly at the bubbles forming around the dishes. The water turned mildly orange. She watched in silence. Whatever dreams Sophia had cherished as a young woman slowly withered away over the years, as sink after sink filled and drained. Her life blended with the lives of countless other mothers, resigned to the whim of tedious chores, the ones that returned every day, mocking a woman's potential and intelligence.

Beth hid in the hallway watching her mother. She longed to say that she was sorry and to take over washing the dishes. But she did not, due to pride or shame; she never really determined which. She left her mother alone on the anniversary of the accident, alone to soak in the soapy water and the hateful words of teenage irrationality.

"Hello? Cat got your tongue?" Mary asked, bringing Beth back into the present.

"I saw a jewelry shop in town," Beth blurted out. "I need to get a ring resized, a very special family heirloom. Is the jeweler reliable?"

Mary sighed and smiled. "Ah, good old Kenny McLeary. He's an odd one, but he's an exceptional jeweler. I've never seen a more meticulous man in my life, hunched over that bench night and day. But he's got a creative side, too. Maybe you'll understand his language. You're an artistic type." She ran her finger along the rim of her wine glass. "There is not much to go by. The man hardly says a word to anyone, except in the course of business. Shy as a field mouse, that one. I often wonder what secrets lay beneath that innocent exterior."

"So I can trust him with my ring?"

"Absolutely. It will be flawless, nothing less. And while you're in there, treat yourself to a custom brooch or pendant. The man is a genius. See, he keeps a little notebook. When he meets a customer, often times a stranger passing through town. . ." She swished her hand through the air and said, "I recommend him to all my guests. Anyway, when he meets someone, he looks them over and scrupulously enters notes in a little book, like a journal. Later he delivers a masterpiece so suited for the individual you would think he'd have known them all his life. It is like he can look inside a person, read them, you know?"

Beth nodded. She pulled her cardigan closer around her chest. She did not like the idea of a man being able to see her with some kind of intimate intuition, making private notes in a little jeweler's diary. "I certainly don't need the man to *read me,* just measure my finger, for God's sake."

"I'm just saying. If you ever want to spoil yourself."

Beth frowned and looked away. She certainly wasn't going to spend her mother's inheritance on a personal luxury. Her mother never treated *herself* to anything frivolous. It would not be right. No, she would wait until her own business brought in enough money for such an indulgence, if she purchased one at all.

"I'll just get my ring resized, thank you very much," she said with defiance.

Mary smirked with an air of knowing something undisclosed. She leaned back in her chair and took a sip of wine.

Lou popped his head around the corner, a grin upon his face. "My guy in Portland found the parts I need. He'll be Fed-Exing them to me. I'll get them in the morning and should have you up and running by noon."

Beth looked up. "Wonderful." She turned to Mary. "In the meantime, may I help you with dinner?"

Beth followed Mary into the kitchen, feeling a bit out of her element. She never was much of a cook, but she followed directions very well. Under Mary's careful supervision, a lasagna and a Caesar salad were on the table by six o'clock.

Mary chattered throughout the dinner, but Beth's mind drifted in and out of the conversation. Her thoughts were filled with new ideas. She reviewed the day's sights and sounds as she satisfied her healthy appetite with bites of lasagna and garlic bread. Beth caught her reflection in the window and surprised at how serene, and even youthful, she looked. Barely a week had passed since she bid farewell to the adobe-dotted hills of Albuquerque, but her journey had already transcended the geographical distance.

Chapter 4
Follow Me

Beth awoke on Friday morning, briefly disturbed by the memory of the firefly racing at an unnatural speed toward her bay window. She glanced around the room for a moment, trying to get her bearings. *The bed and breakfast,* she remembered, and she breathed a sigh of relief. Brushing away her anxious feelings, she decided to greet the day with enthusiasm. After all, she was eager to set up the studio, paint a preliminary draft of *The Virginia Point Cove,* and possibly unpack her gardening gear. The pitiful little garden would need attention soon. There were too many things to do.

After she showered and ate breakfast, she attempted to offer Mary some financial compensation for her stay at *The Cove.*

"Nonsense. Just paint me a hell of a picture."

Beth bought a few staples at the grocery store on the way home, put away the milk and cheese, and ran upstairs to the studio. The morning sun gave the room a warm and inviting glow. Beth hummed softly and returned to the task of assembling the drawers, which would hold various sizes and types of paper as well as large sheets of canvas.

Lou puttered around the house clanging tools against pipes, but he did not disturb Beth. She found his presence somewhat comforting. After about forty-five minutes, Lou called up the stairs. "Beth?"

"Yes?" She jumped to her feet and headed down the hallway.

"Everything should be good now."

"You're the best, Lou. Thank you," she said as she descended the stairs. "You will bill Mr. Thompson?"

"Yes, ma'—" he began. "Ahem. Yes, and don't you worry about old Rod. He'll pay me. And if he don't, I'll just come collecting a painting or two from you." He winked at her, waved hastily, and made his way to the door.

"Thank you for your hospitality the past couple of nights."

"Our pleasure," he called over his shoulder as he walked along the stepping stones leading to the gravel drive.

Beth returned to the studio. Once the drawers were set up, she unpacked the remaining things and hauled all the empty boxes to the side of the house. By then it was late morning, but she wanted to get a little work under her belt before lunch. She pulled out her preliminary sketch of the bed and breakfast and arranged it neatly on one of the easels. On the other easel, she put a thick piece of eighteen by twenty-four inch, acid-free paper. After that she mixed colors on a palette and stood back, looking at both the sketch and the empty piece of paper. The first go would be for practice. She would need to visit *The Cove* again at sunrise, make more details on her sketch, and soak in the radiant colors highlighted by the early morning sun.

Beth found she captured the light better when she painted from the images she tucked away in her mind. The sketch helped her fill in the details. Her habit in high school had been to make a detailed sketch of the object in the room and then turn her canvas away when it was time to paint. At first it drove her teacher crazy, but as her obvious talent emerged, he allowed her the space to practice her art in whatever fashion suited her.

That morning in the studio, she planned to experiment with color. On the following day, if she was ready, she would head over to the bed and breakfast just before dawn. Hopefully, Mary would be busy with her new guests and not notice her. Beth needed to focus when she worked, and she did not wish to be hustled in for breakfast with a group of strangers. She made a mental note to excuse herself if invited.

* * * *

Later that evening, an exhausted Beth took a long, hot shower. She pulled on her pajamas and prepared to get into bed. As she passed her window, she saw a shimmer of light near the cliff. The firefly.

Beth's stomach turned over. "Oh no you don't," she said, trying to sound courageous.

Grateful that she had not yet taken down the old curtains for a trip to the cleaners, she quickly crossed the room to pull them shut. As she reached up to grab the left curtain, the firefly flew swiftly toward her and stopped less than a foot from the window. Beth's hand froze. She was terrified, yet fascinated.

"What *are* you?" she whispered.

As if in response, the firefly swooped and danced. After a moment, it began to repeat a pattern – up to the window slowly, followed by a swift lunge down toward the large boulder near the edge of the forest. Over and over again it dove, as if beckoning Beth.

"No!" Beth said firmly, and she drew the curtains closed violently. Unfortunately, they were several inches too short to cover the windows. "Damn." Beth shivered as a deep chill went through her body. She grabbed her large blue sweatshirt and climbed into bed, leaving her three-way bedside lamp on its lowest setting of twenty-five watts. For a long time, she stared at the ceiling. She pulled the comforter way up to her chin and grasped it like a security blanket. She glanced at the clock every now and again – 11:16 p.m., 12:01 a.m., 12:48 a.m., and 1:19 a.m. Sometime between 1:30 and 2:00, she fell asleep.

She was beset by disturbing dreams; rapid firing images flashed before her eyes – a car screeching down a country road, a yellow duck, her father's face. She awoke with a start. *Why am I dreaming about my father after all of these years? Don't haunt me now, Dad, not when I am alone and feeling insecure.* She opened her eyes, intending to get up and grab a drink of water. The firefly hovered two feet from her face. She screamed with her full lung capacity for a full thirty seconds.

The firefly backed up quickly into the corner of the room near the ceiling.

Beth breathed deeply, her heart racing. She pulled herself out of her bed, absentmindedly clutching the comforter to her chest, and she bravely walked toward the floating ball of light. Slowly, the firefly descended to Beth's eye level. She stared at the curious object, which no longer looked *anything* like a firefly. It was round, the size of a large marble, and it was pure light – no wings, no legs, no eyes – just a tiny ball of light.

Beth dropped the comforter to the floor and cautiously lifted her hands to cradle the light creature. She cupped her hands and raised them to within a few inches of the ball of light. Before she could blink, it zoomed straight at the window and through the pane, as if there were no glass. It swooped down by the boulder and hovered.

Beth clutched the curtains and peered out. She shuddered. The "firefly" seemed to be summoning her. Curiosity overcame her fear. She slipped off her pajama bottoms and tugged on a pair of loose, faded gardening jeans. Still wearing the blue sweatshirt, she hurried down the stairs and out the back door.

The light creature remained at the edge of the forest, waiting for her. When she appeared, the creature leapt and twirled joyfully. Then, as Beth approached, it flew north and disappeared in the woods. Beth followed. She slipped on mossy rocks and almost tripped over a fallen branch. She grabbed a tree to catch her balance. Dawn approached, but in the woods, it was dark except for the light of the firefly. Every once in a while, the creature stopped, as if to make sure that Beth was keeping up. They worked their way through the woods for about a mile before the firefly flew out of the trees and into a small clearing at the edge of a cliff. Then, all of a sudden, it plunged down and seemed to vanish. Beth dropped to her stomach and eased herself to the rim. The growing light of day shimmered on the water.

At the bottom Beth saw a small beach, no more than ten feet across, surrounded by jagged rocks on all sides. The surface of the beach, covered with sand and small rocks, appeared to be about two stories down. It formed a skewed horseshoe shape, which tucked into the rocks on Beth's left and slanted down to the bay on her right. The beach dropped off quickly and became rocky near the end of the tiny cove. The tide was receding, within an hour of low tide. One could walk to the edge of the ebbing tide and still not quite see around the jagged cliffs that formed the inlet. At low tide, the beach would be approximately twenty-five feet from the back of the horseshoe to the shore. At an average high tide it would be no more than ten feet deep and probably completely submerged during an unusually elevated high tide.

The firefly flew up to the edge, paused briefly, and dove down to the sandy shore.

"No way. I can't go down there."

The light creature came to a rest within a few inches of Beth's nose. It was beautiful and mesmerizing with a pure, innocent quality to it. Slowly it traced a path along the side of the cliff just a little to the left of where Beth lay.

"You're insane!" Beth cleared her throat. "Although perhaps not as insane as a woman who screams at little balls of light," she mumbled. "Nope. It's barely dawn. I'll break my neck if I try." Flashing a smile, she added, "But I will mark this spot and have a look in the daylight." After gathering a few stones, she fashioned a six-inch arrow that pointed toward the beginning of the path indicated by the light creature.

The ball of light jumped back up over the cliff and began racing in a random, agitated manner around Beth.

"Tomorrow," she said firmly, and she walked back toward the cottage. The firefly followed her for almost twenty minutes before it stopped. Beth looked over her shoulder as she reached the edge of the forest, and she could barely see the speck of light, hovering in the trees.

Beth sighed and entered the house. "I think I've finally lost my marbles." Wearily, she climbed the stairs. She gathered her blanket off the floor, collapsed into bed, and fell into a surprisingly restful sleep.

Chapter 5
Rip Van Winkle

Beth slept in until 9:16 a.m. *Drat,* she scolded herself. She had missed sunrise at the bed and breakfast. She thought about the evening before and concluded that it must have been a vivid and fascinating dream. She remembered seeing images of her father and then following a marble-sized ball of light. It seemed preposterous in the sobriety of day, but she gazed out the window toward the forest and tentatively wondered whether or not there was a secret beach hidden by the rocky cliff. A thin layer of fog lingered in the forest; wispy tentacles slithered in and around the trees. Goosebumps sprinted up Beth's arms, and she hugged herself, trying to rub them away. Then she headed for the shower, determined to wash away the foolish thoughts. While she dried her hair, her cell phone rang.

"Hello?"

"Beth, it's Bobby."

"Hello, Bobby."

"You've made your first sale."

"Are you kidding me?"

"Nope. Our resident hermit bought your flower painting. Who would have figured? But he seemed very pleased with it."

"Mr. Thompson bought my painting?" she asked, entirely confused.

Bobby laughed a deep-throated chortle. "Oh, no, no, no. Mr. Thompson is the town *grouch*. The town hermit is Kenny McLeary, the jeweler."

"Oh really? I. . . I don't know what to say," she stammered. "This is fantastic news."

"Congratulations. Come on down and collect your commission any time."

"I'll be there this afternoon," Beth announced, and she grinned when she hung up the phone.

Hmm, the jeweler. She tapped her fingers on the edge of the sink. *Perhaps it's time to get Mom's ring resized.*

* * * *

Beth approached the jewelry shop a little before noon. At first she was hesitant to go in, but then she gathered up the courage. The door jangled as she entered.

Inside, the small shop was painted a very bright, pure white. A long oak counter separated the waiting area from the remainder of the store, and a small glass case displayed several rings, pendants, and bracelets. To the right of the door, under a spotless window and next to a small table, stood a comfortable couch in earth tones. On the far wall, Beth's flower painting hung proudly.

Behind the counter, a large oak file cabinet stood

on the left, and a door on the right led to a workroom. The workroom, in sharp contrast to the pristine waiting area, was a disorderly configuration of workbenches and scattered tools. A nerdy, forty-something gentleman wearing a pair of thick-rimmed tortoiseshell glasses, sat hunched over one of the benches. Untamed, greasy black hair covered his head. Under a stained blue apron, he wore a rumpled flannel shirt and an old pair of jeans. He stooped over something small, looking at it very intensely through a jeweler's loupe.

After a moment, he looked up, acknowledged Beth's presence with a nod, and walked slowly to the counter. He said nothing but looked at Beth expectantly.

Beth, eager to fill the silence, rattled through her purse. "It's my mother's ring," she stammered, as she dug randomly through an assortment of personal items. "Oh, look. Here it is." She pulled out a small box.

Beth placed the box on the counter, removed the lid, and carefully freed the ring from the soft blue silk in which it was wrapped. The jeweler picked it up gently, handling it like a newborn chick. He turned it slowly in his hands and nodded with appreciation.

"You would like it appraised?" he asked quietly, so faint Beth could barely make out what he said. She caught a hint of a southern accent. He made her feel uncomfortable for some reason. She shivered subtly.

"Oh, no," Beth replied. "I would like it resized. . . to me. I mean, I'd like to have it. I mean, of course, it's mine. I. . . I'd like to wear it." Beth's stomach turned. She knew she sounded hideous, and she wondered why this man made her feel so flustered. She cleared her throat, determined to take control of the conversation and stop babbling. "Can you resize the ring for my finger?" she asked clearly and assertively.

Kenny McLeary did not respond verbally. Instead he unlocked a drawer behind the counter, reached in, and pulled out a ring-sizing tool – a large silver circle with over thirty loops dangling from it, rings of graduating sizes. He glanced down at Beth's hand and flipped through the smaller rings. He separated one from the rest and reached for Beth's right hand. Beth pulled her right hand away and handed him her left hand. If he noticed the awkward movement, he showed no sign of it.

His hands were rough, but his manner gentle. He carefully tried to push the selected ring onto Beth's left ring finger. It was too small, so he did not force it. He chose the next largest ring. It slid on smoothly.

Kenny pulled a small notebook out of the drawer and began to take notes. Without looking up, he said, "Name?"

"Uh, Beth. Beth LaMonte."

"Address?"

"Oh my goodness. I should know that, shouldn't I?" Beth laughed nervously. "I just moved in. I live in Rod Thompson's cottage," she said, gesturing in the general direction of her house. "I'm an artist. I painted this picture you purchased." Beth pointed to the flower painting and smiled awkwardly.

Kenny looked up at the picture, and then he stared at Beth for a moment as if he saw something beyond her physical presence. Beth looked down and away.

He unnerved her. The silence was unbearable, and yet she could think of absolutely nothing to say.

Finally, Kenny broke the silence. "Nice painting."

"Thank you."

"Phone?" He continued to make notes.

"Area code five-oh-five. . ."

Kenny looked up at her, suspicious of the non-local area code.

"It's my cell," Beth explained. "I don't have a new number here yet. I'm sorry. I can just drop by if you'd like, so you don't have to call."

Kenny did not answer her, but he continued to make several notes in his little book. He looked carefully at the ring that had fit Beth, but he scribbled for well beyond the time it would take to write down a ring size and a phone number. Beth tried to peer over the counter, but Kenny's right arm, draped oddly across the page, blocked her view.

When he finished making notes, he closed his book quickly and returned it to the drawer, along with the ring-sizing tool. He locked the drawer and returned the key to his apron pocket. Then he carefully rewrapped the ring and placed it in its box, put the box in his apron pocket, and turned toward the workroom. He stopped suddenly, glanced over his shoulder and said, "It will be a day or two. Thank you, Miss LaMonte."

Beth stared, somewhat befuddled, as the strange man returned to his workbench, adjusted the loupe, and resumed his task. She wanted to say something. Her mouth opened but nothing came out. She turned to leave the store, looking back over her shoulder as the bell jangled. The jeweler did not raise his head, so

Beth continued out the door.

Beth walked toward *Kelp Corner* shaking her head. *I'll just have to trust Mary,* Beth told herself. *If she thought the guy was a lunatic, she would not have recommended him. She said he was weird, but that was just beyond bizarre.* Beth shuddered. *But anyway,* she consoled herself. *It's not like he's going to run off with Mom's ring. If Mary says he's good, then I'm sure he's good. . . I hope.*

Beth collected her payment from Bobby Downy and grabbed a sandwich at the café to take home. She climbed into her car, trying to shake the uneasy feeling that the jeweler had aroused in her. Her mind was preoccupied all the way home. As she turned up the drive that led to the cottage, she glanced toward the rocky shore. She remembered her dream about the firefly. Her shoulders quivered with a slight chill.

I am not going to get spooked out again. First the creepy jeweler, now the phantom beach. I really can't take anymore of this bullshit. She pulled up in front of the house and slammed the brakes. Then she sprinted to the front door as if someone were following her, slipped inside, and locked the door.

Beth sat at the kitchen table and ate her turkey sandwich. Eventually the uneasy feelings were unbearable. She got out a stool and reached into the cabinet over the microwave oven. A bottle of scotch waited patiently. Beth looked at the clock. 2:19 p.m. Shaking her head in self-reproach, she filled a tumbler with ice and poured herself a generous portion.

She walked over to the fireplace and stared at the picture of her mother for a long time. In the photo,

54

Sophia stood left of center, a few feet away from a tree. The sun was in her eyes, and the shadow of the tree spread out behind her, disappearing from the photo on the right. She laughed joyfully while desperately trying to hold on to a sun hat that longed to blow away in the wind. Sophia must have been about thirty when the picture was taken. Beth would have been five at the time, but she could not recall the location in the photo.

Beth took a sip of scotch and a hot coal seemed to slip down her throat and roll around in her stomach. She grimaced.

"I wish you were here," she whispered. "I wouldn't be afraid." She sighed. "I'm sorry I was so rude about the ring. It looked beautiful on your hand, and I'm sure Dad would have been very happy to see you wearing it." She touched the photo lightly. Then she turned away and headed for the couch.

Beth bit her lip. She had no intention of crying. She may well be going crazy, but crying was not an option. She had learned that strategy thirty years ago. Crying brought all the feelings to the surface where they had no business being. They were more easily managed when they were kept in their place, tight and secure, deep down where they belonged.

Beth sat on the couch, sipping scotch, and reading a gardening magazine to distract her mind. As she sifted through the pages, she tried to picture some improvements she might make in the cottage garden. She hoped the glass of scotch would last until evening, but she poured another just after 5:00 p.m. At 6:03, she yawned and stretched and looked out over the bay toward the islands.

Although blissfully sedated by alcohol, she remained cautious. The sun would not set until after 8:00, but Beth got up and closed the blinds on the bay window. It was obvious the blinds had rarely been closed. A layer of dust clung to the edges, although the slats themselves were dust free. Beth shrugged. "So what?" she mumbled. "I need my privacy." She made her rounds and closed all the curtains in the house. She draped a dark sheet over the rod above the window in her bedroom to cover the gap. The cheerful, sunny day was successfully blocked out long before darkness set in.

Beth went to the kitchen to grab a glass of water. She was very tired and a little drunk. In a haze, she glanced over at the spice cupboard. Before returning to her room, she grabbed a bottle of garlic salt. She opened the container, placed it near her bedroom window, and laughed. A somewhat playful, without abandon, alcohol-induced laugh echoed throughout the cottage.

But her mood snapped briskly from gaiety to despair. "Leave me alone!" she shrieked.

Then she tumbled into bed in her clothing and fell into a drunken sleep.

* * * *

The hangover was not quite as bad as Beth expected when she pulled herself out of bed on Sunday morning. 8:27 a.m. Again, she had missed dawn at the bed and breakfast. She felt it was critical to capture *The Cove's* essence when the sun rose. She would need to set an alarm for 4:00 a.m. in order to keep that appointment, and she was not sure why she avoided making the commitment. Of course, *things that go flitting in the night* clearly had something to do with her break in concentration.

Beth stretched and looked toward the sheet-covered window. She saw the container of garlic salt and reached to pick it up. On the bottle it said, "garlic salt, coarse, ground with parsley." Beth shook her head and chuckled.

"I guess it was the parsley that did the trick. No glowing marble last night."

Beth was in moderate denial about the potential loss of her sanity. She put the lid on the garlic salt and returned it to the kitchen. There, she opened the curtains and was greeted by a thick fog that enveloped the forest. She could barely see the boulder at the edge of her yard. She felt somewhat comforted by the fact that sleeping in had not caused her to miss anything. She would not have been able to sketch the bed and breakfast after all.

Nonetheless, she resolved to make the best of the day. She decided she would sketch Old Charlie and perhaps do a little painting in the afternoon. She packed a sack lunch, grabbed a blanket and her sketching supplies, and headed out at a little after ten. Beth drove along Lighthouse Road and found an excellent viewing place about a quarter of a mile from Old Charlie. There she sat on the blanket and watched as the lighthouse emerged from the fog, standing proudly on its rocky perch. The Lighthouse Preservation Society had repainted Old Charlie in 2003, a bright white with a red stripe just below the watch room deck. The body of the lighthouse, a gently sloping cone, flattened out near the top where a sturdy railing encircled the hexagonal lens room. The attached house was also painted white with red trim and shutters. It appeared to be somewhat disjointed. The stylistic differences between the original keeper's house and several additions made over the years were apparent, but it had charm, and it seemed to impart its fascinating past to those who drew near. Beth imagined strong keepers hauling containers of oil up one hundred narrow steps. She lingered for about an hour, sketching several drafts before packing up.

On the way home, she decided to drive back into town and visit the jewelry store. The sooner she got her mother's ring back, the sooner her apprehension would dissipate. It was possible Kenny finished it. After all, he had said a day or two, hadn't he?

The shop was closed when Beth arrived. On the door was a picture of Rip Van Winkle, his long beard flowing to the ground, with a caption that said, "Gone Hiking." Old Van Winkle carried a walking stick, and he was covered with jewelry – rings on all of his fingers, bracelets up his arm, several pendants around his neck, and brooches hidden in his beard. The drawing was quite good. Beth felt a little envious. Sketching people was not her strength. But she appreciated the quirky jeweler's offbeat sense of humor.

Well, you'd better return before twenty years with my ring.

Maybe this goofball is not so bad after all, she thought as she drove away smiling.

Chapter 6
Acadia

Kenny McLeary rested on the flat surface of a large jagged rock in a grove filled with birches, oaks, aspens and evergreens. Thick trees and saplings mingled among an assortment of wildflowers, while rocks decorated with yellow lichen and a variety of mosses rested in the undergrowth.

It was a perfect day for a hike in Acadia National Park. The fog protected Kenny's anonymity in the early morning. By the time the fog lifted, he sat safely tucked away in the forest. His dark green backpack lay on the ground by his feet. Moss grew around the base of the rock and along the crevices formed by its sharp angles. About twenty feet from the edge of the grove, Jordan Pond shimmered in the late afternoon sun.

Kenny held a sketchpad and a charcoal pencil in his lap. He stared out over the water for several minutes before returning to the task of sketching what appeared to be designs for a pendant or brooch. At one point he picked up a long stick lying by his feet and began to stir the needles and leaves in a curious looping pattern.

The sounds of laughter and twigs crunching beneath hikers' feet startled him. He jumped nervously then quickly covered his sketchpad as if someone were looking over his shoulder, but the path was thirty yards behind him and he was essentially invisible to the intruders. They continued on their way, but Kenny closed the sketchpad and stashed it in his backpack protectively.

He walked down to the edge of the pond, picked up a rock, and held it tightly in his left hand. In a sudden flash of rage, he threw the rock as hard and fast as he could into the water. The rock landed with a huge splash, startling the hikers who had passed moments before – a little retribution for their rude interruption of his peaceful afternoon. The lake aggressively spewed out water in the wake of the rock's impact while ripples gently radiated toward the shoreline. As the ripples drifted closer, a calm washed over Kenny. Embarrassed about his outburst, he wished he could control his anger, but it always seemed to triumph at random, unpredictable moments.

Was he becoming his father?

Since the jeweler vowed to live alone, no child would ever have to learn the answer to that question. Secure in that fact, Kenny found peace.

As the sun fell low in the sky, he packed up his belongings and headed out of the grove toward a trail that ran along the east side of the pond. He walked slowly, taking deep breaths and relishing the smells of the forest.

Chapter 7
Muse

Beth spent the afternoon mixing colors and taking a stab at painting the lighthouse. She was not entirely unpleased with her work, but as the evening wore on, she decided that her fatigue and hunger were handicaps, so she found a stopping point and put the paints away. Later, after dinner, she sat in the clearing and watched as the sunset transformed the bay into a sea of pink and orange. Then twilight embraced land and water with a soothing silver-blue.

Beth returned to her house and took a long, hot shower, attempting to rinse away her growing sense of trepidation. She walked into her bedroom wrapped in a large, blue towel, drying her hair with a small hand towel. The firefly floated silently in the center of the room. Beth screamed. But her fear quickly turned to anger. "Stop it. Stop it!" She stamped her foot like a child. "Get out of my house *now* and *never* come back."

The light flickered for a moment, then it slowly drifted toward the window, pausing briefly before slipping through the glass. In an instant Beth felt cold and empty, as if a wave of disappointment had washed over the room. In the void left behind, she whispered, "Wait."

Beth ran to the window, cupped her hand over her eyes, and peered out. The little creature of light was nowhere to be seen. She threw on some clothing and ran downstairs. The full moon was just beginning to rise. Beth looked into the woodland, but she saw only shimmering shadows of trees. She sat on the boulder, glancing around furtively, hoping to catch the glimmer of a dancing light. She waited, restless, for over an hour.

But the firefly never appeared.

* * * *

Before going to bed, Beth set her alarm. Sleep came in unsatisfactory fragments throughout the night. Disturbing moments, interspersed with incongruent scenes of sand and waves, plagued her dreams. The dream-Beth wandered peacefully along a beach, soft waves splashing on the shore. Then the sound of screeching tires caused her to turn in panic. As her head swung around, the headlights of an unrestrained vehicle blinded her. Suddenly she realized she was no longer on the beach but in some kind of forest, entangled in the branches of a tree. She stood on broken twigs and dead leaves, surrounded by mossy rocks, ferns, and a variety of trees. Her bare arms were scratched and bleeding. Then, in a flash, the car spun out of control and she was bombarded with an array of images – her father's smiling face, a rubber duck, a steering wheel, her father's face twisted in anguish, another duck, distorted and irregular. . . and the sound of a woman screaming with fear. Or was that her own voice? Several times throughout the night, Beth awoke in a sweat, breathing quickly. She looked around the room, oriented herself, and took several deep, slow breaths before reluctantly lying down on the pillow to try again. Sometime after 2:00 a.m., she finally reached a peaceful state of unmemorable dreams and gratifying sleep.

She jolted when the alarm blared at 4:00 a.m. A slight uneasiness clouded her spirit, but she shook the feelings and rushed to get ready and over to *The Virginia Point Cove* before sunrise. She glanced out the window. No fog. At 4:39 she headed out the door, her sketching supplies secured in a light brown canvas tote she had purchased in Albany.

She ran to her car, pleased that she had finally gotten her act together in regards to sketching the bed and breakfast. But as she reached the car door, she looked back toward the forest. A faint light appeared on the horizon. Beth froze with her hand on the car door. A moment later she sighed, set down the tote bag, and entered the woodland heading north.

After searching for an hour, checking out every clearing she saw near the rocky edge, she found it – a six-inch arrow made out of stones. She crawled on her stomach and peered over the rim. Radiant in the new light of day, the miniature, private beach greeted Beth. It lengthened with the ebbing tide. It looked even more inviting than it had three evenings before.

Beth tried to remember the path traced by the firefly. She studied the rocks. Once she felt comfortable that she was familiar with the first couple of footholds, she eased herself gently over the edge, feet first. Carefully, feeling for a secure hold with every movement, Beth maneuvered down the twenty-foot cliff step by step. When she reached the bottom, she jumped on the sand, threw her hands in the air, and shouted, "Yes!"

She looked around and all at once a sense of serenity overcame her. She felt completely removed from civilization. It was just the sand, the water, the sun coming up on the horizon, and her. All the apprehension of the previous few days seemed to melt away as she stood mesmerized, her long shadow scaling up the side of the cliff.

After a while, she brushed away a few rocks and sat down on the damp sand. Then she removed her tennis shoes and socks and stretched her toes. How long had it been since she had wiggled her toes in the sand? She could not remember. With all the hustle of the job, the divorce, and the move, she had forgotten what it felt like to come to a complete stop, to take it all in with no agenda whatsoever. For over an hour she sat silently, doing nothing but watching and breathing.

Later that morning, her stomach had its own agenda. Reluctant to leave, she came up with a plan. She returned to the house and gathered the makings of a cold breakfast – a bagel, some fruit, and a box of crackers. Then she rummaged through the garage until she found a box marked "camping," and she pulled out her backpack. It had been years since she had used it last. She packed the lunch, her sketching supplies, a towel, and an ice-cold water bottle.

Afterward, she returned to the beach.

She spent the better part of the morning and the early afternoon sketching the islands off the coast and reveling in the tranquility of the secret beach. The tide pushed her into the tip of the horseshoe for about an hour, but it turned back around 12:15 p.m. Just after two, Beth returned to the cottage. She placed her sketches in the studio and admired the work she had accomplished. The beach was an inspiration she had not anticipated.

"I'm sorry, little firefly," she whispered, remembering her hostility of the previous night. Beth sighed. Her mind reeled. Was she coming to terms with the idea that the firefly was not a figment of her imagination? Could she ever really know for certain? She shrugged and exited the studio, humming softly.

* * * *

Following an afternoon snack, Beth headed into town to visit the jeweler again. *I hope Mr. Van Winkle found his way home.* She chuckled.

When she approached the shop the drawing was gone and an "open" sign was in its place. She entered the store, causing the bells to jangle. Mr. McLeary stood at the file cabinet. He looked up when she entered. No smile was forthcoming, and if he recognized her, his face did not reveal a clue. He slipped silently to the back room and returned with the box. He gently removed her mother's ring from the silk and placed it on Beth's left ring finger. It was a perfect fit.

Beth stared at the ring. It looked strangely

misplaced on her hand. She removed it and examined it carefully. The refitting was flawless, not a mark or a bulge, as if it had never been touched.

"Oh, this is truly amazing. Thank you so very much."

Beth smiled broadly and brought her gaze to Kenny's face. Looking at Kenny McLeary was like staring into a white sheet. Nevertheless, for a brief moment something more animated flashed. Beth quivered. She was not certain if what she saw was benevolent or malevolent. It passed so quickly, it could have been an eerie black or a deep midnight blue. It came and went in an instant. Afterward, the blank, white sheet glanced away. He pulled out a receipt book and began to figure her total.

"You have truly found your calling," Beth announced.

No response.

"Although you also sketch a mighty fine Rip Van Winkle," she said, giggling awkwardly. She fumbled with the ring, sliding it back on her finger.

Kenny punched some numbers into a calculator.

"I thought it was pretty funny. I got a good laugh out of it." Her voice took on an unnatural, clumsy tone. "Yup, I was a little worried you'd run off with my mother's ring. . . Then I'd have to go and hunt you down," Beth stammered nervously. "And that would be a disaster, because I'm a slow climber," she explained. "Yup. Would probably take me twenty years just to find you, and then you might be—"

"That will be forty-six even," Kenny said, interrupting her.

"Oh, ah, yes." Beth paid him cash and he nodded

silently, handing her the box and silk wrapping. Beth fumbled with her purse. "Thank you so much. . . ah. . . yes, you do beautiful work. . . Okay. Goodbye then."

"Thank you, ma'am," Kenny said quietly, and he returned to the file cabinet.

"What's with all the ma'am stuff?" Beth grumbled after she left the store. "Can't a woman get any respect around here?" She snickered at the irony of her own joke and glanced back toward the jewelry shop. Through the window, she saw her painting glowing proudly on the wall.

At least he's got taste, Beth thought. *Even if he is a little creepy.*

* * * *

The firefly did not return for several days. Beth set aside the guilt and enjoyed her newfound enthusiasm. Her creative energy flowed continuously. She finished the painting of the lighthouse, finally sketched the bed and breakfast at dawn, and spent many hours on the beach renewing her spirit. She spent some time weeding and planting, and she repaired the dilapidated rock wall that bordered the garden. She began planning an inventory for her upcoming website, and she was no longer overwhelmed by the thought of the effort required to make it all happen.

On Thursday morning, three days before her fortieth birthday, Mary called. Beth ran down the stairs and looked frantically for her cell phone.

"Hello?"

"Beth?"

"Yes."

"Oh, hello, dear. This is Mary. I'm just checking in on you."

"Oh, I'm doing fine, thank you."

"Are you lonely out there at the cottage? Would you like some company?"

Beth hesitated for a moment. She really did not want to be disturbed. Her creative energy was abundant. It seemed a shame to stifle it with a social meeting. On the other hand, Mary had been kind to her in a time of need, and she could be a potential business reference. *The Cove* had dozens of visitors every year. If Beth did not fracture the delicate ties beginning to grow between herself and Mary, she could expect to get many referrals.

"Ah. . . some company would be. . . great," Beth said finally.

"Tell you what. I'll drop by tomorrow with lunch. I'm making a ridiculously huge pot of chicken soup today. I don't know what gets into me. I guess I'm accustomed to feeding a horde of Navy boys, even after all these years."

"If I'm hosting, you really shouldn't be providing the lun—" Beth began.

"Nonsense," Mary interrupted. "I just invited myself over. Don't be silly. What am I going to do with all of this soup? Even if the whole town were sick, I'd never be able to get rid of it."

Beth grinned, picturing Mary standing in the kitchen with a stained apron, her forehead sweating, surrounded by scraps of chicken and celery. "All right," she said, surrendering. "I would enjoy that very much."

Beth was pleased with the arrangement. She

would have the rest of the day to be in her own personal space, and she could mentally prepare for gossip and soup when morning came. In addition, Mary's pending visit inspired Beth to work on the painting of *The Cove*. And so she spent the afternoon in the studio fine-tuning her strokes. Every once in a while, she peered out the window toward the private beach. She was not going to share her secret. It was too precious to disclose, too indulgent to give up. No, it was her beach, she decided. After all, how would she explain how she found it?

She pictured the expression that would appear on Mary's face if she told her about the firefly – perhaps a look of bewilderment combined with the excitement of acquiring the best nugget of gossip ever divulged. Beth laughed at the thought.

"She's my little muse," Beth announced to herself. All of a sudden, it had a gender and a title. "She has not visited since I spent the first day at the beach, so she must be content to know I finally found it." Beth did not want to acknowledge the fact that she had demanded the light creature leave and never come back. She was too pleased with her achievements to sort through the unpleasant details of their last encounter. What's more, she was relieved that she no longer considered herself crazy.

At first, the supernatural experience gravely concerned Beth, but as time progressed she convinced herself that it was a normal occurrence. A muse was a perfectly acceptable explanation in her mind. Why not? *Everybody has one,* she told herself as if it were just a matter of fact.

She returned to the studio. "My muse, my beach."

Chapter 8
The Fissure

That night, as Beth dressed for bed, she noticed the firefly hovering near the edge of the woodland, its radiance subdued by the twilight. No longer dancing in circles, it seemed to quiver, reluctant to approach.

"Oh, silly little thing," Beth murmured, shaking her head. "I'm not mad anymore," she called out the window.

The creature did not move. It floated five feet above the ground, waiting patiently, almost hopefully.

"I suppose I must say thank you," Beth mumbled unenthusiastically, unable to admit to herself that she still found the creature somewhat troubling – muse or no muse. She put on her old jeans and a light windbreaker, grabbed a flashlight, and wandered slowly toward the forest.

As Beth came within five feet of the firefly's position, it took off with great speed into the forest in the direction of the private beach, zigzagging through the trees.

"Oh, I'm too tired to play games tonight." Beth

sighed.

But she quickened her pace and followed the creature nonetheless. When the firefly reached the clearing, it dropped swiftly over the edge. Beth clipped the flashlight to her belt and followed, hoping that by now her feet knew the way. As she descended, the beam of the flashlight bounced, forming strange shadows amongst the rocks.

When she reached the ground, she turned around and found the creature hovering at her eye level, two feet away. In an instant it shot upward, about halfway up the cliff, and disappeared into a small fissure, roughly a foot and a half long and eight inches high.

"Now what?" Beth asked.

The firefly darted out and then back into the crevice.

Beth sighed. "I can't get up there, you know," she explained with a slight irritation in her voice. Then she took a deep breath and calmed herself. "Listen. This is an amazing beach. I am so thankful that you shared it with me, truly I am. In the space of a few days I've made tremendous progress in my work, thanks to this beach. Thanks to you. . ."

The firefly popped out briefly, made a small circle, and then returned to its hiding place.

"More secrets? A hidden treasure perhaps?" She beamed. "I suppose it wouldn't hurt to take a look if I can manage it." She propped the flashlight up in the sand, steadied it with a rock, and examined the face of the cliff leading to the miniature cave. Adjacent to the fissure there was a large, relatively flat stretch of rock against which she might lean while reaching into the hole. Beth cautiously climbed the cliff, carefully

71

testing each foothold before continuing.

Once she reached the fissure, she leaned back against the flat area. It felt cold on her back. She steadied herself and apprehensively put her hand in the opening. She touched something and pulled her hand back in alarm.

"My God, there really is something here," she exclaimed.

She reached in again and pulled out an object approximately twelve inches long, ten inches wide, and five inches high. It appeared to be wrapped in several layers of plastic. Whatever hid inside the plastic was hard and shaped like a rectangular box, and it weighed about twenty pounds. It was not awkward to hold, but it would be impossible for Beth to bring it down while she negotiated the cliff. She sat for a moment, feeling the package and trying to discern its contents, while carefully balancing on the flat section of rock beside the fissure.

The light creature swirled happily around the beach, darting now and again over the water. The moon had not yet risen, so the firefly's reflection on the water was especially magical.

"A treasure indeed. You are full of surprises, Firefly," Beth announced.

She carefully returned the box to its hiding place and scrambled down the cliff as quickly as humanly possible with her weak climbing skills. Then she crawled up the rocks leading to the exit and ran to the cottage. Less than forty-five minutes later, Beth returned wearing the backpack, and she repeated the tedious climbing in reverse. Balancing herself on the flat section next to the fissure, she carefully placed the treasure in her backpack and made her way back to the cottage.

Beth sat on the floor in her living room and placed the package on the coffee table. She stared at it for a long time, almost afraid to touch it. In her peripheral vision, she could see the firefly hovering just outside the bay window.

"Don't come in, please. I'm spooked out enough as it is. . . but thank you. . . I think," she whispered.

Beth reached for the salt covered package and set it in her lap. Carefully she unwrapped the plastic, which turned out to be several large, dark green garbage bags wrapped and layered. The bags seemed fairly crisp and worn, but Beth could not discern whether that was due to age or the harsh sea air. Under the layers of garbage bags, she found a sturdy, dull silver box with a lid that lay flat, not overlapping along the sides. It looked like a very simple cashbox. A small latch flipped closed over a loop and a faded gold padlock secured the box. Beth shook out the garbage bags, but she did not find a key.

She turned the box around several times and attempted to twist the padlock with her hands. Eventually, she grabbed a pair of pliers and a screwdriver from her kitchen junk drawer. She tried prying off the lid with the screwdriver and twisting off the latch with the pliers. After forty-five minutes of struggling, she set the box down in defeat. The latch was bent and the box was scratched up, but the small lock stood firm and the lid remained flat. Beth went to the garage and returned with a pair of hedge clippers. With her otherwise fruitless efforts, she had made a large enough gap to fit the nose of the sheers between the box and the latch. She snipped the sheers impatiently, eventually cutting the latch on one side. After about twenty minutes of straining and cursing, she was able to twist the latch around the ring with her pliers. Even though she eventually lifted the lid, the little gold lock stayed intact hanging on its loop.

Inside she found an opaque plastic Tupperware container. She sighed.

"What's next? A set of nested matryoshka dolls?"

She cautiously pulled up one corner of the Tupperware. It contained a faded, cloth-covered book decorated with sunflowers. Beth turned it on its side. The edges of the pages were gold and slightly crinkled from dampness. She flipped through the pages at a glance and noticed curvy handwriting in blue ink. She opened the front cover of the book. On the first page, in the same handwriting with swirls and loops, it read: "Katherine's Diary."

Beth closed the cover gently and let out a long, slow breath.

"A diary. All this effort over a diary."

Beth stared at the cover for a long time. She glanced out the window. The firefly was gone, but a gibbous moon rose on the horizon.

"Would I want someone to read my diary?" she asked herself as she turned the diary around in her hands. She opened the front cover again. "I would guess by the handwriting that this is probably the diary of a young girl. . . maybe one of Mr. Thompson's previous tenants. I should return it to her. That is the right thing to do."

Beth sighed, rose to her feet, and walked over to her mother's photo, clutching the diary against her chest.

"I miss you, Mom."

She gazed at the photo for several minutes, wondering what her mother would do in this situation. She speculated that her mother would come to the same conclusion. Respect the girl's privacy. Return the diary. So, she brought it upstairs to her bedroom. Then she put it in the bottom drawer of her dresser where she kept letters and birthday cards, most of them sent by her mother, few of them answered or even acknowledged.

* * * *

Sleep came quickly, although plagued with disturbing dreams. The last image she saw before she awoke at 6:17 the following morning was a bright yellow, rubber duck tumbling down a hill.

She sat up and rubbed her head. Waking up with a headache was not an ideal way to start the day but she gently eased herself to the side of the bed. Then an unexpected memory flashed through her mind.

Three days following her father's fatal car accident, Beth threw away her favorite bath toys – a large rubber duck, several smaller ducks, an old shampoo bottle, and a blue sponge shaped like a whale. She declared that ten-year-olds did not play with bath toys. In truth, she had warm memories of her father sitting at the edge of her bath when she was four and five, playing with the rubber ducks. He would push them under the water and let them pop up again. He made silly voices for the daddy duck and all the little ducklings. Sometime before she turned six, he stopped sitting with her when she bathed, but she still enjoyed playing with her ducks, remembering the fun they had together, and recreating their adventures.

After her father's death, she suddenly despised the toys. Subsequently she marched into the garage and threw them away. They lay next to the coffee grounds and orange peels, looking up at her sadly. She averted her eyes and placed the metal lid tightly on the garbage can. From that day forward, she took showers.

Beth quivered as the memory flooded her brain, washing over her with a sadness she had not felt for quite some time.

Why had I forgotten that? she asked herself. Then she scanned her brain and realized she could recall very little from her pre-teen years. She could not even remember her eleventh or twelfth birthdays. It was as if those memories were erased or hidden away somewhere safe. The sad recollection of the bath toys did not make Beth eager to dredge up the others, so she promptly tucked that memory away, dressed, and thought about what to do with the day.

She knew Mary would be coming around noon with chicken soup. The afternoon was shot. All the same, she didn't feel very inspired to sketch or paint so the morning was wide open. She looked at the dresser drawer that held the diary and came up with an odd idea.

It was a chilly, foggy morning. Beth dressed warmly and left the house a little after seven. She headed for Rod Thompson's house, which was located five miles inland at the furthest edge of the township.

It didn't surprise Beth that Rod had chosen a house distinctly isolated from its neighbors.

At the corner of Sears Road and Main Street an Irving gas station and an antique store vied for the attention of travelers. Beth headed north at that juncture, looking for Glen Road, a winding street which led to the Thompson house. Along the way, she passed an incongruent assortment of houses. Several late nineteenth and early twentieth century homes with elaborate gardens presented themselves with pride. Some homes needed a fresh coat of paint or a few repairs, but they were still charming. A brown shingled house from the mid-fifties, its yard filled with lobster traps and buoys, made Beth smile. She passed a bright pink house with a matching pink barn, and she chuckled, while next door, an old gray trailer with a dent in the roof and a rusted truck in its unkempt yard made her cringe. A quarter of a mile past the trailer, the road turned and a meadow filled with purple lupine came into view, enchanting Beth. She wished she had thought to bring her camera, but then she reminded herself, *this is not a sightseeing mission.*

She almost missed the entranceway to Rod's house. The mailbox at the side of the road leaned to one side and a digit of the address was missing. But three of the numbers matched, so Beth figured she probably had the right place. She drove cautiously up the dirt road. Rod's once white house was dingy and in desperate need of a fresh coat of paint. It appeared to have been built around 1960. The left side of a railing, which bordered the twenty-foot long porch, tilted forward slightly. No flowers adorned the property and the grass was littered with weeds. Several untamed bushes dominated the front of the house and a large maple in the center of the yard towered above the pitiful display. All the curtains were closed, and the house seemed dark and uninviting.

Beth parked her car at the end of the driveway and approached the door tentatively. A faded, tarnished brass mail slot curled open on one side. It would clearly be a liability during inclement weather. "He doesn't need a mail slot," Beth mumbled. "Why doesn't he just board it up?" She shook her head and mounted the steps.

She knocked quietly, waited two minutes, then knocked a little louder and rang the bell. No one came to the door.

"Mary did say he doesn't answer the door. But perhaps he simply isn't home."

She wandered around the side of the house and peeked into the backyard. Another flowerless, weed-infested yard met her eyes. In addition, a ten-foot wide swamp filled with reeds and cattails languished near the back of the property. She ventured a little farther, her heart pounding. The windows on the back of the house were also curtained and dark.

Beth sighed and returned to her vehicle. She sat in the car, her hands on the steering wheel, gazing at the house. An eerie feeling washed over her as the dark windows stared back. She started her car, quickly spun around, and headed down the driveway.

As she turned left to go back toward town, an idea struck her.

"Perhaps he is at the marina," she said to herself. "What did Mary say the name of his boat was?" She thought for a moment. *"The Big Blue?"*

Chapter 9
The Bottomless Blue

The Virginia Point marina lay at the bottom of the hill where Main Street met with Shoreline Road. One dock facing southwest provided six slips for residents and seasonal visitors. A separate, smaller dock was equipped with a fuel station. Behind the fuel station on the other side of Shoreline Road, a small store offered boatmen groceries and basic supplies.

A fifteen-foot motorboat, *Jaws,* from Bar Harbor, Maine, occupied the first slip on the left. The second slip, typically reserved for boats passing through, stood empty. Two yachts from Virginia Point rested in the slips on the right – a forty-five footer named *Jessica's Sunset* and a thirty-five-foot cruiser bearing the name *Where's Shamu?* elaborately painted in the shape of an orca. A third boat, parked in the furthest slip on the right, was a fishing vessel from Rockland named *Lob And Stir.* And on the last slip to the left with its own, private access dock, a striking, thirty-five-foot sloop bobbed gracefully with the morning tide. *The Bottomless Blue.*

The Bottomless Blue was the most captivating

vessel in the harbor. White with blue trim and teak accents, it floated peacefully – its sails neatly wound; its deck recently polished. Sheets, halyards and lines were meticulously coiled or otherwise tidied up. That the sailboat was well maintained and never neglected was obvious, even to a novice. Apparent to all that saw her, the owner loved *The Bottomless Blue* like a child.

Tentatively Beth approached the vessel. "Hello?" she called. "Mr. Thompson?" There was no response. She waited a minute before trying again. "Mr. Thompson?"

Slowly a man emerged from the cabin, squinting in irritation.

Beth waved from the dock. "Are you Rod Thompson?" she asked pleasantly.

"Who's asking?" the old man replied.

"Beth LaMonte at your service. Finally, I meet my landlord." Beth gently touched the side of the sloop, admiring its beauty. Rod Thompson scowled at her hand with an intensity that almost burned. Beth withdrew quickly in alarm.

His response was brusque. "I do not consider it a *service* that you interrupt me this morning. What is it that you want? Didn't that plumber fix the pipes?"

"Yes *Lou* fixed the pipes, sir. I am quite pleased with his work," she replied tartly. "And I would hardly wait a week if he hadn't," she added under her breath.

"Well," Rod huffed. "What on earth do you need, woman?"

His harsh tone and disrespectful manners shocked Beth. *Woman? I would prefer ma'am if it came down to a choice. What is wrong with this man?* Then Beth became aware of something more disconcerting than his rudeness. It was as if the air all around them took on a dark chill from the moment he stepped onto the deck.

But Beth was not intimidated. "I want to ask you a question, if I may," she ventured.

"Do I have a choice?"

She cleared her throat. "I found something, a book that belongs to a former tenant of yours by the name of Katherine. I should like to return it."

Rod's eyes narrowed and his brow tightened. He stared at her for a second that seemed to drag into minutes. "I have had no tenants by that name," he snapped. "And it is none of your business who and where are the people that lived at the cottage before you. It is not your place to go meddling in the lives of others. Pay the rent and mind your own affairs."

Beth did not move a muscle.

"Go along and don't bother me. The rent is due by the fifth of the month. Please put a stamp on it and stick it in the mail. I don't like unexpected visitors." He retreated into the cabin and swiftly pulled the hatch closed. There was a loud thud, and then all was quiet.

Beth remained on the dock. Her heart pounded and her hands shook unexpectedly. For a moment she froze, as if in fear. She could not move. After a couple of minutes she was able to shake the creepy sensation and compose herself. She turned, walked briskly to her car, and drove away from the dock as quickly as possible.

Chapter 10
With a "K"

Mary arrived a little after twelve o'clock laden with a large pot of chicken soup, a box of crackers, and a jug of apple juice.

"Goodness, let me get that for you," Beth said, as she answered the door and relieved Mary of the apple juice and crackers. She placed them on the kitchen table next to the bowls, plates and spoons that she had already arranged.

Mary carried the soup straight into the kitchen and put the pot on the stove. She turned the burner on low.

"Would you look at this place." Mary strolled out of the kitchen and walked around the living room. "You are settling in very nicely." She wandered over to the fireplace and picked up the photo of Beth's mother. Beth jumped nervously. She wanted to snatch it out of Mary's hands. Mary, whose home was decorated with family photos, seemed curious as to why Beth had only one picture displayed in her living area. "Is this you, dear?"

Beth's brow crinkled slightly with surprise. It had

never occurred to her how much she looked like her mother. She stammered for a moment. "Nuh. . . no, that is my mother."

"Very lovely," Mary replied. "Do you have any current photos of her?"

"She. . . she died recently."

Mary turned and a look of gentle compassion fell over her face. "Oh, I'm so sorry to hear that, Beth. My condolences, truly."

With loving care Mary returned the photo to the mantle and Beth's anxiety faded. An awkward silence lingered as the two made their way back to the kitchen. Mary stirred the soup while Beth fidgeted with the table settings.

Eventually Beth blurted out, "I met Rod Thompson this morning."

"Oh, really? Isn't he a charmer?"

"Man, you weren't kidding. The guy is. . . he's a downright asshole, that's what he is."

Mary laughed loudly and slowly stirred the soup. "Oh my, you've nailed that one on the head. What happened?"

Beth hesitated for a moment. Reluctant to tell Mary about the diary, she concocted a believable lie. "I found a box of clothing in the garage marked 'Katherine's.' It looked like a young lady's clothing. I thought she might be missing it. So I asked him for the address of a previous tenant named Katherine and he blew his stack like I asked to see him skinny-dipping or something."

Mary cringed. "Please don't put such images into my head right before lunch."

Beth giggled. "Sorry. . . but I don't know why he

got so mad. He said I should mind my own business about the previous tenants. He gave me the creeps. Do you remember a Katherine living here?"

Mary looked up at the ceiling briefly, as if recalling the names of the last couple of families she had known. "No. There was John and Cindy Messinger. That was the couple that lived here eight years, divorced, you know. Their kids were Timmy, Jennifer, and Joseph. The last family, hmm, the ones from New Jersey. What was their name? Kingsley. June, Brent, and their daughter Ashley. No Katherines."

Beth sighed. Perhaps the diary belonged to someone just passing through, or someone who lived elsewhere and knew about the secret beach. She hadn't thought about that possibility. "Any girls named Katherine living in Virginia Point that you remember?"

"Hmm, is that with a 'C' or a 'K'?" Mary fetched the bowls, filled them, and carried them to the table one by one.

"A 'K'."

"Oh. That's not it then. There is a teenager named Cathy with a 'C' who lives on Pine Lane two blocks from me. But I don't recall any Kathy with a 'K'."

Frustrated, Beth said nothing and sipped her soup.

"You can just give the clothing to the Good Will. Goodness if it is a young lady's clothing, surely she's outgrown it by now. Besides, why would a girl living on Pine Lane keep her clothing in your garage? Perhaps it was a friend or a cousin of the Kingsleys or even the Messingers. In any case, I doubt anyone is missing it."

Beth had not thought through her cover story very carefully. Of course it sounded ridiculous that she would desperately want to return a simple box of clothing to a phantom Katherine who may or may not have lived in the house in which it was found. She chastised herself. But the lie just seemed safer than sharing the diary with Mary. Mary would want to read it and tell everyone about it. That didn't feel right to Beth. It seemed too intrusive.

"You're right," Beth said, forcing a smile. "I guess it is a little silly. But it gave me a good lesson, Rod Thompson 101. There is something seriously wrong with that man."

"I told you. Didn't I tell you?"

"Yes, only I didn't realize just how creepy he was. Perhaps he murdered this Katherine and threw her body into 'the bottomless blue,'" Beth said mockingly.

"Oh now, wouldn't that be delicious?" Mary said.

Beth shuddered. She hardly found such an idea *delicious*. She didn't even know why she had said it. All of the late night rendezvous with a glowing marble were starting to affect her state of mind.

"Anyway," Mary said as she crumbled some crackers into her soup. "If you really want to find this Katherine, you should ask my mother, Abigail. She'll be here on Sunday. And she knows everything about everyone in this town."

"Oh, really? More so than you?"

Mary laughed. "Yes. . . much to my chagrin."

* * * *

Abigail Glenn was an energetic, elderly woman.

She had turned the third-generation family home into a bed and breakfast after her youngest daughter, Mary, married Lou and moved to Norfolk. When Abigail was in her mid-fifties, her husband of thirty-five years died of lung cancer, but she continued to run the inn with warmth and success. Upon turning sixty-one, she decided to move to a retirement community in Palm Beach. At that time, Mary and Lou returned to Virginia Point to take over the bed and breakfast. Every summer, June through early September, Abigail came to visit. She typically flew into Portland, and drove the coastal route to Virginia Point. Throughout the rest of the year, she enjoyed a busy and social lifestyle in Palm Beach: swimming, playing golf, hosting a book club, walking dogs for several clients, and volunteering at the assisted living facility a few blocks away.

Abigail was slender and somewhat athletic, her short silver hair tastefully accented with faint red highlights. She stepped swiftly up the walkway of *The Virginia Point Cove* wearing tan pants, a matching blazer, and a cream t-shirt. When Mary opened the door Abigail dropped her bags, ran up the stairs, and embraced her daughter.

"Welcome!" Mary said. She stood back. "Would you look at you, all tidied up and sophisticated. You've become too good for us humble folks in Virginia Point."

Abigail waived her hand. "Oh, cut it out. You know this will always be my home."

Mary grinned. "And you are welcome anytime, night or day." They hugged again. "How was the drive?"

"Absolutely beautiful as always," Abigail replied as she stepped back. She glanced behind Mary and saw Lou approaching to greet her. "Good morning, Lou," she said warmly.

"Abigail. It is great to see you," Lou said. "Let me get your suitcases." He slipped by the gushing ladies and retrieved the discarded bags at the foot of the stairs.

"Come in, Mom, come in," Mary insisted, as she pulled Abigail through the doorway. "I've got tea all set up, and there's someone I want you to meet. Our new resident artist."

"Is she the one who's going to paint the inn?"

"The one and only." Mary led her mother into the sitting room where Beth and a tray of pastries were waiting.

Beth stood up hastily, smiled awkwardly, and reached out her hand. "Hello, Mrs. Glenn. I'm Beth LaMonte."

Abigail grasped Beth's outstretched hand and shook it enthusiastically. "Oh please, young lady, call me Abigail. Very nice to meet you."

Beth smoothed her skirt and sat down on the couch. She picked up her tea and sipped it quietly. Abigail and Mary poured themselves a cup and fussed over the pastries before making themselves comfortable – Mary on an armchair, and Abigail on the couch next to Beth.

Abigail leaned toward Beth. "So, tell me all about yourself."

Beth pulled back slightly. Then she related a very brief, impersonal version of her background, her decision to paint, and her move to Maine.

Abigail pursed her lips to one side, furrowed her brow, and examined Beth thoughtfully. Finally she said, "I'll have to get the real story out of you later." She waved her hand dismissively and took a sip of tea. "Anyway, how do you like Virginia Point?"

Beth was taken aback by Abigail's frank analysis of her reticence. Her mouth hung open for a moment before she caught herself and tried to stammer her way out of the embarrassment. "I. . . I'm having a lovely time here. I believe I'm finding a true home."

"I'm so glad to hear that," Abigail announced with gusto as she raised her teacup in the air. "Here's to women coming into their own."

Beth looked around the room. Mary raised her teacup. "Here, here."

Beth fumbled for a moment, raised her glass, and smiled shyly, nodding to each of the ladies in turn.

Mary changed the subject. "Mom, our Beth has some questions about a missing damsel she's trying to locate." She raised her eyebrows and grinned mischievously in Beth's direction.

Beth stammered. "Yes. . . ah. . . I was wondering if you know a previous tenant of Mr. Thompson's, someone named Katherine?"

Before Abigail could answer, Mary blurted out, "We think maybe old man Rod's stashed her in the depths of 'the bottomless blue.' And I'm not talking about the boat, if you get my drift." Mary raised one eyebrow. Beth resisted the urge to put her head in her hand.

"Oh, shame on you two!" Abigail exclaimed. "You read too many novels. Katherine is Rod's daughter. He loved her like no one on this earth."

Beth's heart began to pound rapidly.

Mary looked on in disbelief. "His daughter? Why didn't he just tell Beth?" Then she rolled her eyes, remembering Rod's unpleasant personality and his withdrawal from the realm of human beings. "Anyway, what do you mean by he *loved* her?"

"They fell into a huge rift years ago, in the mid-seventies, when Katherine was still in her teens. . . over a boy, of all things. Her father didn't approve. She was a typical teenager, of course. Things got ugly and she moved out, disappeared. As far as I know they haven't spoken since. Oh, it is a shame. I can't really blame the poor thing for leaving. Rod was far too protective. But to sever all contact? I've never understood why folks do such a terrible thing."

"So do you know where she went?" Beth asked.

"No, I'm afraid not, or I'd have hunted her down myself. Rod's become a bitter old man ever since. I tried to be a good neighbor to him, bring him out of his shell. But he's a stubborn one. He became mean and nasty tempered, seemingly overnight.

"See, his wife died before Katherine even started Kindergarten. But I'll give him credit. He was solid as a rock, I tell you. Went right into the business of raising a child alone. He doted on that girl. . . but he also smothered her. He was so afraid something might happen to her. It is a wonder the poor girl could even breathe.

"Anyway, it is one thing to be lovingly protected as a motherless child, but it is quite another to be stifled as a teenager. Katherine rebelled. Rod snapped. He couldn't accept her defying his authority. He was angry. She was determined to live her own life, so one day she was gone. She probably left with the young man. . . and Rod hasn't seen her since.

"And Rod was already laden with more than his share of heartache. His father committed suicide right before his eyes when he was only thirteen. Jumped off the lighthouse balcony."

Beth recoiled in shock. Mary looked down and away. She tapped her foot nervously.

Abigail continued. "*The Bottomless Blue* is just a substitute for all that the man has lost – a father, a wife, a child. He has no one. Nobody likes him because he's become so disagreeable. He doesn't *want* friends. He won't let anyone in that stone-cold heart of his."

Mary glowered. She glanced in Beth's direction, but Beth was engaged in the story, which seemed to further irritate Mary.

"He used to run a car repair shop. Everyone depended on him to fix their troubled vehicles. He was a fine member of the community." She paused. "Now he fixes boats, which is also a great service, but he works typically for strangers who come and go. And he is not at all friendly to them or to the locals who need his assistance. He's gone sour. I have tried to reach him. I remember what a nice man he was when Katherine was young – a strong, decent man. But there is a shell of a person where that man used to be. I can't perform miracles. What can I do?"

Mary chimed in. "No one expects you to do anything, Mother. He's dug his own grave. It's not your responsibility to pull him out."

"I know, but have a little compassion, Mary."

Mary huffed. "No, I don't have any compassion for

a stuffy old stinker. . . no matter what he's been through." She sighed. "Oh, all right. I'll cut him a little slack. . . maybe tell less incriminating stories about him in the future." She winked at Beth.

Beth sat silently, sipping her tea. Her mind drifted – away from the chatter, away from the present – to a world unknown to her. Virginia Point in the nineteen-seventies, a capricious young girl, a protective father. It was a sad story. Even so, something about the whole thing warmed her heart. She had to stifle the urge to smile as a bittersweet wave washed over her spirit.

* * * *

Beth returned home in the late afternoon, still daydreaming about a rebellious teenager named Katherine and her hard-to-fathom loving father, Rod Thompson. She almost stumbled on the stairs, her feet knowing where she was going, her mind not fully accepting what she was about to do. When she reached the top of the stairs she remembered something that had entirely slipped her mind.

June 18th. It's my birthday. She pondered for a moment. *Why did I forget? Is it because I was afraid to acknowledge it, or is it because it doesn't matter anymore?* Her mind scanned over the changes she had undergone in less than a week. Ever since she set foot on the beach, she had become a new person, filled with ideas and surges of creativity. She no longer felt old. She felt as if life were just beginning. She smiled and took a deep, cleansing breath. Then she walked straight over to the dresser drawer and took out Katherine's diary.

She fluffed her pillows, propped them up, and made herself comfortable on the bed. Then she opened the front cover to the page that said *Katherine's Diary.* There she paused for a few moments before turning the page to the first entry.

> *Friday, July 11*
> *Dear Diary:*
> *That sounds so silly, "Dear Diary." I've never had a diary before. Well, I did have one when I was twelve. It was sparkly silver with a small, flimsy lock on one side. I got it for Christmas. But, you know, I never wrote in it. And really, who knows where that diary got to over the years? Besides, it was the diary of a little girl. And I'm a young woman now, almost seventeen and a HALF! I'll be a senior this year. I thought you were much more suitable and sophisticated for a teenager of my advancing years. Anyway, I had to share this with SOMEONE. Sarah has been moody lately, and we haven't spoken in over a week. So you are my new friend, Diary, and I expect you to keep all my secrets. . . even if you don't have a lock.*
>
> *So, so, so. I ramble. You're wondering, "What is the story already? Say something interesting." Right? Well, here it is.*
>
> *A very cute boy started working for my father this week. Well, he is not exactly a boy. He has stubble on his face. But you would just DIE if you saw him. Shaggy, sandy*

blond hair to his shoulders, green eyes, gorgeous tan, broad shoulders. Very broad shoulders. He could probably lift his motorcycle in the air if he really wanted to. Today he was wearing a white tank top and blue jeans. Not the flared blue jeans that the ridiculous boys at school (who think they are so chic) wear. No, these were regular Levi's, a man's jeans, you know?

Anyway, I walked into the shop. Dad was supposed to take me to lunch. I peered into his office and he was on the phone. So I wandered around the garage, and I saw these jeans and sneakers peeking out from under the hood of Bob's green Chevy. I knew that Jimmy had taken off last week. (His mom is in the hospital. Long, sad story. I'll tell you sometime, but first things first.) Anyway, I knew that Jimmy was supposed to be gone, so those legs kind of scared me at first.

"Jimmy?" I said quietly.

The jeans emerged from under the car, rolling out as fast as a Hot Wheel. I come to find out they were attached to a gorgeous hunk of a guy. I couldn't believe it. I almost gasped. I put my hand to my mouth just in time, thank God.

"Uh, hi," I stammered. I was a complete bumbling idiot.

But he just grinned. Oh, the most adorable smile. I practically melted on the spot. He pulled himself up, nodded his head ever so slightly, and said, "Hi. My name is John. I just started working here for Mr. Thompson." He pointed toward my dad, who noticed us talking and seemed to, out of the blue, rush to end his phone call. I heard him throw in a couple of "alrightys" and "okay thens." What a surprise. He treats me like I'm ten. God forbid I talk to a boy.

I held out my hand and quickly spouted off, "Katherine Thompson. Nice to meet you."

He chuckled and showed me his greasy palms as an excuse for avoiding my handshake. Of course I giggled, a STUPID giggle. I hate my laugh. I must have looked like such a 9th-Grader. I picked my brain for something clever to say, and, of course, nothing came to me. Then Dad came rushing over, put his arm around my shoulder, and whisked me away.

"I'm taking my daughter out to lunch," he hollered to John, without even looking at him. There seemed to be a particular emphasis on the word daughter, as if he were drawing an imaginary line on the garage floor. I twisted my neck for one last look at Mr. Cutie-Pie, and he smiled, a carefree, full of life, smile.

Well, Diary, you don't have to ask. I've got the likes really bad. I can't wait to see him again. I think I'll find an excuse to pass by the garage Monday on my way to Jeanie's Ice Cream Parlor.

I should wear my tube top. On the other

hand, I don't think Dad has ever seen my
tube top. I better save that one for another
day. But I'm definitely going to curl my hair.
And wear eye shadow.

Well, must go. I have a busy day to plan.
Thank you for listening, Diary. It feels good
to have a secret friend.
Love,
Katherine

Beth looked up from the page and gazed into the distance. Memories of childhood crushes washed over her. She thought about Todd, the blond-haired stud she had been afraid to talk to in tenth grade. He barely knew she was alive. But all the same, she doodled his name on the inside of her homework folders and daydreamed for hours. She cut out photos from teen magazines of any boy that looked like Todd. She was silly and obsessed, but it had felt wonderful. And then, of course, there was Josh from eighth grade. He had noticed her first and asked her to the end-of-year eighth grade dance. She was quite smitten with him, but his family moved out of town before she started high school. She often wondered what it would have been like to start high school having a boyfriend. Then she realized she might have missed out on all the crushes that made the teenage years so exhilarating. She even had a crush on her Math teacher when she was in ninth grade. He was, of course, nothing but professional. But there was something exciting about starting the day looking forward to staring into the dark, warm eyes of Mr. Salinas. She heard not a word he said about algebra or geometry, but with a little studying she managed perfect A's. This was especially gratifying, since it impressed Mr. Salinas.

Beth smiled. She cherished her memories. And in that moment she realized that she was quite satisfied to be turning forty. Naturally, as in any person's lifetime, she had endured difficult, sad periods and, perhaps, many moments wasted – things she should have said; things she should have done. Nonetheless, happy, silly, and inspirational days abounded – a whole life of interesting thoughts and experiences. *And there is a whole life ahead of me with many more to come.* She hugged the diary to her chest. Then she looked down and turned the page.

> *Tuesday, July 15*
> *Dear Diary:*
> *Oh what a wonderful time I had yesterday. God was smiling down on me. Dad had to drive to Portland to pick up some parts and supplies, so Mr. Cutie-Pie was minding the garage on his own. He's a hard worker, that one. Already covered with grease at 10:00 a.m., and looking just as yummy as ever. His hair was messy, but in an oh-so-adorable way.*
>
> *I tried to look foxy. I think I succeeded. I saw him look me up and down. It was subtle, but I've got a good eye for these things, you know? I wore my tight pink shirt with the star on the chest, cut-offs, and sandals.*
>
> *Anyway, I told him I was going to Jeanie's Ice Cream Parlor. I was hoping he*

would jump at the opportunity to come along. But he didn't. He was probably worried about my dad. It sure seemed like he wanted to go with. He was grinning and looking at me. I could swear he likes me.

So, I was bold. I brought the ice cream to him. A vanilla cone. We sat out on the mini-wall next to the bushes, the one that separates the garage from the junk-filled back lot. We were very comfortable sitting there eating our ice cream. John talked to me for nearly half of an hour before he noticed the time. Then he rushed back to work and I had to say goodbye.

I asked him all kinds of questions. He has had an amazing, interesting life. He grew up in California. His mom is an actress. I asked what movies she has been in and he shrugged me off, saying she only does bit parts and I wouldn't know her. But I kind of got the feeling there was some bad history there, you know? I wanted to tell him how I wish my mom were still alive, that I barely remember her, but the timing didn't seem right. I didn't want to make him feel bad, like I was scolding him or something. Besides, I wanted to find out about HIM, not go on with my old sob stories.

Anyway, he dropped out of high school when he was sixteen. He bought a motorcycle with the money he'd been saving up from his after school job at a gas station. He said he loves to tinker with cars, loves fixing things.

He said that gave him a sense of accomplishment, that it felt good afterward to wash up, sit down, and feel like he'd really done something. I thought that was so COOL. He's a good man, an honest, hard-working man. I like that.

Anyway, he traveled across the country, staying for a while here and there. He's been in Boston for the past six months. But he said he's looking for someplace that is a little less up and about, someplace where folks appreciated one another, where the pace of everyday life is a little calmer.

I told him, "Well, you sure came to the right place. Ain't much going on around here on a daily basis." He just smiled, a kind of knowing smile, like he's seen a little of everything and knows more about the world than me. He was right, so what could I say?

I went out on a limb and asked him how old he was. Twenty-two! Wow, no wonder Dad is all freaked out. Still, it is not really that old. When I'm out of high school, it will be no big deal at all. It will be like we're the same age practically. . . except, of course, the fact that he's been all over the country, and I've barely set a foot out of Maine in my entire life.

I've been to Boston a few times. And then there was our disastrous vacation a couple of years ago in Niagara Falls. Dad embarrassed me, wouldn't leave me alone. It was like he was afraid I'd fall over the edge of the waterfall and be washed away. He is so smothering sometimes. I'm going to have to keep my "likes" for Mr. Cutie-Pie under wraps. If Dad finds out, he might send John packing, and that would be no good, no good at all.

I guess I must sign off for now. I've got some serious daydreaming to do. Oh, and guess what? I bought a cashbox to keep you in, and it has a small padlock. I'm going to keep the key on a chain around my neck. I'll put you under the bed for now, but Mr. Snoopy-Pants Dad might come looking, so I'll have to find a better hiding place.

Anyway, ta ta for now.
Love,
Katherine

Beth closed the diary and caressed the cover. It looked so fresh for a thirty-five-year-old book. The sunflowers seemed to smile back at her, quietly concealing memories of youth and love.

An urge to paint overwhelmed Beth. She laid the diary on her bed and wandered down the hall to the studio. She anchored a thick sheet of paper to the easel and began to mix colors. No initial sketch, a first for her. She stared at the blank paper for a few minutes, closed her eyes, and envisioned the painting yet-to-be. Then she opened her eyes and began to paint.

By nightfall she had painted the features of a young girl with flowing, auburn hair. It was not outstanding, but it was decent for Beth who had never been comfortable painting portraits. A mood of mischief glimmered in the girl's green eyes. Beth had imagined a young girl who was a little rebellious and full of life. She had captured a hint of such a young lady, but she was not entirely satisfied with the results. She pulled up a chair in the corner of the room and stared at the painting-in-progress for several minutes.

"Not bad for me, I guess. It definitely needs *something*. A lot of work for starters. Then a hand, perhaps on her hair. . . putting in a barrette. Oh, I cannot draw hands. That will be a difficult undertaking." But she smiled nonetheless. She had something, her first human subject. The red-haired, free-spirited young lady was Beth's interpretation of the author of the diary – a girl with passion, a girl from the past.

It was almost 9:00 p.m. Beth glanced outside and gasped. The firefly hovered near the window. It hesitated for a moment before it slipped through the glass and into the room. Beth backed away.

"Did I say you could come in? I thought we had an understanding," she said nervously.

The firefly paused at the portrait and then circled it two times before drifting toward Beth.

Beth continued to back into the corner. "Stop! What do you want? I shouldn't have read it? Then why did you lead me to it?"

The light creature circled the painting again.

"You like it?" Beth asked hopefully, stepping forward and sounding more confident. "Isn't it amazing what you have inspired me to do?" Beth walked toward the painting boldly. "I could never do portraits, but look, here it is. I am so lucky I found you, really. . . and the beach, and the diary." Beth's words flowed hastily from her lips. "I mean, my very own, personal muse. Who would have guessed?"

The firefly began to circle the painting rapidly and repetitively. Beth stepped away. The firefly flew so fast it almost blurred into a stream of light.

Beth's shoulders dropped and her face conveyed disappointment. "You're not my personal muse, are you?"

The firefly hovered, waiting.

Beth pondered. "You are here on behalf of Katherine? An angel, perhaps?" Beth pulled her hand through her hair and sighed. "You want me to find her," Beth stated with some reluctance.

The firefly continued to hover patiently.

"That is not a very convincing answer," Beth said, pointing at the firefly. "But I suppose an angel is much more socially acceptable than a muse." She tried to sound cheerful. "Let's see. Abigail seemed to believe that Katherine ran off with her boyfriend. What was his name? Mr. Cutie-Pie?" Her voice quivered nervously. Her feeble attempt at humor did not calm her anxiety. "Okay, John."

The firefly backed away slowly.

"So I need to find John."

The light creature reached the glass and passed through it silently.

"Thanks for all the useful advice," Beth called sarcastically as the creature drifted away. She stood at the window and watched it go.

"Why me?" she whispered.

Exhaustion overcame Beth, so she retreated to her

room. The diary was on her bed. She picked it up as if it were a soiled tissue and placed it on top of her dresser. Then she shuddered and climbed into bed.

* * * *

That night, dozens of dream images inundated Beth. They blended, overlapped, and dissolved when she awoke with a start on Monday morning. She remembered dreaming of high school, long linoleum-lined halls that smelled of old mops, and cute boys. The passionate redheaded girl from Beth's painting made an appearance here and there, laughing joyously.

Just before dawn, a haunting nightmare slithered around the frivolous dreams and suffocated them. Again Beth walked along the beach. Again she heard the screech of tires. As she turned toward the headlights, she found herself caught in the branches of a tree in the forest. This time her father emerged before her, silhouetted against the light. In a fit of rage, Beth began throwing things at him, things which appeared from nowhere – the infamous rubber duck, a stick, and a pinecone. She shrieked, "Why didn't you come home, asshole?" She continued to throw things – another duck, a branch, and finally a rock. When the rock pierced her father's shadow, he blurred and disappeared. Then the headlights raced toward her and she bolted up in bed.

It took her several minutes to shake the fear and anxiety which plagued her tired spirit. She looked over at the dresser and saw the diary. She retrieved it, propped herself up in bed and found the next entry.

Wednesday, July 16

I hate my life! Dad is impossible. I want to run away from home. Maybe I will. Maybe I will do just that. Dad is such a smothering butthead. I hate him. Okay, no. I love him, but he needs to just be cool sometimes. He's all strung up like a fly in a spider's web.

Obviously he found out. I must have been too happy. God forbid I be happy, Dad. Is that too much for you? Ooh, he's such a pain in the ass.

Anyway, this morning I snuck into Dad's car and pulled out his lunchbox. I hid it in the pantry. Brilliant. Then I'd have an excuse to walk to the garage. "Oh, Dad, you forgot your lunch." Well, I thought it was brilliant, but Dad has a memory like a steel trap. He remembered putting the lunch in the backseat, because he had some tools lying there that he forgot to put away. So when I showed up with the lunch, he KNEW something was fishy.

We had a big fight in his office. I kept glancing over my shoulder, thoroughly embarrassed, hoping Mr. Cutie-Pie wasn't listening. But he heard the whole thing, I'm sure. At least the yelling part. Heck, they could probably hear it a block away.

The looking over my shoulder only made Dad madder. "What are you up to, young lady? Are you bored this summer? Do I need to set you up with a part-time job doing filing for Mrs. Willoughby?"

I kept trying to bring him down to a whisper. "I just thought you'd like to have your lunch. Go ahead and be hungry then," I growled.

But he was not convinced. He spelled out for me how he was certain he'd already put his lunch in the car, that I must have taken it out, and that I was probably looking for an excuse to come down and visit "that drifter." He actually said "that drifter" with an ugly tone. It was very rude. Why would he hire John and then be all judgmental of him? I asked him about it, and he calmed down a little, finally speaking at a regular volume like a normal person for once. He said that John was a fine, hard-working young man, but that he was a LOT older than me, that I was still in high school, and that I'd better keep my mind on my studies and off of boys.

"It's summer, Dad," I reminded him. But then he got all red in the face, and I didn't want to go through another bout of him yelling at me, so I slipped out of there as fast as I could and ran all the way home.

It's not fair. It's simply not fair. I hate him sometimes. He is such an overbearing monster. I am so embarrassed. I'm sure John is laughing at me. I wish I were dead. I wish I could live my OWN life. I'm tired of him being on my case all the time. He's raised me like a canary in a cage. If Mom were still alive she would understand, I'm sure of it.

She was a girl once too. Why are fathers so impossible?!

I'm going to go to my beach now. I want Dad to think I ran away from home. That will teach him a thing or two, won't it?

Love,
Katherine

"Don't run away, Katherine," Beth said out loud. Then she promptly dressed, ate breakfast, and drove to the marina.

Chapter 11
Taking Charge

Rod Thompson was meticulously cleaning salt deposits off the electric winches on *The Bottomless Blue* when Beth pulled up in her car. He stood, quickly disembarked, and strode down the dock as if to prevent her from stepping on. He was decidedly irritated.

Beth held her head high and walked toward the intimidating man.

"Good morning, Mr. Thompson."

"I thought I told you to leave me alone," he barked.

Beth ignored his response. "I know who Katherine is."

Rod's face contorted in anger. "Don't you *ever* say that name in my presence again. Do you understand?"

"It's just that I feel that—"

"Are you deaf? Jesus Christ, woman, leave me the hell alone!" He crossed the distance between them and pushed Beth so hard she fell down. "Unless you want to find yourself looking for another place to live." He turned to walk away.

Beth gasped in surprise. "What did you do to her? No wonder she ran away, you *monster*."

Silence fell over the marina as Rod stopped in his tracks.

Beth could feel the air change. She scrambled to her feet, ran to her car, and did not stop to look back. She sped up Main Street and drove for miles until she found an obscure, dirt road. She followed it for about ten minutes and came to a rest in a clearing filled with smooth stones. A small lake covered with a thin layer of fog could be seen just beyond the clearing. Grass and brambles surrounded the edge of the lake, and they seemed to continue to grow beneath the surface of the water. Beth looked around. Behind her, beyond the smooth rocks, a forest of trees – both deciduous and evergreen – blocked her view of the road and any surrounding property. Numerous young trees were cracked in half or broken at the base, lying on the ground or entangled in other trees.

Beth grabbed a jacket from the backseat, emerged from the car, and sat on a large rock near the lake. She took deep breaths, drawing in the damp, foggy air. As she rested, the fog dissipated and she could see the far end of the lake, which was no more than two hundred yards away. A patch of reeds rustled ten feet from the shore.

Along with the fog, Beth's head began to clear. Her mind traced the interesting and amazing events of the previous two weeks as her heart slowed down and her breathing returned to normal.

Then she thought of the red-haired girl, and an odd impulse urged her to move.

* * * *

On her way back home, she stopped at the jewelry shop. When she entered, Kenny was in the back, but he had a good view of the front door, and he glanced up when she walked in. She cleared her throat and announced, "I would like to commission a barrette from you." She hoped to appear sophisticated, but she knew she sounded ridiculous.

Kenny approached the counter, looking at her with interest, yet saying nothing.

How can you run a business without saying hello to your customers? Beth wondered. Then she spoke out loud, a little less pretentious. "Do you make those? Barrettes, I mean. Nothing real fancy, no jewels, maybe something silver attached to a comb. Yeah, that's it. A hair comb, not a barrette. Could you do something for under one hundred dollars?" Beth chased away the reproachful voices in her head that reminded her to respect her mother's money. *It's a business expense,* she justified.

Kenny nodded, mumbled an "uh-huh," and unlocked his customer journal drawer.

Beth saw what he was doing, and she clarified. "It is not for me, actually. It is for a teenage girl. So if you're making notes there," she said, gesturing to the little book Kenny had removed from the drawer, "then write down 'passionate, capricious redhead.'"

Kenny's face took on an expression that looked almost like a smile. No, it wasn't a smile, it was more like a stifled air of amusement.

Is he laughing at me? Beth asked herself incredulously. *Well, Mister-with-the-notebook, I could have a snicker or two at your expense, couldn't I?* Beth remained quiet for a moment, eyeing Kenny suspiciously as he made a few notes in the journal.

"Thursday," he said, his eyes averted.

Slightly perturbed, Beth asked, "What's Thursday?"

"I'll have it for you on Thursday," he said dryly, glancing up at her.

She grinned mischievously. "See? I knew you could make a full sentence."

Kenny's eyes flashed that mysterious color Beth had seen the last time she was there. She still couldn't tell if it was black or midnight blue, but for a moment he came to life. It unnerved her slightly, but she held his gaze. Then, in an instant, the life vanished and the well-guarded façade took its place once again.

Beth took a step back from the counter and turned to go. "I'll see you Thursday," she said slyly as she exited the store. Pausing for a moment, she waited for another reaction, but Kenny walked, unfazed, back to the smithery.

* * * *

When Beth returned home, she found her cell phone on the kitchen counter. A message from Bobby Downy politely asked when she would deliver another painting. He said he had several people look with interest at the lighthouse.

Beth sighed feeling flustered. She had the lighthouse to finish, the bed and breakfast to paint, and a website to set up. Yet, all she felt like doing was painting the girl. Such an endeavor wasn't sensible.

Deadlines and time management were essential tools for a successful artist. Beth put the diary away in her bottom dresser drawer and went to work.

After making good use of the day, she allowed herself to surf the Internet in search of art supplies. A flexible wooden hand, precisely what she needed, popped up on *misterart.com*. Smiling, she grabbed her purse and placed an order.

Later that evening Beth closed the curtains to avoid the firefly, averted her eyes from the dresser, and went to bed, vowing to make the most of Tuesday.

Chapter 12
Flashback

Late Monday night, after wrapping up several repair projects, Kenny McLeary began to design a hair comb for an unknown red-haired girl.

Out of wax, he fashioned a dogwood flower with three leaves. He delicately sketched veins on the leaves and ripples on the petals. Then he created a small, raised border around each leaf and petal. The border would remain silver. The leaves would eventually be painted a dark, olive green, and the petals white. A small yellow rhinestone was to be set in the middle to form the center of the flower. The thin, sterling silver ornament would be attached to a clear plastic comb, the type he normally used to create pearled wedding hairpieces for gushing brides.

Sometime on Wednesday, while Kenny multitasked between creating a new pendant, designing a ring, and casting the dogwood in silver, he knocked a toolbox off one of the benches. It crashed loudly on the ground and tools clattered and rolled in several directions. Kenny jumped with a start. He crossed to a chair at the far side of the room and took several deep breaths to quiet his pounding heart.

Occasionally loud crashing sounds gave rise to unpleasant flashbacks. He tried to keep them at bay, but sometimes they caught up with him.

That afternoon the memory of a terrible evening interrupted his creative endeavors. He was eight years old, sitting at his desk putting decals on a model airplane. It had taken him two months and considerable detailed attention to finish the model, and he was quite pleased with himself. He sat quietly in his room, admiring his accomplishment.

Kenny's mother was drunk, talking loudly in the kitchen across the hall from his bedroom door. His door stood ajar and he heard her cracking jokes and laughing hysterically. His father was also drinking, but he was less jovial. Something his mother said perturbed his father, and the man went into a rage.

"Watch your mouth, you trashy slut," he screamed.

"Settle down, Mack. I was only joking."

"You want to talk back to me? I'll give you something to complain about."

Young Kenny froze and did not breathe for a moment. The tension in the air almost suffocated him. He could hear his father slamming kitchen cupboards.

"Clean up this mess, bitch!"

Dishes crashed and broke in the sink.

Kenny heard his mother pleading. "No, Mack. Stop. Please."

Kenny slipped stealthily to his door and closed it as quietly as possible. But his father must have heard him. Loud, stomping footsteps came barreling toward Kenny's bedroom and the door flew open. His father towered over him with a two-day beard, reeking of sweat and alcohol. He wore a stained t-shirt and gray sweatpants.

"What are you doing in here? Are you listening to us?"

"Nuh. . . nothing. . . no, sir."

"Are you still working on that stupid toy?" his father asked, gesturing toward the model airplane.

"Yes, sir. I'm just finishing up." Kenny tried to smile, but he was shaking. "The decals are drying."

"What a stupid waste of time. Doesn't your mother give you enough chores?"

"No. . . ah, yes. . . I mean, I do my chores. I bought this with my own money, and I only work on it during my free time."

"Don't get smart with me," Mack barked. "You have too much free time. This weekend you need to clean out the garage."

"But I did that last month."

"What did you say?" His father stepped briskly toward Kenny and shouted in his face.

Kenny tried to hold his breath against the smell. He said nothing.

"I *said* what did you say?"

"Uh. . . nuh. . . nothing," young Kenny responded, quivering.

"Nothing, my ass, you little punk." His father reached for the airplane.

"No!" Kenny blurted out.

Mack turned in fury. "Are you saying *no* to me? I can't look at this piece of shit plastic you wasted your time on?"

"No. . . uh, I mean yes. . . sorry."

In a matter of seconds, which passed in slow motion in Kenny's memory, his father's face transformed into the image of a deranged beast, fire engine red with a grimace from hell. He threw the airplane as hard as he could across the room against the far wall. It shattered into several pieces. Kenny stood rigid, his chin up, looking over – not at – the wreckage.

His father laughed. "I guess it's back to the drawing board." He continued to laugh as he exited the room and slammed the door behind him.

Eventually Kenny crossed the room, kneeled on the floor, and gathered up the pieces. He loosely arranged them into their proper shape. He could hear his parents arguing in the kitchen. Then he heard his mother screaming and crying. He threw the airplane into the garbage, lay down, and put a pillow over his ears.

The older Kenny pushed the memory out of his mind, mangled it and buried it as deep as it would go. Then he stood, crossed the room, and began to gather the scattered tools.

Chapter 13
Sleuthing

Early Tuesday morning Rod Thompson set out on *The Bottomless Blue*. He threw the dock lines loose, put the engine in reverse, and backed out carefully, correcting for wind and current. He slipped past the breaker wall at 5:06 a.m. He was not seen in Virginia Point again until the following week.

* * * *

Beth worked diligently all day. She finished the painting of the bed and breakfast by noon, and by dinnertime *Old Charlie* stood proudly, drying in the fresh air that wafted through an open window. Beth absentmindedly closed the blinds before sunset. But the diary seemed to sing like a siren from her dresser drawer, and she was unable to resist its summons.

"Muses, sirens," she mumbled. "I should have majored in Greek mythology." Wearing a slightly guilty smile, she eagerly retrieved the diary from its hiding place. "Where were we?" She opened the cover and found her place.

Thursday, July 17

Sarah is being a real bitch. I finally told her about John and she acted all weird, you know. She says Dad is right and that he's too old. I think she's just jealous, that's what I think. But she's still my friend, so I don't entirely hate her. . . yet.

Well, I'm going to take a walk and think. Thanks for listening.

Love,

K

Friday, July 18
Hello, Diary:

I'm feeling much better today. I've decided to take matters into my own hands. I'm just going to schedule my drop-in visits to the garage for the days I know Dad is running errands. Brilliant, right? I'm going to go this afternoon. Wish me luck!

L,

K

Saturday, July 19
Dear Diary:

It went pretty well yesterday. I hung out with John while Dad was visiting a client, Mr. Campbell. That old fart thinks he deserves house calls. Dad's known him for a long time, so he heads on out there to take a peek under the hood of Mr. Campbell's Oldsmobile every now and again when the old guy "smells trouble."

Anyway, it was fine by me. I got to spend a couple of hours with John. We talked a little. . . about his travels and about my straight A's in history classes. I told him I enjoyed history, especially World War II. That's not typically a girl thing, so I think it impressed him. Sometimes we didn't say anything at all, and it was okay. . . comfortable. I've never experienced that before. It was weird and good at the same time. I handed him some tools when he needed them. We just passed the time.

I made sure I cut out of there before Dad showed up. John grinned at me when I left. I can't tell you how gorgeous that grin is. It made me tingle all over. I think he likes me. I really think he likes me.

Well, that's all for now.
Love,
Katherine

Monday, July 28
Oh, man. What a nightmare. Dad dreamt up a surprise vacation for us the Sunday before last. I feel like I've been gone a month. I really missed Mr. Cutie-Pie. I've got to find some time to catch him alone this week.

Anyway, Dad must be going bonkers. He's just trying to keep me away from John. I know it. We drove north along the coast. It was pretty nice in some ways. But I was edgy the whole time. Dad could feel it, and I think it made him a little sad. I used to love taking spontaneous vacations with him. But this time I was sort of mad, so I didn't care if I was hurting his feelings. He's got to realize that I'm seventeen now. I'm not exactly his little girl anymore. If he doesn't start treating me like an adult, I swear I'm going to go out of my mind.

Anyway, I didn't dare bring you, Diary. Dad is all over me. I'm going to take some time this afternoon to scout out a really good hiding place for you. If Dad reads you, I'm a dead woman.

Love,
Katherine

Tuesday, July 29
How do you like your new hiding place? I'm pretty clever, huh? Dad will never find you now. This is my beach. No one comes here. I've got you wrapped in a Tupperware container inside the metal box to keep you dry. If you start to get crinkly, I'll have to choose another place. But in the meantime, this is the perfect spot.

I'm going to try to catch a glimpse of Mr. Cutie-Pie today. I'll tell you all about it tomorrow.

L,
K

Friday, August 1
Dear Diary:
Sorry I haven't visited for a few days. It is

a little harder to get to you on the beach. If I sneak down here too often, Dad will smell something fishy in the air. I don't need him casing out my private beach.

Anyway, it has been a very good week. I got to visit John twice. Once at the garage, and one morning when he was home sick. I brought him some chicken soup and crackers. When he answered the door, he looked like hell, but he was still cute in his robe with his hair flying in every direction.

At first he did not know what to say when I was standing there. I think he was a little embarrassed. But after a moment, he flashed me his famous grin. I heated up the Campbell's on the stove, and I sat with him at the kitchen table. He kept saying that I should go so I wouldn't get sick, but he never stood up and led me to the door, so I stayed. I'll bet he was just trying to be polite. He seemed to like having me there.

Before I left I did the craziest thing. I invited him to visit my beach this weekend if he felt better. Can you believe I asked him? I told him it was my secret beach, mum's the word, you know. That way my dad won't catch wind of anything. And John will think the sneaking is just to keep my hideout a secret. I really hope he comes. Keep an eye out.

Love,

K

Beth fell asleep with the diary on her chest.

When she awoke, she hastily found a bookmark, tucked it in the pages, and returned the diary to the dresser. Then she showered, got dressed, and headed for the studio. She wrapped *Old Charlie* and *The Cove* in brown paper and packed them neatly in her car. She dropped the lighthouse off at *Kelp Corner*. Bobby Downy was waiting with another commission check.

"Thank goodness. We've just sold the lighthouse and my walls are going to look bare."

Beth grinned. She unwrapped the lighthouse painting and held it up for Bobby to see.

"Marvelous. *Old Charlie*. He is stunning. I'll have him sold by the end of the week," Bobby declared.

"That would be wonderful," Beth said joyfully but discouraging thoughts popped into her head. *Assuming his confidence is well-founded, that means I'll have to complete another painting by Friday. Painting for a living is harder work than I expected.* She smiled, nonetheless. And after a moment, she laughed at herself. *It's a pain in the ass when dreams come true, isn't it?*

She dropped by the bed and breakfast. She was nervous, yet excited, to hear Mary's opinion of her work. Mary, Abigail, and Lou were sitting on the patio when she arrived. Lou answered the door and led Beth to the ladies, who were eating sandwiches and chatting joyfully.

"Oh my stars!" Mary exclaimed when she saw Beth. "Is that it? Is that my painting?"

"Uh, yes, but—"

"No buts. Unwrap it. I'm on pins and needles."

Mary's excitement exacerbated Beth's anxiety. "If you don't like it," she explained, "I can always sell it at

Bobby's and paint a new one."

"Nonsense. I haven't even seen it yet. You will have to work on your salesmanship skills if you're going to make a living out of this, dear."

Beth unwrapped the painting with the back facing Lou and the ladies. Then she turned it around slowly. There was complete silence for a moment and Beth's stomach lurched.

Finally, Mary gasped. Her eyes started to water. "It is gorgeous," she whispered. "It is exactly what I wanted," she added with gusto. "Good show."

She stood up and took the painting in her hands. Then she handed it to her mother and gave Beth a huge hug. Lou and Abigail fawned over the painting for a moment. Then Mary snatched it from their hands and whisked it to the entryway. Down came the painting of the starfish, and up went the painting of *The Virginia Point Cove.*

"Lou," Mary shouted.

Lou ran after Mary. Beth and Abigail trailed close behind.

"We need to put the nail a little higher. What do you think?"

"I agree," Abigail said.

Beth stood quietly, not offering her opinion. She was slightly embarrassed, but glowing. A special feeling welled up within her, a feeling of accomplishment coupled with hope for personal significance.

"I'll get my toolbox," Lou hollered as he left the room and headed toward the garage.

Mary continued to gaze at the painting. "What do I owe you, dear?"

"Oh, uh. . ." Beth stammered. "Bobby is selling them in his shop for three hundred twenty-five."

"I'll pay three hundred seventy-five then."

"But—"

"I promised you top dollar, and I don't go back on my word. When you become famous and start selling them for thousands, I'll brag to all my friends about what a *steal* I got." She pointed to the painting and grinned proudly.

Shortly after the painting was properly adjusted, Abigail announced that she was going to take a walk. "Would anyone like to join me?"

"No, thank you," Mary said. "I'll clean up the patio."

"I would like to come," Beth piped up. She thought it might be a perfect time to ask some questions about Katherine. She had defaulted on her promise to the firefly that she would locate the young lady. Beth did some quick math in her head. *I guess she is hardly a "young lady" anymore. She is older than me, for goodness sake.* The idea struck her as odd, since she only knew Katherine through the diary's giddy, teenage narration.

Beth followed Abigail out the door. She ran to catch up with her. Abigail maintained a quick gait. Beth envied the spry woman and her accomplishments. *She has a loving family she can visit as well as her own life in Florida. And she is in great shape,* Beth realized as she struggled to keep pace. Beth imagined Abigail in Palm Beach, celebrating her golden years, content in her solitude, complete with her achievements. She wondered if such a day would come in her own life. Then she realized that she was already closer to that goal than she had been only a few weeks ago. She set aside her envy and thought about the author of the diary.

"Did Katherine have red hair?" she asked suddenly.

"No, not really. She had brown hair." Abigail laughed. "But she certainly had the temperament of a passionate, Irish redhead. So I suppose you could say she had a redheaded spirit."

Beth was somewhat disappointed. She had hoped that she had telepathically captured the true image of the diary's author. It was a ridiculous idea, but then, so was seeing floating balls of light. Perhaps it was enough that she had been inspired to paint a portrait, and that she was having an unexpected success. It was a whole new avenue for her painting career. Plus, being able to capture the essence of someone might be as important as accurately drawing his or her physical image. Beth pondered for several minutes before asking her next question.

"Do you remember the boy's name?"

"Oh, gee. It was Josh or Joe—"

"John," Beth corrected sharply, but caught herself. "Perhaps? Do you know his last name?"

Abigail raised her eyebrows slightly. "You are correct. It was John. John Higgins. I remember that because it was the same last name as my favorite teacher. Good old Mr. Higgins."

"Do you remember anything interesting about John Higgins? Can you guess where he might have gone if he ran away with Katherine?"

"No, I'm afraid I don't have any ideas," she replied. "But if my reasoning serves me well, it appears that someone is planning a little detective work." Abigail smiled broadly. "Are you going to find Katherine, bring her home to her father, and restore love and tranquility to Virginia Point?" she asked, teasing.

Beth blushed. "No. . . yeah. I guess I want to find her. I don't expect it will change the crazy man down there by the dock," she said, gesturing in the general direction of the marina. "But it will make me happy," she admitted.

"Good for you. And don't underestimate the power of love and blood. If Katherine came waltzing into town, that may be just enough to melt the old buzzard's ice cold heart."

Beth laughed. As they walked, she asked Abigail about Florida, and the elderly woman relayed detailed, animated stories. Abigail asked Beth about her past but Beth offered only restrained, emotionless answers.

* * * *

That afternoon, Beth spent a considerable amount of time looking on the Internet white pages for a Katherine Thompson in Maine. She also tried Katherine Higgins and John Higgins. The number of matches overwhelmed Beth. She called most of them. They all claimed they had never lived near Virginia Point. It was possible that one of them was lying, but it was also possible that Katherine had an unlisted number. Besides, if a person was cautious enough to lie about his or her history, then clearly he or she did not want to be found. And it did Beth absolutely no good trying to find someone who didn't want to be found. Still, she attempted to call every Katherine Thompson, Katherine Higgins, and John Higgins she was able to locate in Maine before giving it a rest and preparing something to eat.

As she ate, she realized that Katherine and John could be anywhere. If they had run away, they probably would not have stayed in Maine. They may not have even remained in New England. John was from California. Would they have moved to the west coast? Beth shook her head, realizing it could take weeks to call every match across the United States. It seemed hopeless.

After dinner she took a walk along the road, heading north. Then she crossed through the forest toward the coast. Just before sunset, Beth found her way to the private beach. The sand was cold and she had no blanket. Mesmerized, she sat staring out at nothing as the islands slipped into silhouettes. Soft hues of orange danced on the water and pink caressed the clouds as the sun descended somewhere behind her field of vision. The sea was tame. Barely a ripple could be distinguished on its glassy surface. It was tranquil, a tranquility that Beth craved after days of chaos and concerns. Reluctant to leave, she lingered long after the sun set.

She thought about Katherine's invitation to John. Had he come to the beach? There was one way to find out. Beth stood and brushed the sand off her pants. When she looked up, the firefly floated a few feet away.

"Hello," Beth said wearily. She pulled her hair back with one hand and stared at the creature. For some reason, that night, she didn't find it frightening. "I'm not having much success, you know." She stared impatiently at the firefly as if, somehow, she expected it to answer. "No one wants to lay claim to being Katherine Thompson from Virginia Point. But I have barely scratched the surface. I don't have enough clues. Am I missing something?" She sauntered down the beach and touched the wet sand with the toe of her shoe. The firefly followed her to the water's edge.

"Anyway, I'll try again tomorrow. Maybe California. But right now I'm tired, and I'm going to bed." She said this as if instructing a toddler that it was *mommy time*. The firefly shot over the edge of the cliff. Beth climbed up. When she reached the top, the light creature was waiting.

"Going to walk me home, huh?" Beth said with a whimsical tone. "That is very gentlemanly of you. . . or gentlecreaturely." Beth laughed and walked slowly back to the house, her hands in her pockets, the firefly floating protectively at her side.

Beth slipped into the house without looking back. The firefly hovered in the clearing. Beth noticed it when she closed her bedroom curtain. She waved tentatively. Then she grabbed the diary and propped herself up in bed.

Saturday, August 2

I'm really tired of Sarah. I'm not telling her anything anymore. She is so self-righteous. She thinks she knows everything.

I told her about my visit to John's house, and she went berserk. She told me I "need to get on the pill or something." As if chicken

127

soup could get me pregnant. John is being a perfect gentleman. And well, maybe I should start taking the pill. You never know when it might come in handy.

I did not tell her that I invited John to the beach. She doesn't even know about the beach. It is my secret, and it's going to stay that way. At least until I share it with John. Then it will be our secret.

Ooh. I can't wait!
Love,
Katherine

Monday, August 4
Did you see him? Ha ha. He was here yesterday. And, oh, what an amazing day it was.

I knew Dad was going sailing with Frank Willoughby. So that gave us an opportunity to sneak down to the beach. He hid the Honda up the road in the forest just in case Dad came home early or something. Maybe someday he'll take me for a motorcycle ride. That would be very cool.

I climbed down first. It was fun to spy on him as he came down. His arms gripping the holds, his gorgeous butt swaying as he descended. It was just plain yummy.

We sat and looked out over the water, saying very little for a long time.

Then he leaned over and kissed me. He smelled and tasted so good. I'm blushing just thinking about it. His lips were soft. And. . .

well. . . here's the thing: I've never French kissed before. I thought it would be kind of creepy. But. . . well. . . it wasn't. His tongue was so gentle and. . . whew. I didn't know kissing could be like that. I remember when Tommy Sanders kissed me at the "Freshman Ball." Bletch. That was so awkward. But not Mr. Cutie-Pie. He was really sexy.

We kind of made out. I think. Only we were just kissing. A lot. It was really nice.

We're going to try to meet here again on Thursday.

I can't wait. My lips are tingling in anticipation.

Bye bye,
Katherine

Beth caught herself touching her lips and letting her fingers caress the side of her neck around to the front of her throat. She took a deep breath and allowed herself the sensuous feelings, which had long been absent. She continued to read.

Friday, August 8
Dear Diary:

I'm in love. I am completely and totally in love. I'm going to marry this John Higgins. Mrs. Higgins. Mrs. John Higgins.

He visited the beach again yesterday. We made out. I mean we really made out this time. He touched my breasts. I thought I was going to melt into him right there on the spot. Oh, he feels good. He tastes good. I can't get enough of this.

I can see why Sarah suggested I get on the pill. She's a smart girl even though she's a pain in the ass. I'm going to have to arrange a visit to a doctor. Real, real soon. . . because if he touches me like that again, I'm going to go all the way. I swear. I won't be able to help it. He is the hottest thing in the world!

Smooooch.

Love,

Katherine

For a moment, Beth struggled with an unpleasant memory that wanted to surface. She closed the diary abruptly without replacing the bookmark, set it on the bedside table, and curled up on her bed facing away from the diary. She chased away the bad thoughts and focused on Katherine and her lover caressing on the secret beach that Beth now called her own. She willed herself a dreamless sleep and was rewarded with an uneventful night.

In the morning, Beth made more phone calls. There were a dozen dead ends and two disconnected phone numbers. She redialed several people who had not answered the day before. Then she moved on to the California white pages. Surprisingly, she got through to everyone she called, but she found no Katherines from Virginia Point and no John Higgins that had traveled across the country on a motorcycle when he was in his twenties. Finally, she came to the end of her list.

The last phone number belonged to a Katherine Higgins in California. Beth dialed it with an air of resignation. The phone seemed to ring for an eternity. Beth almost hung up, but at the last moment she heard a click.

"Hello?"

"Is this Katherine Higgins?" Beth asked, conveying as much enthusiasm as she could muster.

"Just a moment."

After several seconds a woman picked up the phone. "Hello," she said. "Who is this?" The woman sounded as if she were in her seventies.

Beth's heart sank. But she offered the woman the same speech she gave every other potential Katherine she had spoken with over the previous twenty-four hours. "Hello. I am Beth LaMonte from Virginia Point, Maine. I'm looking for a Katherine Higgins or a Katherine Thompson who grew up here in Virginia Point."

"I'm sorry, dear. I'm afraid I cannot help you. I've never even visited the east coast."

"Okay," Beth said, all the joy draining out of her in one breath. "Thank you for your time."

"Good luck with your search. I'm sorry I could not have been of more help. Goodbye."

"Goodbye."

Beth sighed, hung up the phone, and set it on the coffee table. She had made over fifty calls in less than a day. Fifty phone calls and not a clue, not one single bite. The thought of moving on to the other forty-eight states made Beth weary.

She wandered over to her mother's photo. "What now?" she whispered. She felt the tears that were longing to burst forth pressing at the edges of her eyelids. One tear broke through her defenses and rolled silently down her cheek. She grabbed a Kleenex, blew her nose, and lay down on the couch. She was emotionally exhausted.

"What now?"

Chapter 14
Melody

Kenny McLeary examined with admiration his latest achievement, the dogwood comb for Beth LaMonte.

This would have looked beautiful on Melody, he thought. All at once, images of Melody popped into his head; images he would rather not have coming to call on such an otherwise peaceful Thursday morning.

Melody was a flamboyant woman with dark auburn hair. She was passionate, yet volatile. She would light up a room when she entered it. Everyone, male and female, would turn and gaze in her direction. But her mood could turn in an instant, and she would explode like a pack of firecrackers. She was especially dangerous when she was drinking.

Kenny dated her when he was in his early thirties. He was a very shy man, and Melody waltzed into his life, changing everything. She was on fire. She made life exciting, horribly dysfunctional, but exhilarating at the same time. He found her intoxicating. Of course, much of the time she was intoxicated. It may have been his mother he sought in her. But, nonetheless, he loved her like he loved no one. Her beauty and passion blinded him. He idolized her.

But she was cruel.

She appeared in Kenny's life just after he opened the jewelry store in Virginia Point. Right off the bat, she seduced him into designing a piece of jewelry, a pendant, for which she never paid. He waived her debt and asked her to dinner. It was the first night on a roller coaster ride that lasted for three years.

On Valentine's Day just before their third anniversary, Kenny planned to propose to Melody. He designed the most lovingly intricate ring he had ever created. It was simple, yet elegant, embracing a precious, one-carat marquise cut diamond that he went into debt to obtain. He grilled a salmon, set a table with candles, and poured two glasses of champagne.

Melody arrived drunk, laughing gregariously. She stumbled into the room and saw the beautifully set table in the candlelight. She dropped her purse by the door. "Hey, Romeo, what do we have here?" She made a beeline for the champagne. She took a sip. "Eww. A little sweet for my taste." She took several gulps anyway.

Kenny smiled shyly and led her to a chair. He was very nervous. In some ways he longed to get it over with, but he wanted the moment to be right. He served a plate of salmon on a bed of rice with lightly steamed broccoli on the side. Melody dug in before Kenny even sat down.

"Good," she said between bites. She guzzled the champagne and poured herself another glass.

Kenny looked around nervously and forgot his

composure. He knelt down beside her, snatched the box from his coat pocket, and popped it open near her face.

She stared for a moment at the ring and at Kenny. Then, guffawing hysterically, she shouted in disbelief, "You want to marry me?"

Kenny stammered. He had not expected such a reaction. "I. . . uh. . . yes." He wiped his brow and tried to steady his shaking knee. "Will you marry me?" he blurted out.

"Of course not, silly."

"Why?"

"Haven't you noticed I've been away a lot lately?"

"I thought you were working on a big project."

"Well, it is a *big* project, if you put it that way." She threw her head back and giggled uncontrollably before her mood shifted to disgust. "I'm seeing someone, you idiot." She took a large gulp of champagne. "Someone who fucks a whole lot better than you," she added with a hateful grin. "I only stick around for the jewelry. . . and that looks like a handsome piece." She reached for the ring.

Kenny snapped the box closed and pulled it away. What kind of wimp did she think he was that he would give her the ring after that sordid confession? He felt rage well up inside of him. He stood up and glared down at Melody. She continued to laugh. She had ruined everything. He wanted to spit in her face. He wanted to push her chair over and watch her struggle to gain her balance. The desire to strike her overwhelmed him. It choked his senses. Hatred coursed through his veins, rushing like a river in spring filled with freshly melted snow. He looked down at the table.

Suddenly in a rush of motion that passed as a blur before Melody's eyes, he grabbed the table and flipped it over. Dishes crashed and broke. The champagne bottle hit the wall with a thud. The candles toppled and sputtered out on the wood floor. Melody screamed. She stopped laughing. She looked up at Kenny, and for the first time, he saw respect in her eyes. He approached her and she jumped up and stood behind her chair. He wanted to pick her up and throw her against the wall. He wanted to hear her scream and cry. He wanted her to pay for the pain she had caused him. He tried to push back the feelings of rage, but they consumed him.

He grabbed her forcibly by the arm. She was at his mercy. He knew it. More importantly, *she* knew it. Then as abruptly as he grabbed her, he let go, pushing her arm away from him as if it were diseased. "Get out," he screamed. "Get *out!*"

Melody ran for the door, not even stopping for her purse. She ran down the path and into town. As soon as she could find a phone, she called her new boyfriend. In the meantime, Kenny gathered up her belongings, including her purse, and he threw them out on the front lawn. For hours he cursed, pounded pillows and furniture, and gathered Melody's things. Just after sunrise, he fell asleep. He had somehow stilled his temper during the night. He did not break anything other than the dishes; he made no holes in the walls. And he had not hurt her.

As exhaustion welcomed him into sleep, he took comfort in that fact. He had wanted to hurt her but hadn't acted upon his impulses. Perhaps this was the line which distinguished him from his father. Nevertheless, at that moment he vowed to remain single and aloof. The turbulent relationship frightened him more than being alone.

Melody was not seen in Virginia Point ever again. Her things lingered on Kenny's front lawn for over a week before he gathered them and put them out with the trash.

* * * *

The jangle of the bell rescued Kenny from his unpleasant memories. He quickly placed the comb on a bed of soft cotton in a forest green box, and he walked toward the front counter.

It was Beth LaMonte.

"Hello," she said. Her characteristic enthusiasm seemed dampened, as if clouds had passed overhead.

Kenny presented the box to Beth. He was still shaking from reliving the horrible night from his past. He steadied himself against the counter and waited for her reaction.

She looked up at him expectantly and then back at the box. She opened it slowly, gently removed the comb, and held it in her palm. She stared at it for a long time and Kenny grew anxious. His pulse quickened; his breaths shortened.

Beth was speechless. She took in the delicate design, the beautiful colors, and the intricate veins and ripples which brought the blossom to life. She pictured it in the imaginary Katherine's hair and shook her head in disbelief. Then she shrugged her shoulders. "It's perfect," she whispered in complete astonishment. "How could you possibly create something so perfect?" she asked.

Kenny pursed his lips. It could have been taken for a grimace or a smile. He looked at Beth for several seconds without moving a muscle.

Beth saw the elusive window open again, the one in Kenny's eyes. This time it stayed open for more than a brief flash. *Definitely midnight blue,* she noted to herself. Behind the façade, she saw it – something brilliant yet damaged, almost fragile. For some reason on that day, at that particular time, he let her see it. He let down his guard briefly and let her in long enough to catch a glimpse of it.

It comforted him. In that moment when he doubted his sanity, when he wondered whether or not he was a bully or a human being, it was a welcomed recess, a confirmation that he was more man than monster.

"I'm glad you like it."

"Like it? I *love* it. It is as if you took the essence of something right out of my mind and cast it in silver. It is truly wonderful," she said, beaming graciously.

Kenny offered her a faint smile. Then he put up the barriers once again.

Beth continued to fawn over the comb. "I don't know how to thank you."

"Seventy-nine, ninety-nine, plus tax."

Beth laughed. He looked visibly hurt. She stopped laughing.

"Sorry." She cleared her throat and handed him one hundred dollars. "Keep the change and. . . thank you," she said as she turned to go.

"You're very welcome." His voice was clear and

steady.

His momentary confidence pleasantly surprised her. She nodded politely before slipping out the door.

Chapter 15
Obsession

The comb brought out a whole new level of obsession in Beth. She spent the entire day painting the red-haired girl. By late afternoon, she was on her third attempt, with two half-finished paintings propped up against the wall. The first was her original painting. She started from scratch the moment she arrived home with the comb, but her portrayal of Katherine's hand was rudimentary if not dreadful.

The wooden hand mannequin arrived via two-day mail in the early afternoon. At that point, she promptly set aside the second painting and began again. This time she secured a stretched canvas to the easel. The third endeavor was impressive. She started with the eyes, and moved on to the shape of the face. She took a break and repetitively sketched the mannequin hand, which she positioned as if it were grasping a hair comb. Once she felt comfortable with her basic understanding of the shape and perspective of the hand, she continued to paint.

She worked all day, stopping reluctantly to grab quick snacks.

It was one day past the solstice, so the sun didn't set until almost 8:30. Beth took advantage of the daylight as long as possible, and then she resolved to quit for the day. She stood back and admired the painting, which was not yet complete but substantial enough to get an idea of how the finished portrait might look. It was beyond her expectation, something she never believed she was capable of producing. She smiled. She had captured the impetuous redhead who danced through her thoughts every time she read the diary.

After gazing at the painting for several minutes, she decided she had earned a break.

The twilight bathed the living room in a warm glow. Beth fetched the diary and sat on the couch. She had recovered from her brief brush with the past, and she was eager to learn more about the captivating girl. She flipped through the diary to find her place. Then she pulled her legs up under her bottom, leaned on the arm of the couch, and read.

Wednesday, August 13

Dad has been stalking me. Every time I turn around, there he is. He's really pissing me off. I haven't been able to talk to John in days. I'm completely heartsick.

Next week I start cheerleading camp on Wednesday. Only, you know what? I told Dad we start on Tuesday. I have a doctor's appointment on Tuesday in Augusta. I'm a little scared. I've never seen a gynecologist before. But I should start my period this weekend, and I'll need to start taking the pill soon. That's what the nurse told me over the phone.

Dad will think I'm going to cheerleading camp. He's going to let me take the car. I have $100 cash stashed in the side compartment of my top dresser drawer. I'll go see the doctor, get my prescription, and be home at around four o'clock. He won't suspect a thing.

He can't stop me. He thinks I'm still a little girl, but he doesn't know anything. I'm a young woman, a sexy young woman. He has got to understand that he can't keep me in pigtails forever. Get real!

Sorry, Dad. That's just the way it's going to be.

Katherine

Sunday, August 17
Dear Diary:
Congratulate me. I've ridden on a motorcycle. Yup. I told Dad I was going to Sarah's house yesterday. As if...

Anyway, John and I snuck away and drove up to Acadia. It was amazing, the whole thing – the drive, the park, the man – it was incredible.

John gave me his helmet. He is such a gentleman. We went zipping up the road and I felt so free. It was like a roller coaster, the air on my skin, the rush in my stomach. I had that feeling where you want to close your eyes because you're so scared but you keep them open because you don't want to miss what's coming next. You know that feeling? Well, of course you don't. Just humor me.

We zoomed up Cadillac Mountain, along roads cut into granite. It was a whole new experience on a motorcycle. You feel like you are a part of nature or something. We stopped at a picnic area overlooking Frenchman Bay. It was very romantic. He kissed me again. I could live in those lips, they smell and taste so good. This time we didn't get too heavy, because we were sitting in a semi-public area, but it was still yummy. Maybe it was more so because those people were gawking at us. It felt a little naughty. But they don't know me and I don't know them. Besides, I'm in love. Who cares what they think?

In the afternoon we rode back. He dropped me off discreetly down the road and I walked home. But I tasted him on me for several hours even after he was gone.

I'm going to the doctor on Tuesday. I'm a little nervous. I wish I could talk to Sarah about it, but I don't feel like confiding in her right now. She's always so self-righteous.

So I guess I'll have to be a big girl. I'll let you know how it goes.

Love,
Katherine

Beth closed the diary, holding her place with her finger. "Sarah," she whispered. "I'll find Sarah."

Chapter 16
Digging Deeper

The following day, Beth decided to visit Abigail and inquire about Sarah. She left the house at a little after nine Friday morning with a look of anticipation and resolve. It was a beautiful morning, so she walked to the bed and breakfast.

An hour later she knocked on the door. There was no answer.

"I should have called first," she mumbled.

After a couple of minutes the door flew open. Mary looked a little frazzled.

"Beth. Come in."

"I'm sorry to drop by without calling ahead."

"Nonsense. My door is always open to you. . . unless I'm in the shower." She grinned.

Beth noticed that Mary's hair looked slightly damp. She felt a little guilty, but she smiled politely and stepped across the threshold. Her painting hung proudly over the sign-in table. A new guest had signed in the night before.

"Oh, you have guests. Perhaps I should come back later."

"Oh, stop it," Mary replied. "They went for a drive. Nice couple from Connecticut."

Abigail came around the corner, freshly dressed, her hair still wet. "Hello. How are you?"

"I'm fine. And you?"

"Things are busy at *The Cove* this morning. And that is just the way I like it," Abigail announced enthusiastically. She looked at her watch. "I think we've earned a coffee break. Let's sit out on the patio."

Mary brewed coffee while Abigail arranged the chairs on the patio. Beth followed, feeling cozy and welcome but slightly sheepish for barging in unannounced. Once the ladies were settled comfortably on the patio, Beth got to the point of her visit.

"Abigail—"

"Yes?"

"Do you know of a Sarah who was about the same age as Katherine?"

Abigail raised her eyebrows and glanced over at Mary.

"Are Sarah's clothes also in your garage, dear?" Mary asked, sounding almost innocent, while taking a sip of coffee.

Caught again. Beth blushed. "No, I just. . . uh. . ."

"Never mind, Mary," Abigail interrupted. "Beth is on a mission. I would hate to interfere." She winked at Beth and Beth squirmed in her seat, embarrassed but relieved.

"So, you are looking for a Sarah." She thought for a moment, then turned to Mary. "Didn't you baby-sit a Sarah when you were around fourteen?"

"Yes, I believe so." Mary looked up at the ceiling and ran some calculations in her head. "She was seven. That would have been in 'sixty-five, correct? I'll be. The math works out. She would have been about the same age as Katherine."

Beth's face lit up. "Do you remember her full name?"

"Oh, gee. It was Whitney or Windler. . . something like that. Mother, do you remember?"

Abigail sighed, thinking. "They sort of kept to themselves. You're right, though. It was something like Windler."

"Do you remember where she lived?" Beth asked, hopefully.

"It was a couple of blocks away. But I don't remember any Whitneys or Windlers at our town meetings in the last fourteen years since I've returned to Virginia Point."

Abigail tapped a finger on the table. "Like I said, they kept to themselves," she said, shrugging.

Mary turned to Beth, her eyes twinkling. "Would you like to drop in for a visit?"

"I would *love* to drop in for a visit."

The ladies drank coffee and chatted aimlessly for twenty minutes. Beth was restless, but she tried to maintain a veneer of patience.

Finally, Mary stood up, placed the dishes on the tray, and asked, "Are you coming, Mother?"

Abigail looked at her watch and hesitated. "No, I think I'll pass. I'm waiting for a phone call."

Mary looked at her curiously before grabbing the dishes and heading inside. Beth trailed after her.

"Oh," Mary said. "Let's bring some strawberries.

Mother, where did you put those strawberries you picked this morning?"

"They're in the fridge."

Mary fetched a worn Tupperware bowl and filled it to the brim.

"Strawberries?" Beth asked.

"You're not very good in the etiquette department, Beth," Mary said bluntly. "If we're imposing on the woman, the very least we can do is bring her some strawberries."

"Oh." Beth felt a little foolish, but she was not entirely certain as to why.

"Let's go." Mary headed for the door. Beth followed her and ran down the stairs, her heart pumping in excitement. Mary led her two blocks behind and then to the right. "It was a blue house. That I remember. The color of a robin's egg. . . on the left."

The ladies walked down the street searching for a blue house. A green car with several splotches of primer rolled slowly along the right side of the road, stopping at mailboxes. Beth assumed it was the neighborhood mailman.

"Hello, Patricia," Mary called, waving joyfully.

"Hey, Mary." A woman leaned out of the passenger window and deposited a bundle of letters in a mailbox.

As they drew closer to the car, Beth observed that it was not an altered, right-side driving vehicle. It was a normal, early 1990s Chevy Lumina with a steering wheel on the left. Patricia sat in the passenger seat, fumbling with a box on the floor, and she steered with her left hand stretched across to the other side. It was not clear from Beth's perspective how the mailwoman handled the gas and brake pedals.

"How does she do that?" Beth whispered in awe.

"Who knows?" Mary shrugged. "So long as the mail gets delivered."

Mary stopped suddenly in front of a white house. She stared at the house and the yard. "Well, it's not blue, but I think this is it. I remember this pear tree," she said, gesturing to the large tree in the front yard. "It was quite a bit smaller back then."

They approached the door and knocked. A young woman in her thirties answered, a baby on her hip and a toddler peeking around her legs. Mary glanced at Beth.

"Hello, my name is Mary Schmidt from the bed and breakfast. This is Beth LaMonte." Mary held out the Tupperware container filled with strawberries.

The young woman balanced the baby in one arm and fumbled with the strawberry container using her free hand. She set it on a table near the door. "Thank you very much." She nodded politely.

"You look busy. I'm sorry to bother you. We're looking for Sarah Windler."

"I'm sorry. No one lives here by that name. But we've only been in this house three years. We bought it from Mr. Swanson. I don't know how long he owned it. I could dig up the phone number if you'd like, but it will probably take me a couple of days to find it."

"No. Please don't trouble yourself," Mary replied.

Beth was frustrated. She very much hoped that the young woman *would* trouble herself, and she was a little disappointed with Mary's response. She decided she would return later and ask her to look for the number.

"Thank you for your time," Mary said to the woman. Then she turned to Beth. "Let's visit the neighbors. I know Mrs. Miller lives here." She pointed to the house on the right. "She's been here forever. She'll probably remember the Windlers. . . or the Whitneys. . . or whomever they are." Mary laughed as they made their way to the neighbor's house.

A woman in her early seventies answered the door.

"Hello, Mary. Do come in." She turned to Beth. "And who is your friend?"

"This is Beth LaMonte. Beth, Louise Miller." The women shook hands.

"Pleased to meet you, Beth."

"And you."

"Beth painted a gorgeous picture of *The Cove*. You should come by and see it. I highly recommend her."

Beth blushed as Mary threw her a whimsical look.

"Did she now? I'll have to check it out then." Louise pointed toward the living room. "Sit down ladies. What can I do for you this lovely summer morning?"

Mary sat in an armchair. "We're looking for Sarah Windler who used to live next door," she explained.

"You mean Sarah Wylder?"

"Yes," Mary replied. "It *was* Wylder."

"W-I-L-D-E-R?" Beth broke in.

"No, W-*Y*-L-D-E-R. But I'm afraid I don't know where she is. She moved out years ago. . . when she went to college. Then her brother left and her parents moved out a couple of years after that."

"Do you know which college?" Beth blurted out impatiently.

Mrs. Miller turned slowly toward Beth, pursed her lips, and thought for a moment. "I believe it was the University of Washington. Yes, I'm sure of it, because I remember thinking, 'Why do you need to go all the way across the country when we have perfectly good universities right here in Maine?'"

Beth smiled. She hoped this new information was the beginning of a trail that might lead to Sarah Wylder and on to the elusive Katherine Thompson. Sarah would know where Katherine went, she hoped. And then Beth would be able to track down the diary's author, putting an end to the mystery. Of course, the plan hinged on a number of ifs, but Beth was excited nonetheless.

The other ladies chatted for a while, but Beth paid little attention to their conversation. She was already planning her next set of phone calls.

* * * *

Mary and Beth returned to the bed and breakfast a little before noon. They were surprised to see Abigail standing on the front porch laughing with, of all people, Kenny McLeary. Mary tossed Beth a curious glance, but Beth didn't acknowledge because she was staring in fascination at Kenny. The pair on the porch had not yet become aware of the two approaching women, so for a moment they continued talking as if no one was watching. Kenny looked natural and relaxed, the laughter entirely transforming his features. Beth barcly recognized him.

Thirty seconds later, Kenny appeared to notice them out of the corner of his eye. He stopped laughing and put on his familiar stoic face. Beth was stunned.

Mary took advantage of the awkward moment. "Hello, Mr. McLeary. What brings you to my abode on this fine morning?"

"Just dropping something off. I'll be out of your hair, ma'am," he said as he quickly brushed past the ladies. He glanced up at Beth on the way, obviously fraught with embarrassment.

Mary called after him. "Oh, do stay for lunch."

"Thank you very much, ma'am, but I must get back to the store."

"Nice to see you." Her saccharine sweet tone lingered while the echo of his receding footsteps faded away.

Livid, Abigail scowled at her daughter.

"What?" Mary asked, feigning innocence.

"Don't *mock* him," Abigail whispered sharply.

The Virginia Point ladies walked to the sitting room. Beth followed slowly, taking one last glance over her shoulder before entering the house.

"So what was that all about?" Mary asked.

"It's none of your business."

"Please, Mother. I'm just bursting at the seams with curiosity."

Beth wanted to admit that she was curious too, but she wasn't sure it was an appropriate time to share such information. So she sat quietly and listened.

"He was dropping off some jewelry," Abigail said finally.

"You're buying jewelry?"

"No, I'm selling it."

"You're selling jewelry?"

"Yes, in Palm Beach."

"Really?" Mary asked with great fascination.

"Yes, *really*. Kenny and I split the profit."

"Well I'll be damned."

"Yes you will if you mock that man in my presence again."

"I only invited him for lunch, Mother. You're so sensitive."

"I saw it in your eyes. You were needling him. You know he doesn't like to socialize."

"He sure was having a nice time with you, now, wasn't he?"

"Kenny and I go way back."

"Really? How come I never knew about this?"

"If you disappear for over twenty years, you cannot expect to know everything that goes on in your old hometown." She glared at Mary, but Mary sat silently tapping her index fingers together. Abigail sighed. "I suppose the only way I'm going to get out of this is to tell you the story."

"I'm all ears," Mary said, grinning triumphantly.

Beth followed the conversation with great intrigue.

"Okay," Abigail began. "Kenny moved here when he was in his mid-twenties. You were still in Norfolk. You barely had time for your mother and her stories." She cast a reproachful glance in Mary's direction.

Mary rolled her eyes.

Abigail continued. "He was a young man with an impressive talent, and he wanted to sell jewelry. He worked out of the house he rented from the Willoughbys. But people around here were a little leery of him, with his southern accent and all. For goodness sakes, Mary, he was a transplant. . . and a wilting one at that."

"I understand, Mother. You've always had a soft spot for the emotionally distressed."

"Yes, and I had a lot of practice with three daughters."

Mary scowled.

"Anyway, I wanted to help him out, make him feel welcome here, so I became his first customer. I bought a silver brooch with three emeralds. It was shaped like a pine tassel, graceful and quite charming."

"I remember seeing you wear that."

"Yes. That was Kenny's work. I recommended him to the visitors who stayed at *The Cove,* and he managed quite well. I sort of took him under my wing. He didn't have any family to look after him."

Mary cocked her head expectantly.

"He grew up in Alabama. His mother was a drunk and his father was abusive. He ran away from home when he was fourteen."

Mary furrowed her brow. She was envious that her mother was privy to gossip unbeknownst to her. "When did he share this with you?"

"When Nana died. I was grieving and he opened up to me. He told me that he had tried to go back and look for his mother, but he was never able to find her. He was living in Philadelphia at the time, working for a jeweler. When he couldn't find his mother, he moved up here and branched out on his own."

Beth looked down for a moment. She tried to imagine what it would be like to have been on her own at the age of fourteen. She remembered how lost she was in her teenage years – angry with her father for not being there, and lashing out at her mother because she *was* there. Her poor mother seemed to take it in stride as if it were her expected burden to absorb, without recourse, all of Beth's hormonal pain and resentment. She felt momentarily ashamed. That afternoon, her opinion of Kenny McLeary changed – from faint amusement to modest admiration.

Mary interrupted Beth's reflections. "So how did you end up in the jewelry business?"

"Oh, now that's a long story."

"I'm listening."

"I'll tell you the short version." Abigail gave Mary a warning glance. "Kenny wanted to open his own jewelry shop. It was the fall of 1994. The Lyndon family was selling *Jeanie's Ice Cream Parlor*. He called me to ask if I thought it was a good idea. I told him that not only did I think it was a great idea, but I would loan him the money to get it off the ground."

"Wait. You were already in Palm Beach. I remember when Kenny opened his shop." She pondered for a moment. "And I remember that you made a big deal of encouraging me to tell our visitors about him."

"Yes. And I also sent you a teardrop diamond pendant that same year."

"You little sneak."

Abigail chuckled. "Anyway, we agreed on a loan payment structure of ten years, but he paid it off in eight. That first year I was concerned. I wasn't sure he would make it. He was doing very well until he met a witch of a woman named Melody."

"Ah, I remember her," Mary said thoughtfully. "She was rather flamboyant – the town drunk."

"Yes, among other things. Poor Kenny. Drunk mother, drunk girlfriend – the fate of a young man with a troubled childhood." She continued with the original story. "Anyway, this Melody was greedy, and she distracted him. He spent more time designing jewelry for her than designing pieces to sell. I pleaded with him during the summers when I visited. I thought about calling the loan, but I just couldn't. He was such a lost soul, and my protective, motherly instincts pre-empted my financial wisdom. Thank God that didn't backfire on me.

"In February of ninety-eight, he decided to propose to that monster. She laughed in his face. She was having an affair. He called me the next morning, distraught. Then, out of the blue, he sent me an absolutely stunning engagement ring. I don't know if he meant for me to keep it. It was an awfully lavish gift to send one's lender. So I sold it and wired him the money. Fifty-three hundred dollars."

"Fifty-three hundred dollars?"

"It was a one-carat marquise diamond, beautifully set. A woman bought it for her grandson. She was encouraging him to make a commitment to his lady friend."

"That's a lot of money."

"Oh, you wouldn't believe how much money some of those old birds have."

Beth bit her lip, trying to keep a straight face.

Abigail continued. "Anyway, Kenny was

flabbergasted. I called him and told him that I couldn't possibly accept such a gift, but that the jewelry business held promise in Palm Beach. We made an arrangement, and he's been sending me a dozen pieces or so a year ever since."

Mary shook her head. "All of this going on right underneath my nose. And I thought I was the queen bee on the gossip chain here in Virginia Point. You've outdone me again, Mother."

"When you pay more attention to *who* people are than what they are doing, you'd be surprised what you learn."

Mary groaned. "All right, Mother. Good advice. . . and *great* story."

Abigail shook her head.

"After all that I'm starved," Mary announced. "Let's make some lunch. Beth are you going to join us?"

Beth looked at her watch and stood abruptly. "Oh," she said, startled. "No, thank you. I had important phone calls to make this afternoon. It is already almost one o'clock. I'd better run, but thank you for the invitation. And thank *you,* Abigail, for sharing your story. Kenny makes a lot more sense to me now. I never imagined he was such a courageous person."

Abigail smiled. "I'm glad the moral of the story wasn't lost on *everyone,*" she said, gesturing to Mary with a shrug that said *what can you do?*

Beth chuckled and said her goodbyes.

She ran almost the entire way, arriving home out of breath. But she immediately grabbed her cell phone, ran upstairs to her computer, and pulled up the University of Washington website. After several phone calls, she reached a young woman in the transcripts department. She explained her quest for a Sarah Wylder who would have enrolled in 1976. The woman on the other end of the phone seemed disinterested.

"I cannot give out information on our students, current or past," she said in monotone.

Beth's heart sank. She should have expected such a problem. "I don't need to know her grades or anything. I would just like a last known number or address. Surely you maintain an alumni database."

The woman was annoyed. "I cannot give you that information, ma'am," she said sternly.

Beth thought for a moment. "What about professors? Could you give me the names of the most popular professors for freshmen that year?"

The transcript assistant sighed. "That is the oddest request I've ever heard. I'll transfer you to the faculty department."

Beth waited on hold for several minutes. She went over the story in her mind. She hoped to draw out a little more empathy from the next person with whom she spoke. Finally, a woman came on the line.

"This is Laurie. How may I help you?"

Beth cleared her throat. "Yes, thank you, Laurie," she began cautiously. "I have an unusual request. I'm looking for an alumna, Sarah Wylder." She blurted out the spelling and other details quickly, before Laurie would have the opportunity to shut her down. "I understand that the school cannot give out information on this woman, but I was wondering if I could get a list of the most popular teachers from the mid-nineteen-seventies. Is that a difficult request?"

There was a long pause. "I could get a list of the staff during that period, but I have no idea which professors were more popular than others – at least from the students' perspective. The most populated classes are not necessarily the most popular. And the professors handling those large, core classes don't really get to know the students on a personal level."

"I suppose that makes sense."

"What did you say her name was, Sarah Wylder? Do you know her major?"

Beth's pace quickened. She might get her foot in the door. "I don't know her major, but could you look it up?"

Laurie sighed compassionately. "I can look it up, but I'm afraid I cannot give you that information. But I'll get you the list of professors. It shouldn't take me more than a half hour. Do you have a fax?"

Beth's shoulders slumped. She had no incoming line and she really didn't want to ask Mary or anyone in town to take a fax for her. Her determination to keep the details of her quest secretive was working against her. "No, I'm afraid I don't."

"I'll mail it to you then," the woman responded cheerfully. She took down Beth's name, address, and phone number. Beth thanked her and hung up.

Twenty minutes later her phone rang.

"Hello?"

"Hello, Beth? This is Laurie from the University of Washington."

"Yes, hello, Laurie."

"I'm getting ready to send you your list," she said. Beth heard a staple gun go off. Laurie sounded a little awkward as she continued. "But I just thought I'd give you the name of a professor I believe will be the *most* helpful. Do you understand?" Laurie seemed to be slightly nervous.

Beth's heart began to race. Did Laurie look up Sarah's transcript? Did she handpick the name of a professor in Sarah's department? The wheels in Beth's brain began to spin. "Ah, yes, I think."

"Are you ready?"

Beth fumbled for a pen. "Yes."

"Peter Stephens. He was a biology professor, retired three years ago. He's a professor emeritus now, and he still has an office in the biology building."

Beth scribbled down the number and thanked Laurie profusely.

"No problem. One note though."

"Yes?"

"You didn't hear it from me."

"Got it."

After hanging up, Beth immediately dialed the number for Professor Stephens. It went through to his voice mail. She left a simple message, asking him to call her when he had the opportunity. Then she set the phone down on the desk, stood up, and stretched.

"I guess that is all I can do for the day," she concluded. She realized she was starving, so she made herself an early dinner and took a walk. She brought her cell phone, a piece of paper and a pen just in case the professor got her message.

She returned home in the early evening. The professor had not called, but Beth faithfully dragged her phone around with her wherever she went. Before the sun set, she spent some time working on the painting. She was pleased with her work. With another couple hours of effort it would be finished, but she wanted to wait until daylight.

As she got ready for bed she thought about the diary. Her life was turning into an obsession over a stranger and now that stranger's seemingly uncompassionate friend.

"Maybe I should give this up."

In the end, her rational side resigned. She propped herself up in bed and gave into temptation once again.

Chapter 17
Severing Ties

Sometime between his eleventh and fourteenth birthday, Kenny's mother ceased to be his champion. When he was younger, she had stood up for him, placing herself as a barrier between Kenny and his father. But such moments of heroism had cost her in the form of breaks and bruises. As she grew weary, she discovered that making Kenny the common enemy channeled the violence in another direction, away from her body. She drank more as the years passed, drowning her shame, and numbing her to the reality of what transpired within the walls of their house.

On Kenny's fourteenth birthday, he awoke to find his mother drunk and comatose, languishing on the couch. She lay face down on a throw pillow with one arm dangling over the edge. He gently pushed her, but she did not stir. That heartwarming spectacle had greeted him every morning for six months or more.

Kenny didn't notice his father enter the room.

"That piece of shit is useless for the day," Mack said, pointing at Kenny's mother. He threw a large basket filled with laundry in Kenny's direction. The clothing landed all over his mother. She looked pathetic – drunken into a stupor and covered with dirty underwear and socks. "So guess who's doing laundry today?" his father bellowed.

Kenny sighed. It was his birthday. His mother probably didn't remember and his father didn't care. With an air of resignation, he slowly began to gather the laundry into a pile.

"I want my socks *white*."

Kenny looked at the socks. Mack wore them around the house, and he often wandered outside without shoes. The socks were dark gray on the bottom with an occasional grass stain. Kenny pursed his lips and said nothing.

"You got a problem?"

"No, sir."

"I thought so." Mack turned away.

Kenny took a deep breath and went out on a limb. "Father?"

"Yes?" Mack looked back, his voice dripping with annoyance.

"It's my birthday today."

"So?"

"I was wondering—"

"What? You were wondering what? Did I buy you a pony? You're not getting anything. I'm between jobs now. We can't afford gifts."

Kenny glanced around. The living room was littered with whiskey bottles and empty cigarette packs. He had a rough idea of what those items cost. He looked at the ground.

"Don't go sulking at me. You're lucky I keep a roof

over your lousy, fucking brainless head." Mack marched down the hall, into the bathroom, and slammed the door.

His father had not worked for almost a year. The rent had not been paid for months. Kenny saw the eviction notices and past due bills when he picked up the mail. There was never anything in the refrigerator except for beer, stale doughnuts, and an occasional carton of spoiled milk. He always scrambled to make dinner for himself, or he sneaked over to a friend's. The filthy house was only barely a roof over his head, and it certainly was not a home.

That morning, Kenny made a decision. And in the split second it turned over in his mind, he felt a sense of personal power he had never felt in his lifetime. Courage welled up inside of him. He had nothing to lose.

He started the laundry and peeked into the TV room. His father was watching television, laughing. The volume was loud. Kenny sneaked into his parents' bedroom and rummaged in his mother's dresser drawers. He found what he sought. Whenever his mother needed to make a trip to the liquor store, she retreated to the bedroom before slipping out the door. She squirreled away grocery money for her stash. Kenny's father was not very good at math, and he never noticed the discrepancy in the budget. Kenny found $130, covered by cheap trinkets and gaudy bracelets, in his mother's jewelry box. He tucked the money in his pocket and went to his bedroom.

He spent considerable time thinking before he carefully packed his backpack with the bare necessities for survival – a flashlight, some matches, a water bottle, and one change of clothing. He kept the money in his jeans pocket.

His mother staggered into consciousness sometime after 3:00 p.m. Kenny's heart jolted because he feared she would need to make a liquor store trip, and she would notice the missing money. He quietly replaced the cash, hoping that it looked like the way he found it. Thankfully, she never came searching. Instead, she and Mack decided to go to their favorite pub for dinner. Kenny held on to the slight hope that she remembered his birthday and they were taking him to celebrate. But he was not invited. His mother had entirely forgotten.

When they left the house, laughing as they climbed into the car, all of Kenny's reservations left with them. He grabbed the money and his backpack, and he headed out of town in the opposite direction of the pub.

Over the following six weeks, he hitchhiked his way up the coast, hanging out here and there until he reached Philadelphia, where he became an apprentice to a sympathetic jeweler. He was a hard worker, and he learned the craft quickly, impressing his boss. Soon he was designing pieces that were very popular. Kenny was well-paid, and over the years he saved and planned for the future.

Sometimes he wondered what became of his parents, especially his mother. But when he went looking for her ten years later, he could not find a trace of her. Mack lived alone. He was drunk and belligerent, and he would not speak to Kenny. Folks from town who should have remembered her played stupid when Kenny asked questions, or they avoided him altogether.

Did she drink herself to death? Did Mack kill her?

Kenny went to the county police. They took down the information, but Kenny sensed that they did not intend to investigate. A chill went up his spine as he walked down the steps of the police headquarters. At that moment he realized that he, himself, had no intention of pursuing the matter further.

Was it fear of what his father might do? Or was it apathy over the fate of the woman who had emotionally abandoned him during his pre-teen years? Kenny asked himself these questions only once. Then he left his southern life behind and moved to Maine.

Chapter 18
Surrendering Innocence

Wednesday, August 20

Well, today was the first day of cheerleading camp.

Oh, you want to hear about the disgusting trip to the gynecologist? Well, why didn't you say so?

Yuck. That was a horrible experience. It was downright humiliating. I had to lie on a table and put my legs in brackets, so he could – oh it was so gross – spread them and poke around in my personal space. I was mortified. I tried to put myself somewhere else in my mind.

After the nightmare was over and I was allowed to sit up and cover myself, we had a lovely little chat about contraception. I'm supposed to take this pill every day, preferably at the same time. On the last week, I take the green pills, have my period, and start again with the next packet. Keep it like clockwork, he said. Sounds easy. I'll know if I took it by looking at the packet.

I'm sort of scared, but I have to be prepared. I know where things are going, and I have to be ready. John will be happy when he hears that I'm on the pill. I'm sure he's used to mature women who understand these things. He doesn't need some goofy teenager that doesn't know anything about birth control.

Okay, yeah, yeah, I know. Sarah was right.
L,
K

Friday, August 22
I'm taking the pill, but I don't feel any different. I suppose that is a good thing. No side effects.

Dad is watching us like a hawk – John at the garage, me at home. I should skip cheerleading camp again. But Dad will notice John's absence. And – God forbid – what if he followed him? Oh, my life is impossible.

I'm depressed now. I'll write later.
L,
K

Tuesday, August 26
Finally, an end in sight. Dad is going on an errand-run to Portland on Friday. I'm going to skip cheerleading camp. It's the last day. School starts on Tuesday. It starts early this year because of stupid Labor Day falling on the first. Can I ever get a break?

Anyway, watch out for Cutie-Pie.
Love,
Katherine

Saturday, August 30
Dear Diary:
I'm a woman now. I did it! I did it with John.

Oh my God. I was so scared. He brought a backpack with a picnic lunch. Of course that came with a large soft blanket. When I saw the blanket, I wondered, and I got really scared. We had a nice lunch. I barely said a word. Then he carefully packed up, put everything (except the blanket) over by the rocks, and laid down propping himself up with one hand on his head. I did the same and then he kissed me. . . for a long time. When he moved to take my shirt off, I sat up and told him I was scared. He had thought that because I was on the pill I wasn't a virgin. When he found out, he became very understanding and gentle. How wonderful he was.

He took my clothing off slowly. I was sort of embarrassed. I tried to cover myself and he delicately moved my hands away. I think I was blushing from head to toe. Then he undressed and I was even more embarrassed. I wanted to look, but I kept turning away, giggling. He thought that was sweet.

Then he laid me down, gently separated my legs, and, well. . . right here on my special beach, we made love.

It was nicer than I had imagined. See I've, you know, played with myself sometimes, so I sort of thought I knew what to expect. But it was way more pleasurable than that. . . the feel of him, the smell of him. It was amazing.

This beach will never be the same again.

Love,

Katherine

Beth slammed the diary closed, threw it on the bed, and began to pace the room. Stopping abruptly, she put her head in her hands.

The Hollywood-style depiction of young love as being gentle and pleasurable infuriated her. It did not happen that way for everyone. Memories wriggled out of their hiding places like maggots on a dead mouse. All of a sudden, Beth despised Katherine and wished she'd never set foot on the beach. As if aware of her anguish, the firefly appeared, floating outside of the window.

"Get out of here," Beth screamed. "I don't want to talk to you tonight!" It was as if the wounded animal inside of her had awoken, with one final breath, to face its foe.

The firefly shimmered and then drifted away.

Beth continued to pace. She thought about how Katherine had pushed her father out of her life. "If only my dad had been there for me," she whispered in resentment. He would have protected her honor, offered her guidance, or at the very least made her less susceptible to the admiration fatherless girls often felt for older men.

His name was Larry. He was almost thirty and

Beth was eighteen. She met him the summer she graduated from high school. He was a bartender where she worked, a real charmer. All of the waitresses had a crush on him. *Flock of Seagulls* hair, tan skin, and a smile that would melt a witch's heart; he was hard to resist.

Larry took an interest in Beth shortly after she began to work at the restaurant. She had indulged in dozens of crushes over the years, but she never had a boyfriend, so the attention was especially alluring. One evening he offered to drive her home after work. Instead they ended up at his place.

They sat on the couch for a while before he made his move. He was rough and unpleasant. His kisses were harsh and he tasted like cigarettes. Beth squirmed. Her resistance seemed to turn him on. She wanted to leave, but she didn't want him to be mad, so she stayed. He pulled her off the couch and led her to the bedroom. She looked back at the door, but he held her arm and coaxed her to follow him, all the while leering at her breasts. Before she knew it, she was in his bedroom, her clothing scattered around the bed.

She closed her eyes and turned her face away from him as he climbed on top of her. His breath smelled; his face was coarse. She wanted to be anywhere else except there, but she wanted him to like her. Pinned and suffocating, she was not at all aroused, so it was very painful. It seemed to drag on forever, and she kept praying it would end. When he finally dismounted, she rolled over and cried quietly.

And that was how Beth lost her virginity.

She saw Larry several more times in the weeks

that followed. The sex was unpleasant every time, but she made herself available anyway. She enjoyed the feeling of being wanted, and she knew he would discard her if she didn't put out.

One evening, when they were lying in his bed shortly after having sex, she looked up and saw Larry's roommate smirking at her, as if he were waiting for his turn. Larry and the roommate exchanged a look that frightened Beth. Larry got up and made his way to exit the room.

"I have to go to the bathroom," Beth announced quickly, her heart pounding.

Larry gestured toward the bathroom door. Beth stared defiantly at the roommate until he turned around long enough for her to pull on her shirt and shorts minus underwear and bra. She thought she saw him peeking over his shoulder, but she focused on dressing as quickly as possible.

Beth locked the bathroom door and struggled with the window. It was a short drop from the first floor apartment to the bushes below. Beth climbed down, scrambled out of the bushes, and ran as fast as she could to the bus stop. She had a few dollars stashed in her back pocket, but she had left her purse behind. Beth watched nervously, looking up the road for the bus and back toward the street where Larry lived. She decided not to wait. She ran for half a mile and hid out at another bus stop. Thankfully, the bus came within five minutes. She boarded the bus, exhausted and relieved.

Beth never returned to the restaurant, not even to collect her last paycheck. Just before she left for Albuquerque, a check for $34.15 came in the mail.

She tore it up on the spot.

The older Beth stared out the window and watched the light creature drift away. She seethed with hatred. The memories continued to surface and she stuffed them down one by one until they were silenced. She slammed her hand flat against the wall two times. Then she raced down the stairs, retreated to the kitchen, and poured herself a drink.

* * * *

During the weekend, Beth avoided both the diary and the painting of the red-haired girl. She took walks, sketched a lighthouse ten miles up the coast, and began to paint the islands visible from her backyard. She stayed very busy, keeping her mind as occupied as possible. At night she had a drink or took a sleeping pill, trying to numb herself to sleep.

On Sunday night she endured a terrible dream. In this dream she flew along a tree-lined road in the late afternoon. The sun was setting. She soared, seeming to turn along with the curves of the road under no power of her own. She heard a car approaching in the distance. She tried to turn off the road, but she had no control over her body. The car continued to close the gap between them, its tires screeching on the curves. It began to grow dark and Beth longed to stop flying and rest. Suddenly, the car came around the corner going eighty miles an hour. Its headlights blinded her right before impact.

Beth jolted up in bed early Monday morning, sweating from the dream. She took another sleeping pill and went back to sleep.

* * * *

At 10:21 a.m. the incessant ringing of her cell phone awoke her. Her head pounded, but she dragged herself out of bed and grabbed the phone off the dresser.

"Hello?" she said. Her scratchy voice was barely audible.

"Is this Beth LaMonte?"

"Yes, who's calling?"

"Dr. Peter Stephens from Seattle."

All at once, Beth grew alert. She fumbled for a tablet and a pen. "Dr. Stephens. Thank you for returning my call."

"What can I do for you?" he asked pleasantly.

"Uh. . ." Beth took a moment to jog her brain and organize her thoughts. "I'm looking for Sarah Wylder. I believe she was a student of yours in the late seventies."

There was a brief pause on the other end. "Ah, yes, Serious Sarah." The gentleman chuckled warmly. "She hated it when I called her that. I was her advisor. Good old Sarah, a brilliant young lady."

Beth's heart quickened and her face flushed. Finally a phone call that amounted to something, a true lead. "Oh, Dr. Stephens, that is wonderful news. Do you happen to know how I would get a hold of her now?"

"I'm afraid we didn't stay in touch. When she started medical school, she hardly had time to phone her mother, I would imagine."

"Medical school?"

"Yes. She went to Ohio State in Columbus. I

suppose if she's practicing you could find her in the American Medical Association listings."

That idea had already raced through Beth's mind. In fact, she realized that had she simply Googled Sarah's name to begin with, it would probably have shown up on a website. Beth wanted to kick herself for not thinking of it. She pulled up Google and typed in *Sarah Wylder*. The charming professor prattled on about Sarah – how diligent she was, and that in spite of being a very serious young lady, she had a soft side that emerged now and again.

With one click of the mouse, Beth located a website for the Cleveland Women's Care Facility. And on staff, Dr. Sarah G. Wylder, a gynecologist.

"I found her," Beth exclaimed. "Thank you so very much, professor."

"You found her already? Oh, you kids and your computers. I hate to think what you'd find if you looked me up."

Beth grinned. "Would you like me to?" She started typing.

"No, no," Dr. Stephens protested. "I think I'd rather not know."

"I bet it's all good," Beth teased.

"That's all right. I'm glad I could be of service. Where is Sarah, by the way? Perhaps I should drop her a line and see if she remembers an old friend."

"She's in Cleveland." Beth read the phone number to the professor. Then they exchanged goodbyes.

As soon as Beth hung up, she dialed the number.

"Cleveland Women's Care, how may I help you?"

Beth was almost giddy. She had to slow her speech. "I'd like to speak with Dr. Wylder please."

"Are you a physician?"

"Oh, no," Beth explained. "It's a personal matter."

"Your name?"

"Beth LaMonte."

"Hold please."

Beth waited for several minutes before the young woman came on the line again. "I'm sorry, Dr. Wylder is with a patient at the moment. Can I take a message?"

Beth paused. Just how much information should she give? If Sarah and Katherine were on seriously bad terms, she may not be interested in talking with Beth. Beth didn't want to lose the opportunity, so she kept it brief. "This is Beth LaMonte from Virginia Point, Maine. I . . . uh. . . Please just give her my number."

The receptionist took down Beth's number. "She'll call you as soon as she's available," the young woman promised.

Beth hung up wondering how long that would be. She glanced at the bottom dresser drawer. The diary summoned her again. With all the exciting new developments in her quest, she could hardly be expected to refuse the enticement. She seemed to have forgotten how painful the last reading had been. Curiosity overcame her reservations. She retrieved the diary, went downstairs to make herself a snack, and then settled on the couch to read. She placed her cell phone on the coffee table along with a tablet and a pen in case Sarah returned her call.

Friday, September 5
Dear Diary:

It has been a busy week. School started. Sarah has been weird. I don't know if she can tell, but I don't feel comfortable sharing it with her. I guess I am kind of walking around like a woman with a secret – an amazing, beautiful secret. All these girls at school, they seem like children to me now.

I am going to try to get together with John this weekend. It is a lot harder now that school has started. It is even worse than when Dad was looking over our shoulders. On the other hand, maybe I could skip. . . No, Sarah would notice, and the school might call Dad. I'd better play it safe. If he finds out, he'll send John away. I could not bear that.

Love,
Katherine

Friday, September 12
Dear D:

Sorry. It has been hard to get time to write. I saw John on Sunday. Dad was sailing, so we took another trip to Acadia. John drove Dad's car. Not with permission, of course, but Dad doesn't give me any freedom, so sometimes I just have to take without asking.

John pulled off to the side of the road along the way and we did it in the back of the car. It was even better. It got kind of steamy in the car. We were sweating on Dad's leather seats. Serves him right.

Anyway, I am totally in love. If Dad sends John away now, I'll follow him. I'll go around the world just to be with him. He was made for me in heaven. I really believe that. Because nothing short of divine could feel this good.

L,

K

Sunday, September 14

Did I mention that I am in love? John loves me too. I'm sure of it.

We did it again on the beach yesterday. I'm surprised we were able to sneak down here. I gave Dad another "I'm going to Sarah's" excuse.

Oh, the things this beach has seen. I can't stop smiling. Dad noticed. I told him there was a cute boy sitting next to me in my English class. Since he has not seen me hanging out by the garage, I think he buys it. You know, flaky teenager, a new crush every week. He does not realize how grown up I am. He can't accept it, me growing up. It would destroy him, I think. But that is not my problem. If I have to choose, I'll choose John over Dad, so he had better not pull rank on me. He'll be sorry if he does.

Katherine

Friday, September 19

Dear Diary:

I haven't seen John all week. He said he would be gone over the weekend visiting his sister in New Jersey. I guess it is his nephew's birthday. I wish I could go. I would love to meet his family. Unfortunately MY family would disapprove.

I miss him!
Love,
Katherine

Sunday, September 21
It has been a lonely weekend. I can't bear another weekend like this. I miss him. How did I ever live without him? That seems like a lifetime ago, way far away when I was a little child collecting seashells. Now I have much more grown up things to do on the beach.

The pills have screwed up my period. It should have come during the week I took the green ones. But I started a new packet on Tuesday, almost a week ago. So it seems that now my period is suppressed altogether. I know that I followed the directions correctly, and I didn't miss any pills.

I don't want to have to go back to that dreadful doctor. This is a real pain in the ass.

Bye for now.
Katherine

Friday, September 26
Dear D:
I snuck out of class on Wednesday, and I went to John's place. I couldn't bear any more days apart. We made love in his bed. You wouldn't believe how good his bed smells. I thought I was going to die of happiness. It was

a soft bed, too. Softer than the beach. Ha ha.

Hopefully we can get together again this weekend.

    L,

    K

Sunday, September 28

I couldn't get a hold of John on Saturday. I don't know if he went out of town again. He would have told me, wouldn't he?

Sarah and I got together in the afternoon. I finally had to tell her. The truth is, I wanted to ask her about the birth control pills. She knows about these things.

She was kind of bitchy about it. She sighed at me. Apparently, she is still a virgin, so she has nothing to be self-righteous about. But she was glad I was smart enough to take the pill. She actually said that: "smart enough." I could have slugged her. Anyway, she said that the pill is supposed to make my period very regular, so she didn't know what was wrong. She said that I should go back to that doctor. I don't want to go. I really, really don't want to go.

    L,

    K

Friday, October 3

My period still has not started. I am on week three of my second pack. Something is wrong. I couldn't possibly be pregnant because I've been taking them faithfully, the same time every night. However, I can't let the pills end my period. I won't stop taking them either. I can't exactly ask John to wear a condom now. That wouldn't be fair.

I've made a doctor appointment for Tuesday. Sarah and I are going to ditch class and she'll take me. I'll let you know how it goes.

    L,

    K

Beth's stomach turned over in circles and she felt like she was going to be sick. It may as well have been the summer of 1990 when she noticed her own period had been absent for weeks. In the wake of her repulsive relationship with Larry, she found herself alone, with a terrible secret. She set the diary aside and tried to suppress her thoughts. But there was no holding them back. Beth and her painful memories stood face to face. The afternoon she went to the doctor. The shock. The anger. The self-hatred. And the morning she took the bus to downtown Minneapolis, unbeknownst to her mother. A day that irrevocably changed her life.

She didn't need those all-too-familiar, disparaging voices to interrogate her now. It was what needed to be done at the time. She knew it, but that did not make it easy, nor did it fill the hole that had taken residence within her ever since that day. She never told anyone, not Bill, not even her mother. Would her mother have given her different advice? Would her life have been better. . . or worse, had she made a different decision? It was pointless to ask such questions. But after twenty-two years, she wondered why the aching never went away. It was not fair what had happened to her. Was it? As much as she wanted to blame some force outside of herself, she knew that it was her own weak self-esteem that had put her in that dreadful position in the first place – forced to choose between one nightmare or the other. And with such admonitions, the voices plagued her until she shut them up and pushed them away.

She grabbed her cell phone and called Sarah Wylder's office again.

"Cleveland Women's Care, how may I help you?"

"Hi. . . uh. . . this is Beth LaMonte again."

"Hello, Ms. LaMonte."

"Yes, hello. I'm sorry to bother you, but I was wondering, is Dr. Wylder available yet?"

"She got called over to the hospital. One of her patients went into labor."

"Labor, right. Okay. So when will she be back?"

The young lady laughed. "That is entirely up to the baby."

Discouraged, Beth did not appreciate the joke.

"I'll give her your message, Ms. LaMonte."

"Thank you."

Beth put her head in her hand and sighed. She set the cell phone on the coffee table and stared at it for several minutes before picking up the diary. On its pages, she read the words she already knew were written.

Tuesday, October 7
Dear Diary:
I'm pregnant.

Only Sarah knows. And now you. Please don't let Dad find out.

I'm scared, and I'm angry.

I guess I was supposed to take the pills for a month and use extra "precaution" until I started my second pack, preferably my third. I asked the doctor why he conveniently left that part out of our little talk. He became rather belligerent and said that he told me, but I just wasn't listening. I KNOW I was listening. He DIDN'T say that. I told Sarah he barely said two words to me, that he spent more time sticking his hands all over where they don't belong than talking to me.

She said, "That's why men shouldn't be gynecologists."

It's too late for that piece of wisdom.

I have to talk to John. I have to get him alone. But I can't be too weird or Dad will know something is up. But he'll know eventually. . .

Oh my God.

John, I need you!

L,

K

Thursday, October 9

Diary:

Everything is falling apart.

I was finally able to catch John alone. I knew Dad was going on an errand-run, so I skipped school.

God help me I'm going to die this minute!

John was mad at me. He actually yelled at me. He's never yelled at me. He called me stupid. I'm so ashamed. He said he thought I knew what I was doing and that it served him right for fucking a stupid child.

I'm not a stupid child. It wasn't my fault. The doctor. Oh my God. What am I going to do?

Katherine

Friday, October 10
Dear D:
Sarah says I should get an abortion and get on with my life. I don't know what to do. I guess she's right.

I'm scared.
L,
K

Monday, October 13
My life is over.

John's gone. Dad says he wasn't at the garage on Friday, and that he didn't come in today. I tried not to show any expression. He left because of me.

Mom died thirteen years ago. Thirteen years on the thirteenth. I hardly remember her. Dad assumed I was sullen all day because of Mom's death. We went to her grave. But I was numb inside. I might as well have been lying in the grave right next to her, in the barren plot of land Dad purchased thirteen years ago. My final resting place. . . my *destiny.*

I've lost everything on the thirteenth. Everything.

I wish I was dead.

No. I wish I was never born.

Beth turned the page. It was blank. Then she flipped through the book. There was nothing else written. The last words hung in the air as if a large, harsh bell had been rung, and its discordant sound lingered. "I wish I was dead. No. I wish I was never born."

Beth held the diary to her chest, her eyes watering.

"Oh, Katherine, what did you do?" Beth looked toward the clearing, the place where she first saw the firefly. Even though it was mid-morning, her mind conjured up the image of the graceful creature, glowing in the dark of night. Beth did not want to believe that Katherine was dead or, even worse, that she might have killed herself. Katherine's paternal grandfather had committed suicide, so there was a family history. *Furthermore,* Beth thought. *Rod Thompson isn't exactly a shining example of mental health.*

She looked down at her cell phone and had to hold back the overwhelming urge to call Sarah Wylder a third time. Instead, she grabbed the phone and walked to the secret beach. She spent the entire day on the beach. She didn't eat or work. She just sat, sorting through her memories of that unpleasant summer, wondering about the fate of Katherine, and making peace with the choices she herself had made. Beth considered the naïveté of her youth and found a way to forgive herself for wanting to be loved by a man more than she wanted to take care of herself.

In the late afternoon, she slowly climbed the cliff. She was hungry. She looked at the time. 4:47 p.m. Sarah Wylder had not returned her call.

"Damn." She hit redial on her phone and listened to it ring. The Beth-on-a-mission emerged after a day of self-reflection.

"Cleveland Women's Care."

Beth took a deep breath and tried to remain calm. "Is Dr. Wylder in, please?"

"Who's calling?"

Beth bit her lip and paused for a moment. "This is Beth LaMonte."

The friendly voice on the other end of the line turned sour. "Ms. LaMonte, I have given Dr. Wylder your message. She will call you when she's available. Typically she catches up on her phone calls at the end of the work day, so she'll probably call you this evening."

"Thank you," Beth said in defeat. She had become a liability to her own quest.

* * * *

Beth tried to go to bed early. She could not sleep. She got up at 11:00 p.m. to take a sleeping pill, and she saw the firefly hovering in the clearing. She pulled on some clothing, grabbed a jacket, and walked out to meet it. She marched up to the light creature, saying not a word. She stared at it for a long time. Then she wandered toward the cliff and sat down about six feet away from the edge. The firefly drifted behind her.

"I don't know what you are. I don't know what I can give you," Beth said finally. She gazed up at the sky. There was no moon and a million stars seemed to overwhelm the darkness. She shook her head in dismay. "Why do you haunt me and dredge up all of this stuff? I don't need this in my life right now." She put her head in one hand. Then she sat upright and hollered at the light creature. "And just for the record. . . *I* didn't commit suicide. I had the courage to face the consequences of my actions and the difficulty of my choices."

Beth picked up a rock and rolled it around in her hand.

The firefly began to drift away north, slowly, toward the secret beach. It slipped into the trees and disappeared.

"Yeah, you run now," Beth shouted after it. "You run and hide. Leave me here to sort through the Pandora's box you've opened." Beth stood up. She threw the rock as far as she could, not a decent throw. It bounced off the rocks and tumbled helplessly down the side of the cliff before reaching the water.

* * * *

The flying dream interrupted Beth's sleep almost hourly. With each pass of the dream, the car seemed to be moving faster, but its headlights grew dimmer. Just before she awoke for the day on Tuesday morning, the headlights were dim enough that she could make out the image of her father at the wheel. He looked terrified.

Beth jumped out of bed and ran from it as if it were filled with snakes. She screamed in anger, a growl that started low and crescendoed into a piercing cry of desperation.

Chapter 19
Quest

Sarah Wylder sat in her office on Tuesday morning sorting through charts and paperwork before her scheduled appointments began. The waiting room was already filled with women and shrieking toddlers. Dr. Wylder tried to concentrate. She looked at her watch.

Her receptionist buzzed.

"Yes?" Sarah responded wearily. She was tired before the day had even begun. How did she let her life get this hectic and out of control?

"Dr. Wylder, I've got that Beth LaMonte on the phone again. She insists she talk to you. She called a jillion times yesterday. It is about Virginia Point, Maine. I don't even know where that is." Her receptionist had a tendency to ramble and throw in unnecessary details. It was annoying, but her talents outweighed her quirks. "Anyway, now she wants to hold. Can you believe it? She says she wants to hold until you are ready to talk to her. I told her, 'We can't keep a line tied up that long.' Doctor, I know you're busy, but this woman won't leave me alone until you speak with her. Could you please take the call? I'll owe you a batch of chocolate chip cookies."

A tired smile briefly crossed Sarah's face. Then she took a deep breath, puffed up her cheeks, and let it out slowly. Finally, she said, "I'll take it, Rachel. Line one?"

"Yes. Thank you, thank you, doctor."

Virginia Point, Maine. Sarah had not gone back since she packed up the Chevy and drove to Seattle thirty-six years ago. Her parents had moved to California, her brother to New York. She had visited New York and Los Angeles dozens of times, but she never felt the desire to visit Virginia Point, Maine. Everything she had there was gone. It was a provincial childhood. When she left, she was ready to leave her hometown behind. Who could possibly be looking for her from Virginia Point?

She picked up the receiver. "Hello. This is Dr. Wylder."

* * * *

"Dr. Wylder!" Beth exclaimed. "Thank you for taking my call." She was so excited she found herself shaking. A night of interrupted sleep and disturbing dreams did not put her at her best.

"How may I help you?"

Slow down, take your time, Beth said to herself. "My name is Beth LaMonte. I live in Virginia Point, and I'm looking for someone you may have known when you were in high school. Katherine Thompson."

A long silence ensued before Dr. Wylder responded. "Yes, I knew Katherine Thompson."

189

Beth's stomach turned upside down. She bit her lip, trying to choose her words carefully, but everything came out jumbled. "Do you happen to know how she ended up? I mean, what happened to her? Where she is?"

"Katherine was a mess. She could have *ended up* any number of different places."

Beth did not know what to make of that response. "Uh—"

"Listen, I have no idea what became of Katherine Thompson. She got pregnant. She dropped out of high school. . . are you writing this down? Because the list of Katherine's screw ups goes on and on."

Beth was shocked by the woman's callous tone. "She was your friend, wasn't she? Don't you care what happened to her?"

"She was a cheerleader and I was a feminist. I mean, how far is that relationship supposed to go? We were friends as children, but we grew apart. She only came to me when she needed something, and she *always* needed something." Sarah's voice was harsh and intimidating. "She was a disaster. I wanted more out of life."

Beth frowned. "You don't know anything about what happened to her?"

Dr. Wylder groaned and remained quiet for a moment. "I don't know what else I can tell you. She started seeing a jerk who worked for her father. I warned her to take precautions, but she got pregnant. I told her she should get an abortion and move on with her life. And that was that."

That was that? Hardly. That is not such a casual decision to make. Beth stifled her urge to tell the doctor a thing or two. First, it would be counterproductive in her effort to get information on Katherine. Second, she never approached the topic with anyone.

"Anyway, she called me a month later—"

Beth sat up straight and interrupted. "A month later? She called you a month later? Are you certain?"

"Yes. She said that she was 'moving on with her life.' I figured that was her way of telling me that she had had an abortion, and that she was leaving Virginia Point and her troubled past behind her. I told her I was happy to hear things were working out."

"Did she tell you where she was?"

Sarah sighed. "She told me she was working for a dentist, a Dr. Bennett or Barrette or something in Bangor. She wanted me to know in case her father came asking about her."

"Did he?"

"No, he did not. And then I graduated and moved on with *my* life."

Beth tapped her pencil on the tablet. "Do you think Katherine was suicidal?"

"She was awfully depressed the last time I saw her. I mean, I'm assuming you never actually met her. This was an emotional roller coaster of a girl. She could have been suicidal one minute, and she could have been flying on a kite the next. But the last time I *spoke* with her, when she was in Bangor, she sounded fine."

Beth felt relief wash over her. Maybe she was wrong about Katherine. Maybe she didn't kill herself. And then it was all a matter of finding her and bringing her home to mend the conflict with her father. Beth could offer Katherine some personal *I've-been-there* understanding about what happened and help Katherine heal. She chided herself. Such a fairy tale was a bit far-fetched to hang her hopes on.

"One more thing," Beth said hastily.

"Yes?"

"Did Katherine have anything to do with your career decision?"

Silence.

"I'll be sure and tell her *thank you* on your behalf when I find her."

Sarah cleared her throat. "Is that all, Ms. LaMonte?"

"Yes," Beth said faintly, a little sheepish for her smart-alecky comment. "I appreciate your time."

"It's been a pleasure," Sarah responded dryly.

They hung up and Beth stared absentmindedly at the pencil holder on her desk. Katherine hung over her head like a hammer on an anvil. "Can't I let this go and move on with my life?" She sat for several minutes contemplating the answer to that question. Then she shook her mouse and her computer screen flickered and lit up.

Chapter 20
Bangor

Beth spent an hour on the Internet looking for a dentist named Bennett or Barrette. She had no luck. She checked the surrounding area as well. Still no luck. "Maybe he's retired," she mumbled. So she started calling dentist offices one by one. On the eighth phone call, she got a bite.

The receptionist at Dr. Fox's office said, "Well, Doctor *Benning* worked here. He's been retired for four years."

Benning, Bennett. This could be it, Beth thought. "Oh, Benning. Of course, I'm sorry. My memory fails me sometimes. I don't suppose you could give me his address. We've been out of touch for a while. I wanted to send him some photos of my grandchildren." Beth cringed privately. *Grandchildren?* Now that was a good one.

"Sure," the receptionist replied helpfully. "Just a moment."

She's lucky that I'm not an old, scorned girlfriend, Beth thought, snickering.

The receptionist came back on the line and gave

the address to Beth.

"Thank you so much, young lady," Beth replied, laying it on thick.

"You're welcome. Have a nice day."

Beth hung up. "I'm going to have a *great* day."

Fed up with the telephone, Beth decided she would attempt to visit the retired dentist in person. Bangor was a little over two hours away. She could make it a pleasant day trip and get away from Virginia Point and the cottage for a while. So she showered, dressed, ate a quick snack, and headed out – driving directions in one hand, purse in the other. She figured she would get into town before 1:30.

She arrived at Dr. Benning's house at 1:17. Built around 1920, the two-story, white house was well shaded by a pair of oak trees in the front, and a large spruce in the back. Forest green awnings accented all of the windows visible from the road. Wild blueberry bushes ran along the right side of the house and roses bloomed near the steps leading to the front door. A two-person bench and a small glass table occupied the left side of the front porch, while a large potted plant sat on the right.

Beth took a deep breath and rehearsed what she would say. Then she walked slowly, but confidently, to the door. A pleasant gentleman in his seventies answered, dressed in gardening clothes. His slightly tousled hair gave him an air of warmth. Beth felt immediately at ease in his presence.

"Forgive my attire," he said. "I've been weeding the strawberries. What can I do for you?"

"Hello, my name is Beth LaMonte. Are you Dr. Benning?"

"That would be me. Come on in, young lady."

Beth smiled. She enjoyed being called *young lady* every once in a while. She followed the gentleman into a sitting room overlooking the backyard. Several gardens filled with strawberries, vegetables, and clusters of bushes were visible from the floor-to-ceiling trio of windows. A gray-green couch sat against one wall and two reupholstered, antique chairs framed the windows. The curtains were pulled aside with tiny tasseled ropes, while a large gray-green silk cloth was dramatically draped over the curtain rods. A cherry wood coffee table, littered with books and magazines, sat halfway between the small fireplace and the couch. As Beth entered the room, a sleek, orange cat peered out from under one of the chairs, cautiously observing the new arrival.

Dr. Benning gestured toward the couch. "Have a seat." He sat in the chair closest to Beth. "Now what can I do for you today?"

"I'm from Virginia Point. I'm trying to locate a woman who used to live there. I have a few of her possessions I would like to return. Her name is Katherine Thompson. Do you know her?"

Dr. Benning sighed softly. "Ah, Katherine. She used to work for me. I guess it was decades ago. She was a lovely girl." Dr. Benning looked out the window as if, momentarily, he was no longer present.

"Does she still live in Bangor?" Beth asked hopefully.

"I'm afraid I don't know where she is. One day she disappeared. Never even called in to quit, never said goodbye. . . very unusual. We have not seen her since."

Beth's shoulders slumped. "About how long did she work for you, do you remember?" she asked, hoping that Katherine had given herself time to become stable and healthy before moving on.

"At least two years. The baby was a year and a—"

"Baby?"

"Susie, her daughter."

Beth reeled as a flood of emotions she could not sort out washed over her. *She had the baby.*

Dr. Benning continued, "She must have been pregnant before she took the job. I didn't know. She started to show sometime between Christmas and New Year's, and she tried to hide it. Honestly, I was as dense as a doorknob. She pulled it off on me, but my wife waltzed in one day to take me to lunch and blurted out, 'Katherine, when are you due?' You should have seen the look on Katherine's face. Oh the poor little thing, she turned as white as a sheet. Linda, my wife, has a way of not beating around the bush."

Beth smiled, enjoying a sense of warmth and tranquility she had not felt for days. It was as if Katherine had become a part of her, and Katherine, in all of her passion and chaos, challenged the reclusive, detached person that Beth had become. Katherine and her adventures made Beth feel alive on some level which had been extinguished since she was nineteen.

"Linda took Katherine under her wing and helped her get prepared for the baby's arrival. We're Susan's godparents," he said with a warm smile. "But we haven't seen Susie since she was one and a half," he added sadly. "Katherine was very secretive about her past. I hired her on an impulse one afternoon. She struck me as intelligent and honest, and I was short-staffed. I never asked her where she was from, so I didn't know where to go looking for her when she left. It broke Linda's heart, not to get to say goodbye to Susie."

Beth sorted through her emotions, trying to take in the details of Dr. Benning's story. As she gazed absentmindedly at the bird bath in the backyard, a dignified woman in her late sixties appeared in the hallway. Her smooth, shiny, silver hair hung about her shoulders. She wore a brown sweater and tan pants, and she walked gracefully on her long legs. Everything about her appearance smelled of old money, yet an air of acceptance and warmth radiated from her person. She was carrying a bag of groceries, humming softly.

"Hello, Wyatt. Who is your guest?" Without waiting for an answer the woman set down her groceries and marched gregariously toward Beth with an outstretched hand. "I'm Linda Benning."

Beth stood up, stepped forward, and shook the woman's hand. "Beth LaMonte."

"Beth is looking for information about Katherine," Wyatt Benning informed his wife.

Linda gasped, dropped the *how-do-you-do* face, and exclaimed, "You've found Susan!"

"No, I'm sorry, ma'am. I'm afraid I didn't even know about Susan. I have some of Katherine's possessions. . . I mean I live in her old house. . . I, ah. . . I'm trying to find her." Stumbling over her scattered assortment of half-truths, Beth felt uncomfortable, inauthentic.

"Her old house? Where?"

"It's in Virginia Point, but I—"

"Does anyone in Virginia Point know where they are?" Linda demanded. Then she took a deep breath. "No, of course not, I'm sorry. Otherwise you wouldn't be here. Give a woman with a broken heart a bit of leeway, if you could, Beth."

"No problem, Mrs. Benning. I'm sorry if I raised false hopes for you."

"Please call me Linda," she said. "Anyway, it's not your fault. After all these years, I still drop my britches at the mention of their names." She laughed sadly and her eyes drifted away. "I just wish I could have said goodbye." Linda crossed the room and sat in the other antique chair. The orange cat jumped immediately into her lap. She stroked him as he turned in circles, trying to rub her chin.

Beth bit her lip and looked at her feet. Then she sat down again, still looking at the floor. Eventually she looked up and posed another question. "Could you tell me a little about the days leading up to her disappearance? Was she depressed?" She cringed slightly, hoping the last question would not open unhealed wounds.

"Oh, dear, I wish I could tell you," Linda said. "I was in New Haven for several months. My mother had a stroke in the fall of seventy-seven. She needed constant care." Linda pursed her lips to one side and shook her head. "She never recovered. She died mid-February the following year."

"I'm sorry to hear that."

"It was a very difficult year." She looked up at the ceiling as if trying to recall a series of events. "I tried to call Katherine a couple of days after Wyatt said she had disappeared. She lived as a boarder with a dreadful woman named Eleanor Sharpe. I called every day for weeks. Once I thought that someone answered the phone and then hung up. Wyatt tried to visit several times. The house was always dark.

"On the day I got back I ran over to that house. I saw someone slip from the front room into the kitchen, so I continued to knock and ring the bell until she finally answered the door. It was Eleanor. She said that Katherine and Susie had disappeared in November. One day they were there, the next day they were gone.

"I asked her if they had moved out, you know, taken their belongings. She acted kind of weird about that question. She stammered for a moment. Then she said that they had taken some things and left others behind. Eleanor gave the abandoned items to the Salvation Army because she needed to rent the room, she said. I suppose it made sense, but the woman gave me the willies. I always wondered if she got into an argument with Katherine, or threw her out because she had a baby. No one knew she was pregnant when she moved to Bangor. But wouldn't Katherine have come to Wyatt or me?"

"I would imagine so," Beth said. The details disturbed her. It seemed very likely that Katherine *would have* come to the adults she trusted the most. Why didn't she? It was not a pleasant question to consider. Beth looked up and noticed that Linda Benning wore the same expression of unease.

"Could you give me Eleanor's address? Is she still around?"

"I believe she still lives in that same house, yes. She'd be about eighty by now," Linda pondered. "I don't think it will do you much good to talk to that woman, but I shouldn't let my cynicism damper your quest. Maybe you're the angel I've been waiting for all these years," she said sadly. Linda left the room briefly and returned carrying a small note card with Eleanor's address. "Oh, and please take my card as well." She fumbled in her pocket, searching for a business card. "Wyatt and I make floral arrangements now."

Wyatt stood up. "I couldn't bear the thought of a complete retirement. What would I do all day? Watch the grass grow?"

"I promise I'll call you if. . . no, *when* I find them."

Linda smiled at Beth. It was a smile weighted by a look that said *I've already exhausted the possibilities.*

"We look forward to hearing from you, Beth," Wyatt said, casting a stern glance in Linda's direction.

"You will," Beth assured him.

* * * *

Eleanor Sharpe's Tudor stood at the end of a long drive, about two miles from the surrounding neighborhood houses. It was a striking, well maintained home, mostly brick. Chocolate brown strips of wood accented its white gables. A large brick chimney to the left of the arched doorway dominated the front, and a forty-five foot red maple shaded the right half of the house. Its leaves rustled softly as Beth walked up the path and rang the bell.

A young woman answered the door. She looked

tired and disgruntled. She sighed. "May I help you?"

"Is Eleanor Sharpe home?"

"She really doesn't want visitors right now."

Beth inspected the young woman. Her brown hair was unkempt but clean. She wore thin, white cotton pants, and a blue striped cotton shirt. She stood with one hand on her hip. Reading the body language, Beth surmised that the young miss was the person who would not welcome visitors.

Beth stepped forward slightly and spoke loudly, glancing up the stairs to the right of the entryway. "But I've come all this way just to see her," Beth said, hoping her voice resonated throughout the house.

"Who's there, dear?" an elderly voice called from somewhere upstairs.

The young woman glared at Beth. "Who exactly *are* you?"

"I'm Beth LaMonte from. . ." Beth paused for a moment. Eleanor Sharpe had avoided the Bennings decades ago when they came looking for Katherine and Susie Thompson. It was not likely that a full disclosure of Beth's true mission would gain her entrance into the home. She rattled her brain for a plausible fib. She had told so many in the previous two weeks; they ought to have come naturally. Finally she said, "I'm a friend of her grandson." Keeping her fingers crossed that Mrs. Sharpe actually had a grandson, Beth clenched her jaw and waited.

"Send her up, dear. Send her up," an enthusiastic voice rang from upstairs.

The woman in cotton rolled her eyes, stepped aside, and made an overtly sarcastic gesture swishing her arm from the door toward the stairs. "Come right on in," she said, making no attempt to conceal the disdain in her voice.

She led Beth upstairs to the first door on the right.

Excessive floral prints overwhelmed the bedroom. Lavish dark wallpaper covered with roses made the room feel small and somewhat oppressive. Lilacs adorned the bedspread and matching window coverings. The thick curtains remained partially closed, giving the area a gloomy atmosphere. A long, white, antique dresser with curvy legs sat by the wall next to the closet. It would have been beautiful, except that the paint was chipped and an assortment of scarves, brooches, and lotion bottles cluttered its surface. With a little daylight and a tad less flash, the room might have been considered cozy.

Mrs. Sharpe looked pale and weak. She sat propped up in bed with a book in her lap. A glass of water and a half dozen medicine bottles lingered on the bedside table. The elderly woman's body was frail, but her eyes were full of life. She eagerly awaited the arrival of her unexpected guest.

"Don't you mind Rebecca. She's a bit of a grouch to strangers, but she's the best nurse I've ever had."

Rebecca gave Eleanor Sharpe a look normally reserved for a parent to a mischievous child.

"Are you Tom's girlfriend?" Eleanor asked, her raspy voice filled with anticipation.

Beth looked back at Rebecca. "Would you excuse us for a moment, Miss Rebecca?" she said in a saccharine tone.

"Why certainly," Rebecca said, an artificial grin adorning her face. She exited and swiftly closed the door behind her.

"So, how is Tom?"

Beth took a deep breath. How long would it take Rebecca to throw her out? She listened, as Rebecca's footsteps grew fainter. Then she admitted, "I'm not Tom's girlfriend."

"Well, then who. . . oh my, is he in trouble?"

"I'm sorry, Mrs. Sharpe. I don't even know Tom. I'm here because I'm trying to locate Katherine Thompson. She was your tenant in the late seventies."

Eleanor's smile faded. Beth looked away, bracing herself for an outburst of anger and an immediate summons to Rebecca. But there was only silence. Beth looked up. The old woman's face seemed to have aged five years in the matter of a moment.

"Sit down," she said in a low growl.

Beth grabbed a wooden, high back chair with a red floral upholstered seat from the corner of the room. She sat down a few feet away from Eleanor's bed.

"So who are you looking for? Katherine or Susie?"

The question caught Beth off guard. "Both, I guess. Initially, I came looking for Katherine. I didn't know she had a daughter."

"If you are looking for Katherine I cannot help you. That irresponsible young woman disappeared one day, leaving her eighteen-month-old daughter behind."

Beth's jaw dropped. "She left her behind?"

"Yes," the old woman barked. "She left her *here* with me, a forty-six-year-old divorcee, trying to make ends meet. A freeloading boarder who needed her diaper changed," she grumbled bitterly.

Beth gasped and her stomach churned. The chill in the air grew more ominous.

Eleanor took a few deep breaths. The emotional outburst left her weary. "I'm sorry," she said in a more civil tone. "It's just that I was so angry. That young girl got herself pregnant, rented a room from me without letting me know she was expecting, and then left that poor child. . . abandoned her. I hated her for it. Stupid, selfish girl."

"Did she leave you a note? Do you think she abandoned her or could she possibly have committed suicide?"

"What's the difference?" the old woman snapped.

"I suppose you are right," Beth mumbled. She sighed. "Did she say *anything?* Who was taking care of Susie that day? Did Katherine disappear in the middle of the night?"

Eleanor cleared her throat. "Conveniently," she said in a flippant tone, "I was taking care of Susie that day. It was a Sunday. During the week Susie either went to Mrs. Luntz's daycare or Katherine took her to work. The dentist and his wife spoiled that undeserving little tramp. Imagine, letting her bring a baby to work.

"Anyway, occasionally I watched Susie. My grandchildren lived all over the country. I enjoyed a baby day now and again." She looked sternly at Beth. "But I wasn't looking for a full-time caregiving situation."

"I understand," Beth said patiently. "Did Katherine say what she was going to do that day?"

"She said she was visiting her father, that she would be gone all day. I was very gracious about it, mind you. I sensed it was important to her. But she was rather melancholy and jumpy that morning, and she gave Susie a big, long goodbye hug as if she intended to be gone for days. Then she rushed out of the house. In retrospect, I thought it was odd. After she disappeared, I wondered. . . did she even have a father to go home to? Where was her mother? Why didn't she want to bring Susie with her? Wouldn't the man want to see his own grandchild?"

"Her mother was dead, and she was afraid of her father," Beth said curtly. "The old man is one difficult individual."

Eleanor narrowed her eyes. "A grandparent *always* wants to know their grandchildren. I can understand him being totally disappointed with that capricious daughter of his, but that wouldn't keep him from wanting to meet his granddaughter."

"Theorize all you want. You don't know Rod Thompson."

Eleanor looked toward the dresser uncomfortably. "If you know him, why don't you ask him where his daughter is?"

"I have," Beth said sharply. Then she toned it down and mumbled, "It's complicated."

"Not nearly as complicated as my life became when Katherine left me with a year-and-a-half-old child. I kept hoping she would return, hoping that there would be a big story about troubles with her father or some other pathetic excuse, but there was no phone call, and she never came home."

Rebecca interrupted unexpectedly. She peeked in and frowned at Beth. "Perhaps your guest should be leaving now," she said.

"I can take care of myself," Eleanor reassured her. "Now go along and polish some forks."

Rebecca scowled, a look that said *life is too short for this kind of treatment*. But she did not respond. She closed the door and walked away.

Beth turned back to Eleanor and continued to press for information. "Did she take her things?"

"Except for her purse, she left nearly everything behind – her suitcase, most or all of her clothing, everything that belonged to Susie. Nothing was missing as far as I could tell."

"I suppose that would be natural if one was leaving on a day trip."

Eleanor retorted, "Or calculated if one was leaving for good and wanted to have the freedom to put four hundred miles between herself and those she left behind before they noticed something was wrong."

"Or irrelevant if someone was planning on committing suicide," Beth muttered in disappointment.

All of a sudden the elephant in the middle of the room whacked Beth over the head. "Where is Susie?"

The old woman looked away – a grim, tired expression on her face.

"Where is Susie? And why didn't you ask the Bennings for help? They were her godparents."

Eleanor sighed, fiddled with the bookmark in her book, and finally spoke. "I was so angry those first few days, I didn't want to talk with anyone, especially not the Bennings. Those folks were part of the problem. They pampered that sinful, irresponsible girl. They contributed to her downfall."

"They certainly did not get her pregnant. Perhaps they were just helping her out, a young girl trying to rebuild her life," Beth said in Katherine's and the

Bennings' defense. "Anyway," she added sharply, "you have not answered the question. What happened to Susie?" Beth stood up.

"Oh, sit down. I'll tell you the story. An old woman knows when it is time to let go of her well-guarded secrets. Who knows how many summers I have left? It is time."

Beth sat patiently, but her stomach churned. She turned her lips inside on themselves and tried to tame her heartbeat with slow, quiet breaths.

"Katherine disappeared on November thirteenth. At first, I thought she was delayed, that she would return. I thought it was unusual that she didn't call, but she was an irresponsible, self-centered girl. Susie and I kept to ourselves. I didn't go out. I didn't answer the phone or the door. We had canned soup for Thanksgiving dinner."

"That was almost two weeks. I still don't understand why you wouldn't ask—"

"Be quiet, young lady. You were not there. You do not know what it was like. To look into those soft green eyes and wonder if you'll ever have to tell that child her mother isn't coming home. I figured if I didn't make a big deal out of it, Katherine would return, everything would go back to normal, and no one would be the wiser. I didn't get along that well with the Bennings. We'd had words about Katherine, unpleasant words. I was worried that if they took Susie, they might not let me see her again."

"The freeloading boarder?" Beth asked sarcastically.

"Don't taunt me," Eleanor replied tersely.

Beth sighed. "I'm sorry. Please continue."

"Susie started to cry more frequently. We were running out of food. So I called my son, Gregory, who was living in New Jersey. I told him what happened, and I asked him what I should do. I figured it was time to let the Bennings take her, but I was so distraught, I needed to hear my son's voice. He told me to wait a few days. He promised to call me back. He warned me not to tell *anyone*. He said it was very important. So Susie and I held out for a few more days.

"One afternoon someone came to the door. As usual I shushed Susie and hid, leaving the curtains closed and the lights off. But a note slipped through the mail slot. It said, 'Gregory sent us.'"

Beth's stomach continued to churn, and she was unable to slow her rapid heartbeat.

"I approached the door cautiously. I peered out the window. A young, well-dressed couple stood at the door. There was no one else in sight. I ushered them in quickly."

"No, no, no," Beth mumbled, shaking her head.

Eleanor gave her a long, cold stare before she continued. "They were a *very* nice couple – young, wealthy, well mannered. . . decent people. They were from upstate New York. They wanted to arrange a private adoption."

"You sold her?"

"What was I supposed to do? Turn her over to the state orphanage?"

"What about the Bennings?"

"The Bennings be damned. They didn't know anything about raising children. They were childless."

"A lot like the wealthy couple, I would imagine."

"Those people could provide for her things she would not get here in Bangor. They wanted a child desperately. The woman fell in love with Susie on the spot. It was perfect for everyone."

"I'm sure it was," Beth said coolly. "How much did they pay you?"

"Five thousand dollars."

Beth raised her eyebrows.

"It was a lot of money in those days."

"I know," Beth grumbled. "What was that you said about being worried that you'd never see her again?"

Eleanor stuck her chin out and said definitely, "I was arranging a good future for Susie."

"What if Katherine came back?"

"She didn't come back."

Beth had no response. She was seething but Eleanor was right about the last fact. Why didn't Katherine return? Did she commit suicide? Did she get tired of single motherhood and run away? The Bennings and Mrs. Sharpe relayed drastically different character analyses of Katherine. Which version was the most accurate? Beth stood up and paced the room.

"How can I find her?" she asked pointedly.

"They went by John and Mary Smith, although I doubt that those were their real names." Eleanor's lips curled up slyly.

Beth put her head in her hands.

Eleanor sighed. "I kept the birth certificate," she said quietly.

Beth looked up, "What?"

"Susan's birth certificate. I found it with Katherine's things when I was cleaning out her room."

"May I have it?"

"Top left drawer of the dresser."

Beth crossed to the dresser and opened the drawer. It was filled with silk handkerchiefs and jewelry.

"On the bottom."

She shuffled past the drawer's contents and retrieved a manila envelope. Inside was a birth certificate. "Susan Elizabeth Thompson, May twenty-third of 1976," she read. Her heart stopped for a moment when she saw the "Elizabeth."

Underneath the birth certificate, she found three letters. She flipped through them. All three were addressed to Rod Thompson in Virginia Point, Maine. Two of them were stamped, but it appeared as if they were never mailed. One of them had been returned to sender because it had no postage, presumably an oversight. All three letters were sealed.

"What are these?" Beth asked, taking shallow breaths. "These were never mailed, I presume," she said as she held up the two stamped letters. "And this one was returned on November eleventh of that year."

Eleanor pursed her lips, a look of indifference on her face.

"Here," Beth shouted as she crossed the room, waving the letters. "Here was Susie's next of kin. Did it occur to you to let him know of the existence of his granddaughter, Mrs. 'every grandparent wants to know their grandchildren?'"

Eleanor stared at Beth coolly. Then she looked away with a hint of shame. "The transaction was already underway, I—"

"The *transaction?* You are a seriously disturbed woman. 'Looking into those soft green eyes,'" Beth said, mocking the elderly woman's voice. "I'll bet you sold her three days after Katherine disappeared. You're full of shit."

Eleanor cast her a look of indignation.

Beth retorted as fast as gunfire. "Don't you look at me so innocent and offended. You make me sick."

Eleanor shifted her head to one side. She seemed fatigued. "I am an old woman who has carried an ugly secret for thirty-five years. I've finally released it. My conscience is clear."

"Oh really? I think a little penance. . ." Beth began. Then she glanced at the woman's feeble condition and added with no compassion, "or *purgatory* is in order before your soul is cleansed."

"Listen, young lady," Eleanor said. "I've given you all I have." She gestured toward the birth certificate and letters.

"Why don't the *buyers* have the birth certificate?"

"Now that would not have been very helpful to them, would it?" Eleanor said condescendingly. "A friend of my son forged a birth certificate for them. Susie is their daughter now, by birth, as far as the government is concerned, even if only on paper."

"And you have no idea what their names are? Or what name was given to Susie?"

"I did not see the final paperwork."

"Can you ask your son?"

"He did not see it, either. I asked him several years later. I wanted to find her myself, but I could not." She looked away sadly.

"Oh spare me the sob story," Beth barked.

"Perhaps you can tell it to your cronies in prison."

Eleanor laughed. "Everyone believes that Katherine took Susan. At this point it is my word against yours."

"Unless Rebecca *quite contrary* was listening." Beth smirked.

Eleanor glanced nervously toward the door. Then she looked back at Beth. "Anyway, the birth certificate and the letters won't convict me, either. I simply found them after Katherine and Susan disappeared."

Beth looked at the old woman with disgust. Eleanor was right. It would be an uphill battle. Although Beth wanted to report this woman and her baby-peddling son, what purpose would it serve now? Wherever Susan was, the young couple had been her parents. She might have had a very loving childhood. Did she really need to be burdened with the news that her parents purchased her? That her mother may have committed suicide or just outright abandoned her? Hell, did she even know she was adopted? It was a whole can of worms that probably did not need to be opened, however satisfying it might be to see the unrepentant old woman squirm.

Beth looked down at the birth certificate in her hand. It would be next to impossible to locate the former Susan if her birth certificate was forged. Was any information on the false certificate the same? Maybe the birth date, but it could be off by several days, if not weeks, and still seem authentic. Was she called Susan? Probably not. Did her new parents ever tell her she was adopted? Would they have given her any clues to her past? Did they even *know* the information on Susan's real birth certificate?

It was a dead end. *Everything* had led to a dead end. No Katherine, no Susan, no trail.

Rebecca peeked in.

Before the nurse could speak, Beth said, "Never mind, Rebecca. I'm leaving." She looked over her shoulder as she exited the room. "Rest in peace, Mrs. Sharpe."

Then she raced down the stairs and out the front door. She sped out of the driveway, the tires throwing gravel in her wake. She drove about five miles before she pulled off to the side of the road, her anxiety at an all-time high. She fumbled in her purse. No anti-anxiety pills.

Beth disliked confrontational conversations, yet she had been more confrontational and openly angry when speaking with Eleanor Sharpe than she had been with Bill during their divorce. In fact, as she recalled, she had barely even raised her voice at Bill. She wondered why she felt so much passion and outrage about two people she never even met. It was as if she were championing them – two women who had no voice in the turn of events.

After sitting in her car for twenty minutes trying to calm down, Beth realized that she was in no condition to drive. So she found a Super 8 and decided it would be prudent to settle in for the night. She hoped she could get some rest and be fit to drive in the morning. She inserted the keycard in the lock and walked into the small, clean motel room. A bathroom and two queen beds with green-and-gold paisley print comforters were on the left. On the right, a television and a small desk stood pressed against the wall.

Beth threw her purse on the bed nearest the bathroom. She crossed the room and opened the curtains, and then she flopped down on the other bed. She stared at the ceiling for nearly half an hour, thoughts racing through her head. Real or interpretive images circled in her mind: Katherine, Susan, Mrs. Sharpe, Rod Thompson, the Bennings, and a young couple from upstate New York – characters from an ongoing saga of the search for the diary's author. Over and over again the details played in her head. She felt like she was suffocating in a melodrama she wished she had never invited into her life.

Suddenly she sat up, grabbed her purse, and dumped it out. She found Susan's birth certificate and Katherine's letters to her father. The letters. Could there be a clue in the letters? Mrs. Sharpe had never even opened them to check. She probably did not want to know. *The transaction,* as she had put it, had already been initiated.

Beth opened one of the stamped letters that appeared to have never been mailed. It was dated May 29, 1976. The other unmailed letter was written on December 24, 1975. She read the December letter first:

> *Dear Dad:*
> *I'm sorry I ran away. I was afraid to tell you the news, which still may come as a shock to you.*
> *I'm pregnant. The baby is due in May. Please call me if you are not angry. I love you and I want to see you. Do you want to see me?*

It was signed "Love Always, Katherine." Underneath her name she wrote a phone number, presumably Eleanor Sharpe's.

Beth grabbed the letter dated May 29, 1976.

Dear Dad:

I am so sorry I have not contacted you. So many times I've started letters that I never finished. I almost mailed you a letter at Christmastime. But I was afraid you would be mad at me. I couldn't mail it.

I don't know how to tell you this, so I'll just come out and say it. You have a granddaughter. Susan Elizabeth. She was born six days ago. I would love for you to meet her.

Please call me, and please forgive me for running away.

"Why didn't you mail these, Katherine?" Beth said in desperation. "Why? So much could have been different."

Beth picked up the last letter, the one with a returned postmark of November 11, 1977. She opened it and a picture fell out. Beth looked at the photo. A young girl, presumably Katherine, held a baby in her arms. Susan had peach fuzz hair, a round nose, and playful eyes. She grasped a small toy and her mouth was open as if in surprise. Katherine wore jeans and a bright yellow t-shirt. Her brown hair was tied back in a ponytail. She looked a little disheveled, but her face radiated joy.

A lump formed in Beth's throat. Here was the

woman whose trail she had been chasing for nearly two weeks. Only two weeks? It felt like months. Beth tried to find a resemblance between Katherine and the red-haired interpretation she had created. After a careful examination of the photo she concluded that any similarity was imagined at best. Beth sighed. Perhaps there was a likeness in essence. She would have to be satisfied with that.

She gently placed the picture on the bedside table and picked up the letter.

Dear Dad:

I am so very sorry. I keep trying to write, but I can't seem to mail the letters. It has been over two years. You must be very worried about me. I am so ashamed about the way I left you, I can hardly bear it. But I am afraid of what you will say when you hear my story.

As you can see from the picture, I have a daughter – your granddaughter. Her name is Susan. She is a beautiful, cheerful child. Oh, how I've longed to tell you. I miss you like you'll never know. Are you mad at me?

I'm sorry, Dad. I'm sorry I ignored your advice. I'm sorry I did not tell you I was pregnant. I'm sorry I waited this long to make it right.

I must come visit. I can't let things remain the way they are any longer. I will drive down this weekend. I will come by myself. I think that is best. I can bring Susan next time.

Love Always and Always,
Katherine

Beth put the letter on the bed. She looked at the envelope and tried to sort out the details. Assuming Eleanor Sharpe was telling the truth, and that was a huge assumption, this letter had been with Katherine's things. It was rejected by the post office on the eleventh. Katherine probably received it on the twelfth. She left on the thirteenth. Surely she would have noticed that the letter was returned due to lack of postage.

"Surely she understood this," Beth whispered.

But what if she hadn't? What if she had seen the return stamp and thought her father had refused to accept the letter? How would she have taken it? As a sign of rejection? Beth remembered what Eleanor had said about the day Katherine left – the moodiness, the long hug for Susan. Beth closed her eyes and tried to pray, tried to comfort herself. After all, the idea was ridiculous. It should have been clear to anyone in her right mind that the letter was missing a stamp.

Anyone in her right mind. . .

Beth neatly returned the letters to their envelopes and reclined on the bed holding the picture. She lightly touched the face of Katherine and then Susan. Afterward she sighed and placed the photo on the bedside table.

Sleep did not come easily, and what sleep she did manage was so inundated with nightmares, it hardly counted as rest. The flying dream was the most prevalent. But it was littered with distorted images of her father's face – sometimes behind the wheel of the oncoming car, sometimes floating in the air. A variety of toy ducks made their appearance, typically falling through the air or rolling down the embankment at the side of the forest-lined road. *Stupid ducks.*

The sun was always setting in her dream. The shadows of the trees lengthened and the road gradually grew darker. As the twilight slipped away, the sense of panic and lack of control escalated. Why couldn't she move off to the side of the road? Why wouldn't the car stop? *Why didn't you come home that dreadful night when I was ten?*

Another duck tumbled down the incline. She watched it go. She could not see to the bottom of the hill. It seemed to go on forever. Small trees and broken branches blocked her view. Moss and rocks briefly interfered with the duck's descent, but it continued to roll until it was lost in the foliage.

As the flying Beth zoomed around one bend, she saw a tattered sign with a picture of a duck and some words she could not distinguish. The sign was posted on the side of a tree in a distinctive patch of the woods. A group of three trees grew near the road. The one with the sign was relatively straight, but the other two jutted out at approximately forty-five degree angles on either side. Beth continued to fly, but the car approached, faster and faster. She saw the driver behind the wheel.

This time it was not her father. It was the redheaded girl from her painting.

Beth jolted and screamed. She sat up in her bed, sweat dripping from her temples. A chill traveled up her spine to the nape of her neck.

Why did I not think of it before?

Chapter 21
Regrets

Rod Thompson returned to Virginia Point early Tuesday morning. He eased *The Bottomless Blue* gently into her slip, cut the engine, and secured her to the dock.

He walked slowly toward land, tired in both body and spirit. Damn that meddlesome woman. Why did she have to come into his life and dredge up buried memories? He rarely thought about Katherine anymore, but even those memories were cool and fleeting. Images of her faded as the years progressed.

He would not see Katherine ever again. She had cut him out of her life. In the first few years, he had hoped she might return. As the years passed, that hope slowly evaporated until, more than a decade later, he became resigned. She was never going to come home. Eventually, when Old Charlie was taken out of service, Rod left the cottage. He could no longer endure wandering within its walls, haunted by the echoes of unfinished conversations.

In the beginning, he asked himself why. Why did she leave? And then, why did she not return? What had he done that was so offensive that she would choose to purge him from her life forever? It was no coincidence the drifter left only a few days before Katherine disappeared. Obviously, she had run away with him. What was his name? Rod didn't like to think of it. It stirred a rage he did not wish to confront. Damn that worthless punk for taking his daughter away.

He had only tried to protect her. When his wife, Lucille, had died of pneumonia at the age of twenty-seven, he vowed that he would never let anything happen to Katherine. He had not taken care of Lucille. He hadn't seen the symptoms; thus he hadn't brought her to the doctor in time. She had always been so strong; he didn't realize how sick she was. He never forgave himself for not being more attentive. He could not bring Lucille back, but in her honor he would protect Katherine no matter what the cost.

No matter what the cost.

The cost was too much to bear. If he had been a little more lenient, would she have stayed? Would she have at least come back when the flash of anger and hormones faded? Was she so afraid of him that she dared not return? He wished that he could tell her not to be afraid, that he would understand. But it was too late.

Rod pulled his car up the drive. He entered his home and locked the door. He did not wish to be disturbed, especially by that intrusive Beth LaMonte. He had no room for people in his life. People had let him down. He preferred to be alone.

He had long since learned to ignore the voices that attempted to remind him of his vow to never become as broken as his father. It wasn't the same. Samuel Thompson abandoned his family, abruptly and without recourse. Rod Thompson, on the other hand, remained, in body even if not in spirit. Should she ever need him, he would be there for Katherine.

He closed the curtains and turned on the television. He allowed the noise to silence his thoughts.

Chapter 22
Look Out For Loons

Beth paced the hotel room waiting for the light of day. She was showered and her bags were packed. As soon as the sun was barely visible, she checked out and jumped into her car. She headed out of town, taking Interstate 95 South.

Beth scanned the roadside obsessively. "It's too populated here," she mumbled, getting off the freeway. She headed back toward Bangor, going north, but she cut off at Interstate 395. She continued southeast until she reached Highway 1A. There, she drove off and on the highway, taking side streets and county roads. At one point, she pulled off and put her head on the steering wheel. "This isn't working," she growled in frustration. "There is no reason Katherine would have taken this route."

Nevertheless, Beth pulled back onto the road, slowing down and craning her neck at every possible side street. She became progressively discouraged with each mile. She was about to drive through East Holden, when something made her turn around. A road led southwest out of town. Her neck tingled slightly.

"This is it," she whispered. Something about the area was familiar. It felt like her nightmare. Her heart pounded as she drove slowly, examining the woods carefully. She passed Dedham and another junction, but she continued south, scanning the forest. Past a lake and a quarry, she drove south, searching. Then, she saw it. She slammed on the brakes and stopped in the middle of the road. There it was, clear as day – a trio of trees in a curious pattern and a sign that might appear like a duck to someone unacquainted with the species.

Look Out For Loons, it read.

Beth stepped out of her car and walked toward the sign. She looked along the side of the slope that dropped off behind the three trees. About fifty feet downhill, new trees, broken branches, and the density of the forest blocked her view. It was identical to the hillside in her dream. Beth felt the blood drain out of her face. She backed up, slowly, toward the car. She fumbled with her hands behind her back. When she found the car door, she got in as quickly as possible and sped away.

The fear associated with the nightmare flooded her brain. Waves of anxiety and flashes of images impaired her driving. She saw a small tackle shop about five miles down the road from the loons sign. She pulled off and parked in front of the store. After she took a few minutes to compose herself, she got out of the car and entered the shop. Beth felt a desperate need for human company to alleviate her fear. No imaginary creatures or nightmares, just a friendly smile.

She was rewarded when she stepped into the store. A young woman in her mid-thirties sat behind the counter reading a book. She looked up when Beth walked in and grinned.

"Good morning," she said. "Are you doing a little fishing today?"

"Oh, no, not today." Beth saw a coffee machine and some pre-packaged pastries near the counter. "I just need a cup of coffee."

"Coming right up," the young woman said cheerfully.

Beth rubbed the back of her neck and turned her head from side to side, stretching the muscles. As she rolled her head in a circle, her eyes passed over the ceiling of the shop. She gasped. "Oh my God."

The store clerk's face creased in alarm. "Are you all right?"

Along the ceiling several configurations of rubber ducks hung from hooks. Each group included a large duck followed by three smaller ducks, strung together with fishing line or some kind of thick thread. Beth just pointed at them.

"You like my ducks?" the young woman said, her face shifting from concern to puzzled amusement.

"Sorry," Beth replied, blushing. "It's just that they reminded me of. . ." Her voice trailed away.

"My father made them. I had a set when I was a child. They actually floated upright in a line," she explained. "When my father passed away, I tried to make more. But the rubber ducks coming out of China these days don't float upright." She laughed. "So they all flip over on their backs. They were ridiculous. I can't bring myself to sell these few that are left, so they are just for decoration."

Beth shook her head. Rubber ducks out in the middle of nowhere. *Nothing should surprise me now.*

The young woman smiled. "I'm Cindy," she said, extending her hand.

"Beth. Nice to meet you."

She handed Beth a Styrofoam cup of coffee. One table with a red-checkered tablecloth and two chairs sat near a window in the front right corner of the store. Beth sat, drank her coffee, and tried to sort through the thoughts and images that flooded her brain.

Let's take inventory, Beth thought, gazing absentmindedly at the highway. *Glowing supernatural creature, reoccurring nightmares of an actual place I've never seen before, and a young mother vanishing into thin air thirty-five years ago.* Ideas she would have scoffed at only a month ago tumbled around in her head, each competing for her attention. She knew she needed to go down the side of that hill. But it was dense and intimidating. Besides, she was afraid. *What if I don't like what I find down there?*

I need help. But who can I trust? Mary will have the whole town buzzing, questioning my sanity. She considered how, exactly, she would tell someone why she needed to go, and which details she should include or leave out. *Who in their right mind would agree to climb down there?*

Suddenly, she jumped up, practically knocking down the chair. She steadied it, threw Cindy an apologetic glance, and headed for the door. "I've got to run."

"Bye," Cindy replied, trying to hide a bemused smile. "Nice to meet you."

"You too," Beth hollered as she exited the store.

* * * *

Kenny McLeary was studying a diamond under a jeweler's loupe at a little after 9:00 a.m. when Beth LaMonte burst through the door.

"I need your help," she cried, her voice filled with anxiety and urgency.

Kenny crossed to the gate, which separated the back of the store from the customer waiting area, and he met Beth near the couch. His shirt wrinkled and his hair a bit disheveled, he stared at Beth with a puzzled expression on his face.

"Listen. I need your help. I have to search through a dense incline on Highway 46 a little over two hours' drive north. I really want someone to accompany me." Beth tried to slow her breathing. "You like to hike, right?"

"Well, yes, but—"

"Kenny, I don't know who else I can trust."

Kenny gazed at her with a frightening intensity. He seemed somehow moved by her declaration. Beth waited several minutes, fidgeting and wondering if she should just depart. Finally, Kenny motioned for her to sit down on the couch. "Tell me what this is all about," he said quietly.

Beth took a deep breath and sat down. She had hoped he would be receptive. But, in truth, she wasn't entirely certain if he would offer help or simply give her one of his standard, unresponsive shrugs. She was pleased and relieved that he was open to her request.

"This is going to sound weird," she began.

"I won't belittle you."

"And you can't tell anyone. Please don't tell anyone."

"Do I strike you as the kind of guy who runs around spreading gossip?"

Beth smiled. "That is why I came to you."

"Go on."

Beth paused briefly. She considered leaving out several of the outrageous details. Who would believe them? If she focused on the dream and the road, Kenny would probably help her, no questions asked. But there was a part of her that wanted to share the entire story. No, a part of her *needed* to share that story, to release all of the secrets that had kept her a prisoner for two weeks. Those bizarre, disquieting secrets could no longer be contained.

Beth sighed. "When I first moved into the cottage, I saw a firefly." Over the course of nearly an hour, she relayed in detail her experiences and discoveries – the secret beach, the diary, the nightmares, her interactions with Rod Thompson, the Internet sleuthing, and her visit to Bangor. She left out most of the personal stuff – her father's accident, the rubber ducks, the painting, and the depth of her fear.

"Are you ready to write me off as a nut case yet?" Beth asked.

"I'm not entirely sure what to think," Kenny responded with a hint of a smile. "But I'm comfortable that you're being honest with me, that you believe you saw and experienced the things you're telling me."

Beth looked at him with a peculiar expression. "What?"

"There is a lot more to you than the man who sulks silently behind that wall," she said, gesturing to the counter. "It's good to hear your voice."

"Thank you." He looked amused. "I take to heart any psychological advice I can get from women who talk with floating balls of light."

Beth put her head in her hands and laughed uncomfortably. "Touché."

"I'm rather impressed with your resourceful detective skills. You've got my attention," he noted. "So what is special about that road?"

"Early this morning, I had another one of those nightmares where I am flying along a road and a car collides with me."

"Okay. . ."

"This time the details of the road seemed. . . crisper. I could really see the outline of the trees and the foliage on the slope. And just before the collision I saw a sign with a duck on it and there were three trees shaped like this." She held up three fingers, trying to recreate the positions of the trees. She looked at Kenny and realized that her account probably seemed like one of those *let me tell you about my dream* narratives. Before, she had only briefly mentioned the car collision dreams. Now she was going into tedious detail. It was the kind of story that normally caused people's eyes to roll, but Kenny did not roll his eyes. Either he was extremely polite or he was truly interested.

"The thing is, Kenny, driving home, I found that very place on highway 46. It was *exactly* like in my dream."

Kenny raised his eyebrows.

"Only the duck was really a loon," Beth explained.

He smirked.

"I mean. . . not *crazy* but a *loon,* the bird, you know? Oh, never mind, this whole thing is ridiculous."

Kenny tapped his fingers together. He seemed deep in thought.

"Is it possible?" Beth asked him hopefully. "Is it possible I'm not crazy and that something is really going on here? That maybe Katherine had an accident on that road? I would never have believed any of this a month ago, this nonsense about psychic dreams, but I don't know what to think anymore. And I *have* to go down there. I have to know. Do you understand? Does any of my rambling make sense to you?"

Kenny smiled. It reminded her of that day when she caught him laughing with Abigail on the porch of *The Virginia Point Cove.* She felt honored that he finally trusted her enough to smile in her presence.

"Believe or not," he said, "It makes enough sense to stir my curiosity. Let's go see what's there." He stood up. "Do you want me to drive?"

Beth was relieved. She nodded her head enthusiastically. "Actually, that would be wonderful."

A little over two hours later, they were standing by the *Look Out For Loons* sign, staring down the incline and into the forest. Beth looked up at Kenny, her eyes noticeably apprehensive.

"Damn. We should have brought a flashlight," she said.

"Never fear. I'm always prepared." He retrieved a large Coleman camping flashlight from the trunk of his car. "Follow my lead," Kenny instructed. And step-by-step they traversed the woodland.

Beth was glad she wore full-length jeans. After half an hour of negotiating the slippery moss-covered rocks and low hanging tree limbs, her arms were badly scratched. When she reached the area where the incline flattened out, she gazed at her surroundings. If anything were there, it would take a search crew to find it. Vegetation, dead leaves, and broken limbs covered everything.

Beth sat down on a log in defeat.

"We can still take a look," Kenny said, reading her thoughts. "If this theoretical crash happened thirty-five years ago, there is going to be very little left of it," he reminded her. "You knew that, didn't you?"

"I guess," she mumbled. She hadn't really thought about it. What *did* she expect to find? A bright blue Chevy glistening in the trees?

They spent another half hour searching the forest floor. Beth sighed, a loud sigh of resignation. Angrily, with no concern for the environment or the animals that made their home there, she kicked a pile of old leaves and moss-covered branches near a young pine tree.

Something flipped.

"Kenny!" Beth shouted as she bent down to examine it.

Kenny negotiated his way to the place where Beth squatted. She turned something over in her hands, a flat rectangle with slightly curved edges. It was bent and covered with a thick layer of dirt. Beth used the side of her hand and then her fingernails to chip away at the encrusted mud. The paint had long since eroded away, but the raised letters and numbers clearly identified the object. It was a license plate.

Beth looked up at Kenny. Her heart pounded so loudly in her ears, she could barely hear herself think. They both looked downhill from where the license plate had rested. Recently fallen trees, a cluster of saplings, and heaps of sticks and dead leaves partially obstructed a very large tree twenty feet away. Beth's eyes began to water and her breathing grew shallow.

"I'm scared, Kenny," she whispered, almost inaudibly.

Kenny gently lifted her to her feet, placed his hands on her shoulders, and firmly said, "I'll go."

Beth bit her lip and nodded her head, unable to respond.

Kenny approached the area and wrestled with the moss-covered deadwood and broken branches that concealed the old tree. Beth watched tentatively, willing her feet to move, but she remained frozen. Haunting questions plagued her. *What really happened? Why would Katherine have driven this way in the first place?* The suicide theory raised its ugly head. If Katherine had indeed died in a crash near the place where Beth stood, suicide was the most plausible explanation. Why else would she be in the middle of nowhere? In 1977, the location would have been barely populated for miles in any direction. Beth looked down. She was disappointed. *Why Katherine? Why?*

She glanced up just as Kenny moved a pile of leaves, uncovering something near the tree. Finally her feet found the power to move. She ran toward him, almost tripping over a jagged rock. Kenny continued to clear the area. Beneath the branches and layers of sticks and leaves rested a few fragments of a car, its make and model long since indistinguishable under years of rust and decomposition. Large and small chunks of glass lay scattered on the ground. Several rusted pieces of metal were marginally identifiable as a door, a trunk, and a bumper. Saplings grew up through the thin sheet of rust that had once been an undercarriage. The rear window, nearly intact, lay askew adjacent to several large, rusted springs – presumably the rear seat. Most of the interior of the car had essentially decomposed, having been pecked and chewed by birds and burrowing animals or simply disintegrated.

Uneasy, Beth watched while Kenny rummaged near the tree, gently lifting what appeared to be the driver's side door. She gasped and closed her eyes. Underneath the door rested a pile of bones, the top half of a skull, and the remnants of a steering wheel. There were not enough bones to comprise an entire skeleton. Beth turned her head away from them, her body shaking.

If her suppositions were correct, the bones were all that remained of Katherine, a vibrant and passionate young lady who had dominated Beth's world for nearly two weeks. The Katherine of the diary had passed away thirty-five years ago, lying in the center of an uninhabited forest. Remembering the picture she found in the letter, Beth shook her head. A young mother in the prime of her life. It seemed so unjust. It made Beth angry. *Did you do this*

Katherine? she thought in disdain. *How could you do this?* Kenny reverently covered the bones and walked around to the other side of the wreckage. When he lifted an unidentifiable slab of metal, Beth could scarcely believe what she saw. Lying on the ground, its original color dulled by dirt and years of neglect, one of the few non-biodegradable objects for miles, was a set of rubber ducks – one large, three small – tied together with fishing line.

"The tackle shop ducks," she said joyfully, running to pick them up. A thousand thoughts inundated her brain. She tried to sort out the information, and as she did, a logical conclusion arose.

"It was an accident," she whispered.

"Yeah," Kenny said matter-of-factly. "I thought that was what we were looking for."

Beth began to ramble, dozens of facts spilling out and overlapping. "Yes, I know but. . . remember the suicide theory. . . you know, she was out here in the middle of nowhere, right? It could have been deliberate. You know what I mean? And remember I worried that she might have killed herself? And I was so angry that she might have left her daughter behind in such a selfish way. It would have been so wrong. . . I was disappointed. I was almost ashamed, really. . . but I couldn't put it all together, and I didn't understand why she took this road. I still don't understand why she took this road." Beth paused for a moment to catch her breath, and she slowed her speech. "But I know now, without a doubt, that this was an accident," she declared confidently.

"How?"

Beth held up the dingy ducks triumphantly,

shaking them in Kenny's face. "Because she wouldn't buy a toy for her child and then deliberately drive off the road ten minutes later, never to be seen again."

"Ten minutes?"

"They sold these ducks at the tackle shop just down the road."

Kenny crinkled his brow. "I suppose it makes sense."

"It makes a whole world of sense," Beth said. But as she spoke her voice cracked. Her throat constricted and her stomach turned. "It makes sense," she whispered, tears falling down her face freely. She grimaced, trying to hold them back. "It was an accident."

Beth turned and walked away from the wreckage. She took several steps before the tears overcame her. She held the ducks against her chest. Then, the woman who'd barely allowed herself a tear at her mother's funeral began to sob uncontrollably. She shrank to the ground, clutching the ducks, cuddling them as if they were a teddy bear. The tears flowed endlessly, interspersed with gasps and almost unintelligible declarations.

"It was an. . . accident," she cried. "It's oh. . . kay, Ka-Katherine. . . It's all right, D-Dad. I'm. . . so sorry. . . that. . . I. . . I was angry, Daddy. I know you. . . didn't. . . mean it. I know. . . it wasn't. . . wasn't your fault. . ." Years of grief came tumbling out, spilling all over an anonymous place in the middle of the forest. Beth sat amidst the dead leaves and broken branches and succumbed to a cleansing that was decades overdue.

Kenny bit his lip and cautiously sat down on the

ground next to her. Beth continued to cry. She mourned the loss of her father and the unexpected death of her mother. She grieved for her failed marriage and the disintegration of a relationship that once held joy and promise. She denounced the unceremonious way she lost her innocence, and she longed for all the human experiences in which she declined to participate out of fear. She wept for the child she might have known as her own who never came to be. She yearned for the life of a passionate young girl named Katherine who had suffered a horrible fate, snatched from the world when she had so much to give. And she cried for the baby girl who looked out the window one afternoon and her mother never came home. Then the cycle started all over again.

For nearly an hour they sat there. Beth's gasps and sobs grew softer as time progressed. Kenny's body was steady and reassuring. He said not a word, not a single solitary word. Yet he provided all the warmth and comfort a human presence could offer that words could not.

In a moment entirely uncharacteristic of him, he bent over and kissed her hair. A single tear rolled down his face. Beth sat up and dried her tears with her hand. Her face was red, swollen and hardly recognizable. But she smiled at Kenny, the kind of smile that comes when all the anger has been washed away.

He helped her to her feet. She made a move to return the ducks to the place where she found them. Kenny stopped her, pushing the hand in which she held the toy toward her chest.

"But isn't this sort of a crime scene?" Beth asked innocently.

Kenny gazed at her with a mixture of tenderness and amusement. Then he shrugged and looked around, pointing to the incomplete shards that indicated years of decay. "Moving the ducks will hardly make a difference now," he said.

Beth laughed, slightly embarrassed. She clutched the ducks and took his hand. Then the two began the tedious trek back to Kenny's car.

* * * *

Cindy jumped in surprise when Beth and Kenny walked into the shop carrying the tattered toy.

"My father's ducks! Where did you find them?"

Beth looked at Kenny. "They were at the scene of an accident—"

"Oh my God. Are the police there?" Cindy asked, picking up her phone.

Beth reached toward Cindy. "Don't call 911. The accident occurred thirty-five years ago. We should notify the sheriff, however. Do you know their non-emergency number?"

Cindy pulled a phone book out from under the desk and fumbled through the blue pages. She wrote the phone number down and handed it to Beth. Beth started to dial. Then she stopped and looked at Cindy.

"Do you remember. . . was your store open on Sundays when your dad was here?"

"Yes, I believe we've always been open on Sundays, but only from one to five."

Beth crinkled her brow. "What about Sunday

morning fishermen?"

Cindy shrugged. "Dad went to church with us. Then we had a nice brunch together. After that, he came here. He was very serviceable to his customers, but Sunday morning was family time."

Beth meandered through her thoughts. It made sense that Katherine had stopped on her way home. The tackle shop was south of the scene of the accident. Did Katherine make it to Virginia Point? That would mean she had visited her father, or at least tried to visit him. But then, wouldn't someone have seen her? Abigail said she was never seen again. Maybe Katherine wanted to be invisible. Or perhaps she chickened out and never drove all the way to Virginia Point. But then, what did she do with all that time? And what was she doing on Highway 46?

"Would you like me to call them?" Kenny asked gently.

"Who?"

"The sheriff's office."

"Oh, yes. Certainly." She handed her cell phone to Kenny. He ushered her to the table by the window and Cindy poured her a cup of coffee.

When the detectives from the Hancock County Sheriff's Office arrived at the tackle shop, Beth was on her second cup. Kenny sat next to her, staring out the window. The older detective was slightly balding with a moustache and a modestly plump waistline. The younger detective had bright orange-red hair and freckles. He was tall and thin.

"You wish to report an accident?" the older detective asked.

Kenny stood up. "Yes, we can take you to the

location. It is a very old accident, sir."

"How old?"

"We're guessing thirty-five years or so."

"November, 1977," Beth chimed in.

The detective raised an eyebrow. "Do you have a specific incident in mind, ma'am?"

Beth blushed and looked at Kenny. How could she explain? She took a deep breath and let it out slowly before launching into the story. "I've been looking for Katherine Thompson who disappeared on November thirteenth of that year. I know she was in this area, so I talked my friend, Kenny here, into helping me scout around. We were lucky. She must have known we were coming and led the way." Beth thought of the firefly and shuddered.

The detective frowned and eyed her suspiciously. Clearly Beth's "led the way" explanation was meeting skepticism. *He can't possibly suspect us,* Beth thought. *I mean, he has to realize Kenny and I would have been children in 1977.* She grimaced, hoping they wouldn't become victims of a long-term investigation.

Beth looked at Kenny. He gave her a significant warning glare, which Beth interpreted meant something to the effect of *do not talk about the dreams or the firefly.* She nodded, almost imperceptibly, in response.

"Can you describe the accident scene?"

Beth turned her head away, trying not to remember the gruesome sight and what remained of a girl whose secret thoughts and dreams Beth had uncovered in a diary. A young lady permanently silenced by an enemy Beth knew only too well –

death.

Kenny turned to the detectives, and, forming a circle that left Beth separated from the three of them, described the scene to the best of his ability. He left out the toy ducks, which were lying on the floor behind Beth's purse, out of view.

The detectives wrote out a lengthy report including as much information as possible about Beth, Kenny, and the suggested victim. They also took down contact information for Rod Thompson. When the younger detective asked about dental records, Beth sat up quickly.

"Oh, the Bennings!" she exclaimed. Then she leaned in to explain. "Katherine used to work for a dentist in Bangor. I'm sure he has her dental records, but..."

"Yes?"

Beth almost told the detectives about the Bennings being godparents to Katherine's baby. But then she realized that such information might start a whole new investigation into the whereabouts of Susan Thompson. For some reason, Beth felt that such an investigation was inappropriate. It was not really her decision to make, and it would probably all come out in the open in the long run, but she felt obligated to protect Susan from the pain such an inquiry might unleash.

"They were very close to Katherine. I want to tell them first. If I give you their number, could you wait until tomorrow afternoon to call them?"

The younger detective looked at the older one. The older detective shrugged. "I don't see why not. We have a lot of paperwork to process. And besides, we don't even have a body yet, presuming what you are telling me is true and we actually find a wreck."

"Oh, it's true, sir. I wouldn't waste your time."

"I hope not," he grumbled.

The redheaded detective smiled playfully at Beth with a nod and an expression that said *he's having a bad day.*

Beth pursed her lips and suppressed a grin.

"Kenny, would you mind going to the Bennings' house after we finish up here? I really need to talk to them, and I would rather it be in person."

Kenny sighed.

Beth sensed he was exhausted. "Please?"

"No problem," he said with a slight edge in his voice.

The detectives completed the necessary reports and Beth and Kenny led them to the *Look Out For Loons* sign.

"It's down there, at about a twenty degree angle from where we stand," Kenny said, gesturing to the left. "A large old tree in a sea of saplings. It will be obvious when you get down there. The site is mostly uncovered now."

"Why didn't you get police assistance in the first place?" the older detective asked.

"We were looking for a needle in a haystack we were not even sure existed. The lady just had a hunch," he said, shrugging. "I didn't want to let her down. We were not positive we would find anything at all."

"Okay. We'll take it from here." He turned to his assistant. "Is this Dedham or Bucksport?"

The young detective looked up the road. "Uh. . . I

believe it's Bucksport."

"Figure out who the hell has jurisdiction and get them on the radio."

"Yes, sir."

* * * *

Beth and Kenny arrived at the Bennings a little after 3:30 p.m. Linda Benning opened the door. She was surprised to see Beth standing on the porch with a gentleman.

"Linda, this is Kenny McLeary. Kenny, Linda Benning."

They shook hands and Linda invited them in. Kenny followed Beth and Linda to the sitting room.

Wyatt peeked his head in from the hallway. "Back so soon?" he said. "Do you have news for us?"

Beth and Kenny exchanged a somber glance. Linda stumbled as she made her way to a chair in the far corner of the room.

"What is it, Beth?" Linda asked cautiously.

Beth hesitated before she said, "We've found the remains of a car wreck."

"Oh my God," Linda shouted, filling in a dozen blanks in her mind in an instant.

"Wait," Beth said. "Please hear me out. We don't even know if it is Katherine yet. It's hard to explain. I. . . I. . . I just had a. . . a feeling. And, well, we found a very old accident. But it was on highway 46, just south of Dedham. I don't know what Katherine would have been doing there."

"Dedham?" Linda exclaimed.

"Yes, is that—"

"Oh my God. Oh my God," Linda said softly, shaking her head.

"What is it?"

"It's my fault. It's *my* fault," she said slowly, visibly stunned. "My grandparents lived in Dedham. We used to visit when I was a child. I grew up in Connecticut, but I cherished summers in Maine with my grandparents – fishing with Grandpa, making blueberry jam with Gran. I told Katherine that was why I moved to Maine after I finished college. Dedham is where I fell in love with Maine, I told her. She must have wanted to visit. What else could it be?"

"Uh. . . that must be it," Beth responded absentmindedly, oblivious to Linda's anguish and misplaced guilt. Beth was too intrigued by the details to be cognizant of the woman's need for reassurance. The pieces started to fall into place. Katherine *did* take Highway 46 intentionally Sunday afternoon, maybe even around sunset. Twilight would have made the road harder to negotiate, Beth reasoned. It may have been an unpaved road at that time. Finally, she had the fragments of a theory that made some sense.

Linda started to cry.

"You can't blame yourself," Kenny said. "And nothing is official yet. They will need to do some investigating and examine dental records."

Wyatt remained steady. "Of course. I'll pull my files," he said calmly.

"It's my fault," Linda continued to say. "I can't bear to imagine it. Poor Katherine. Poor little Susie. They must have been so scared. I hope they died on impact and didn't languish there in—"

"Linda," Beth interrupted. "Susan wasn't in the car."

Linda looked up, completely bewildered.

"Katherine didn't take her along."

"I don't understand."

"Mrs. Sharpe was supposed to be watching her."

"What?" she yelled. "Where the hell is she then?"

Beth took a deep breath and sighed. "Mrs. Sharpe arranged a private adoption." She could not believe that she had used Eleanor's euphemism for selling a baby.

"Private adoption?" Wyatt asked.

Linda looked overwhelmed and confused.

"She sold Susan to a wealthy couple from New York," Beth blurted out rapidly, as if the words would hurt less if they all came out at once.

"What? We were her godparents," Wyatt said indignantly.

"I know. I had a rather detailed conversation with Mrs. Sharpe reminding her of that fact. At first she claimed it was something about you and her not getting along. Then it seemed like she was just doing it for the money."

Wyatt rose from his chair. "I'm going to call the police."

"Wait," Beth pleaded. "I thought about that. First of all, it is her word against mine at this point. Everyone believed Katherine and Susan left together."

"But now you have a crash site, potential evidence."

Kenny interjected, "A baby's bones would have decayed sooner than Katherine's."

Linda grimaced.

"Sorry, ma'am."

"She was one-and-a-half," Wyatt contested.

Kenny shrugged. "I'm not sure that makes much of a difference."

"Excuse me, forensics team," Beth said, scowling. "Can I explain my objections?"

Linda stared at her. Wyatt crossed his arms. Kenny raised one eyebrow.

"Susan grew up with two people whom she believed were her mom and dad. Does she now know her true history? I don't know. But I don't think it is fair for her learn about it from a team of police officers and German Shepherds arriving at her door one random afternoon in summer."

Wyatt sighed. "I doubt they'd bring out the dogs, but I kind of see your point."

"I would like to try to look for her," Beth said, realizing that she had almost nothing to go by. Nevertheless, she wanted to bring some comfort to Linda as well as stall Wyatt's pursuit of justice. "Look how well I did tracking you down."

Linda capitulated. "All right. But don't ask me not to strangle that old woman in her sleep."

"You may not have to. By the looks of her, she could go any day."

"She should be so lucky." Linda sneered.

"Anyway," Beth said, trying to change the subject. "The police will be asking you for information. . ." Her voice trailed off.

"Don't worry," Wyatt said. "We'll hold off discussing Susan for now. But if you don't find her, I *will* go to the police. That woman be damned. I don't care how old she is. She took money for my goddaughter. She will pay for that crime."

"Perhaps we ought to ask Susan what she thinks is best when we find her," Beth said.

Wyatt seemed unmoved, but he relented.

Before they left, Linda hugged Beth for a long time. They exchanged a somber goodbye. Beth and Kenny were halfway down the walkway when Linda called after them.

"Beth."

Beth turned. "Yes?"

"How did you know?"

Beth looked at Kenny briefly. She pursed her lips and answered. "I had a dream."

Linda nodded her head. She seemed to find that answer to her satisfaction. Perhaps all the years of waiting made her open to anything. "Thank you," she whispered.

Beth nodded. Then she and Kenny climbed into his car and drove away.

* * * *

As they turned the corner, Beth cried, "Wait. Would you mind if we visited Mrs. Sharpe?"

Kenny rolled his eyes. "Why do you want to even acknowledge that wretched woman?"

"I want to ask her some questions. I want to know what time Katherine left the house."

"You think she's going to remember that after all these years?"

"She ought to remember if the young lady left around six in the morning or closer to noon, shouldn't she?"

"I suppose. But how does that help us?"

Beth paused for a moment. *Us.* Kenny had progressed from a reluctant assistant to an active partner in her investigation. She smiled. "The tackle shop was open from one to five on Sundays, and it is south of the accident site. So Katherine must have been on her way home. . . theoretically. I just want to understand why she was on that road in the *afternoon*. According to Abigail, no one saw Katherine in Virginia Point after she left. Where did she spend the day if she didn't spend it with her father?"

"How do you know she *didn't* spend it with her father? The old man lives a very reclusive life. Perhaps they spent a day at his house or on his sailboat. It is possible to take a walk in Virginia Point and not be noticed by the gossip squad, you know." He said this with an air of one who was well acquainted with that fact, and had done so many times.

Beth frowned. "I suppose you are right. But I want to see Mrs. Sharpe anyway. Do you mind?" There was a hint of desperation in her voice.

He shook his head and resigned. "I'm in," he said reluctantly.

* * * *

They stood on Eleanor Sharpe's porch for several minutes waiting for someone to answer the door.

Beth whispered to Kenny. "She was hardly fit to travel. There has to be someone in—"

Rebecca opened the door, her clothing rumpled

and her face red and swollen.

"I need to speak to Mrs. Sharpe," Beth said with an air of authority.

"You can't," Rebecca replied, outraged.

"It will only take—"

"She's dead."

"What?"

"You," she said slowly. "*You* killed her. I don't know what you said to her yesterday, but she was all in a fit after you left. She died in her sleep. You killed her!"

"I'm truly sorry for your loss, but I did not kill Mrs. Sharpe."

Kenny tugged at Beth's elbow.

Beth continued. "Was it her heart?"

Rebecca grumbled. "The doctors don't know yet. You had no business disturbing an eighty-one-year-old, sick woman in her bed."

"I didn't mean—"

Kenny tugged at Beth a little more forcefully. "Let's go," he whispered harshly in her ear. Then he pulled her back down the walk.

"Goodbye, ma'am," he said, nodding to Rebecca.

"Bitch!" the young woman cried.

Kenny had to force Beth into the car.

"What are you doing?" she asked.

"Do you want to be part of another police investigation today?"

"Of course not."

"That woman is standing on the doorstep saying you killed the old lady. How do you think that sounds, huh? They don't know how she died, and you were one of the last persons to see her alive. Let's get out of here, *now,* before we end up spending the night in jail."

"Oh. I see your point."

"Damn straight," Kenny mumbled under his breath as he turned onto the main road.

Beth looked down, embarrassed. "I'm sorry. I'm sorry I dragged you into all of this."

Kenny was silent for a moment. "It's all right," he said. "Do you think she died of guilt?"

"Either that or her body decided to hold out long enough to release its secret. . . She didn't have to tell me, you know."

"I suppose."

"Maybe she simply didn't want to take it to the grave."

"Perhaps. Let's just hope the doctor issues her a death certificate that implicates *natural* causes."

"Fair enough," Beth said, chuckling. "But I have nothing to hide."

"Except the fate of Susan Thompson."

Beth sighed and looked out the window.

"Why are you so committed to keeping this a secret? You certainly are not trying to protect Mrs. Sharpe or her son, I hope."

"No," Beth said, thinking it should be obvious. "I'm trying to protect Susan."

"How do you know she wants to be protected?"

"I don't. It's just a feeling."

* * * *

They arrived home around 6:45 p.m. Beth was emotionally exhausted, more so than she could remember being in a long time. She decided to take a long, deserved bath. Quietly, as if someone could see her, she sneaked the ducks into the bathroom and washed them thoroughly in the sink. She carefully painted new white and black eyes on their blank faces. When they dried, she dropped them into the tub. Although dingy and almost colorless, they stared up at her with that comforting, placid expression common in the rubber duck population.

After her bath, she put the letters and ducks in a drawer with the diary. She took two steps before she stopped, returned to the drawer, and pulled out the last letter. She removed the picture and stared at it for a long time. Then she took the photo downstairs and set it on the coffee table. After rummaging through a box in the garage, she returned with a picture frame that used to hold a photo of Bill and her. She carefully positioned the photo of Katherine and Susan. It looked good inside the old frame. Smiling warmly, she crossed to the mantel and placed it by her mother's picture.

Beth found herself suddenly energized, and she went to the studio to study the unfinished portrait of the red-haired girl. It only needed a few more color accents and it would be perfect. She picked up the stunning comb created by Kenny. It looked lovely in her painting. Beth put on her apron, mixed some colors, and began the process of completing the portrait.

She finished sometime shortly after nine o'clock as the twilight slipped away. When she stepped back to examine her final product, she noticed the firefly floating discreetly in the middle of the room. It gave her a start.

"Would you please stop that?" she exclaimed. And with the voice of a woman depleted, she said, "It has been a long, *long* day, Katherine." She paused, surprised by her own words. Then she stiffened and backed up slowly toward the corner of the room. The light creature seemed to retreat as if sensing Beth's fear. Beth took a deep breath and stared for a long time before speaking again.

"Are you Katherine?" she whispered, barely able to make a sound. Her mind stumbled over the possibility that might have already occurred to any other person in her situation, if such a situation even existed. She stood frozen in a state of shock, as if talking to some supernatural ball of light or a character from a Greek myth might be completely normal, while conversing with a ghost was entirely preposterous.

The firefly swirled several times in random circles. Then it hovered a couple of feet from her face.

Beth stepped forward, trying to get a closer look, truly examining the beautiful creature of light. She remembered how the firefly had frightened, yet amazed, her when she'd first encountered it.

The firefly circled Beth's head and then swirled energetically from one end of the room to the other.

"I'm glad you're feeling so lively and cheerful now because you didn't look so good at the bottom of the hill this afternoon." Beth laughed awkwardly.

She stared at the light creature for several minutes. Was this, indeed, the spirit of Katherine Thompson? She was reluctant to accept the idea, because she never believed in God or an afterlife, least of all ghosts. But her other explanations – a muse or an angel – seemed equally as unfathomable. In the course of less than a month, things happened which would forever change how Beth viewed life. It was inevitable. And she could not turn back the clock.

Suddenly, she experienced an unusual feeling of warmth and peace. It was a spiritual peace. She no longer felt melancholy and alone. She no longer believed that her father and mother were irrevocably erased from existence. She somehow sensed their presence, and she found that comforting.

Addressing the firefly, she said, "I wish I could ask you what you did that day."

The firefly made a slow circle.

"Did you see your father?"

The firefly backed up toward the window.

"I don't know this language, Katherine," she said, sighing. "I have to go to bed. I'm exhausted, and I've done all I can do for now. We'll get things straightened out. . . somehow."

The firefly drifted back slowly and slipped quietly through the windowpane.

Beth yawned and went straight to bed. She slept peacefully through the night. The haunting nightmares had ceased.

Chapter 23
Denial

Beth slept until 9:35 the following morning. She had to shake her head and rub her eyes to remember where she was. The previous forty-eight hours felt more like weeks as she went over the days' events in her mind.

She dressed, called Mary, and asked if she could come and speak to her, Lou, and Abigail.

"Of course, dear," Mary responded. "We're just putting on tea. We'll wait for you."

When the four of them were sitting comfortably on the patio with tea and cookies, Beth clarified the purpose of her visit.

"I have some unsettling news."

Mary, Lou, and Abigail exchanged looks of concern.

"What is it, Beth?" Abigail asked.

"There was a car crash—"

"Oh my stars! Who? Where?" Mary cried out.

"No, no. I'm sorry, Mary," Beth interjected. "I think it was Katherine, a long time ago. The police are excavating and running tests."

"Oh, dear. You gave me a terrible fright," Mary said, noticeably relieved.

Abigail tapped her finger against her mug. "The poor girl," she said at last.

"How long ago?" Lou asked. "Do you have an idea?"

Beth chose her words carefully. She did not wish to reveal too much. "Yes, I believe so. She disappeared in 1977." They looked at her dumbfounded. "I've talked with a lot of people over the past couple of days. I found her friend Sarah and her old employer in Bangor—"

Lou interrupted. "Where was the crash?"

"On highway 46."

"Huh?"

"By Dedham—"

"What in heaven's name was she doing out there?" Mary asked.

"Taking a drive, I suppose," Beth replied.

The room quieted for a moment. Abigail looked far off in the distance as if tapping into old memories. Then she turned to Beth. "Does Rod know?"

"No. But the police have his name and number. They will probably contact him soon."

"I have to go over there," Abigail said, standing up. "He can't find out this way."

"Oh, Mother, sit down. The old fart is not going to welcome you into his home with the news that his daughter might be dead."

"How would *you* like to find out?" Abigail snapped.

Beth looked back and forth between Abigail and Mary. She thought the older woman was right. Even if he was unpleasant and rude, Rod should not have to hear it from a stranger. Abigail was doing the proper thing.

"Go then." Mary waved her hand at her mother impatiently.

Abigail turned to Beth. "Beth, how did you learn about all of this?"

Beth pursed her lips. "I found the crash site."

Mary raised her eyebrows. "Really? How?"

"You won't believe me."

"Try me."

Beth knew that whatever she said to Mary would be on the lips of everyone in town before the sun set. "I just had a weird intuition. There was this place on the road, and I decided to investigate." She thought it best to leave Kenny out of it. He liked his privacy and stories about Kenny and Beth in the woods were bound to spread like wildfire. "I don't know, Mary. It just happened."

"Looks like we have a psychic in our midst," Mary said with a look of delicious anticipation. "Perhaps the police can enlist you to solve other old crimes or disappearances."

Beth rolled her eyes. "I've had quite enough with this one, thank you very much."

Abigail turned to leave. "I'm going to visit Rod."

Beth also stood up. "I really must be going as well. I am very tired. The last couple of days have been crazy."

Mary followed them to the door.

Beth went home, grabbed a large picnic blanket, and headed for the beach. There she spent the afternoon. Off and on she cried and slept. She did not realize how many tears she had accumulated over the years. But she did not hold them back. She found that letting them flow allowed her to heal. She wished she had discovered that insight ages ago.

* * * *

When Abigail arrived, Rod's house was dark and the curtains were closed, but his car was parked out front. She knocked firmly on the door, waited several minutes, and knocked again. "I know you're in there, Rod. It's Abigail. Please answer. It's very important." Abigail spent the following ten minutes knocking and shouting until Rod finally opened the door – abruptly and with anger.

"What do you want, woman?"

Abigail took a deep breath. "May I come in?"

"No!"

"Rod, it's important. I wouldn't ask if it wasn't."

"If it's important, why don't you get on with it?"

"I'd really like to come in," she coaxed.

"The answer is *no*. Now be out with it and leave me in peace."

Abigail sighed. "I just thought you should hear it from me."

"What?" he shouted.

"The remains of a car crash have been found. . . an old crash."

"So?"

"The driver did not survive. It uh—"

"Why would I care?"

"It may have been Katherine."

"She didn't have a car," he responded dryly.

Abigail glanced away awkwardly. "The police are going to run tests. They may come by to talk with you."

"Let 'em come, then."

"Do you understand what I am saying?" she asked. Rod's mannerisms and expression seemed as tight and unfeeling as they had been the moment he opened the door.

"Yes, you are interrupting me with a bunch of harebrained ideas and theories that have nothing to do with me, my daughter, or my life," he shouted as he slammed the door.

Abigail stood on the porch for several minutes in stunned silence. Then she returned to her car and drove away.

* * * *

Several hours later, the young, redheaded detective arrived at Rod Thompson's house. This time Rod answered more promptly, but he held the door only six inches open, and he peered out suspiciously.

"May I help you?"

The detective showed his badge. "I'm Detective Douglas with the Hancock County Sheriff's Office. May I come in?"

Rod pursed his lips, trying to hide his disdain. He knew that being uncooperative with the police was not going to help him maintain his privacy in the long run. Reluctantly, he opened the door.

The inside of the Thompson house was dreary. The perpetually closed curtains were thick and dark brown from the inside. Several small lamps with low wattage bulbs glowed throughout the living room – one on each side of the couch and one on the top of a large bookshelf covered with dust, magazines, and books in a chaotic arrangement.

Rod led Detective Douglas through the living room and into the kitchen. Several days' worth of dirty dishes, empty soup cans, and the remnants of microwavable dinners littered the counters. The detective sat down at the kitchen table, discreetly moving a stack of newspapers aside. He pulled out his notebook and pen, and he motioned for Rod to sit across from him. Rod remained standing.

"I'm afraid I have some disturbing news," he began. The detective was nervous. He had never before visited a home burdened with the information he carried that day.

Rod stood above him, tapping his foot subtly.

"Please sit down, Mr. Thompson."

"I'd rather not," Rod growled. Nevertheless, he pulled out a chair and slowly sat down across from Detective Douglas.

The detective took a deep breath and exhaled. "We have identified the body of your daughter, Katherine, as the victim of a fatal car crash. We believe the crash occurred thirty-five years ago."

"It's not my daughter."

"Oh. . . ah. . . you do not have a daughter named Katherine?"

Rod sighed in irritation. "I *do* have a daughter named Katherine, but she did *not* die in a car wreck."

Confused, the detective looked at his notes. "Do you know where your daughter is?"

"No," Rod responded, quiet and bitter.

"When was the last time you saw her?"

"She doesn't have a car."

"Sir. I beg your pardon, but when was the last time you saw your daughter?"

Silence.

"Sir?"

"October thirteenth, 1975."

Detective Douglas inhaled slowly. "Sir, we believe the crash happened in November of 'seventy-seven. If you have not seen your daughter since—"

"She did *not have* a car!"

"We recovered a license plate at the scene registered to a Katherine M. Thompson."

"It wasn't my Katherine."

"Sir," Detective Douglas said as gently as possible. "A lot can change in two years."

Rod stood up abruptly pushing the table and knocking over his chair. "Are we through?"

The detective ran his hand through his hair, bewildered. He did not know how to handle the situation and he wished his partner had joined him. He stood up, cleared his throat, and said, "Mr. Thompson, I will need to know where you were on November thirteenth of 1977."

Rod looked at the detective with an air of outraged defiance.

The detective folded his arms.

Rod left the room and moved toward the back of the house.

The detective grabbed his cell phone. "We can go to the station if you would prefer," he said, as he dialed the number to request backup.

Rod returned carrying a tattered, leather

notebook. He threw it on the table.

Detective Douglas picked it up. *1976 through 1981* was scrawled on the inside cover. The detective leafed through the book. A series of neatly printed but crowded log entries filled its pages. He read the first few entries.

December 3rd, 1976
Purchased on 12/2/76 from John Witherspoon in Miami. Needs paint and minor repairs. Renaming to "The Bottomless Blue."

December 6th, 1976
Laid out a course for the channel marker at Port Everglades. Ended up two miles off course. Forgot to take currents into account. Had to motor-sail last two miles.

December 7th, 1976
Two-foot waves today and winds from the northeast. Was able to sail downwind for three hours offshore between Fort Lauderdale and Miami.

The detective flipped through the pages. There he found detailed accounts of sailing conditions, nautical miles traveled, and ports visited. He searched until he found the specific date in question.

November 13th, 1977
Twelve miles east of Long Key at 16:03. Plan to anchor just outside of Layton before dark. Weather fair. Sunny with mild winds from the north.

He looked up at Rod and closed the book. "May I take this back to headquarters to make copies?"

"Sure," Rod grumbled. "Will you leave me alone now?"

"Yes, sir. I. . . ah. . . I'll return this as soon as I can." He almost said "Sorry for your loss," but he realized that would elicit a whole new wave of outbursts and denials. He reached into his pocket and felt the item he had intended to give Mr. Thompson, but he decided it was best to leave it alone and move on. The man was not ready for any form of acceptance. "Thank you for your time."

Rod said nothing. He marched across the room, opened the door, and motioned for the detective to leave.

On his way out of town, Detective Douglas stopped at Beth LaMonte's home.

* * * *

Beth returned from the beach a little after 3:00 p.m. Her eyes were a tad red, so she washed her face thoroughly in cold water. She was just about to make a snack when the doorbell rang.

"Yes? Oh, hello detective," Beth said warmly.

"I'm sorry to disturb you, ma'am."

"No problem. What can I do for you?"

The detective reached into his pocket. "I have Katherine's personal effects," he said, trying to sound professional. "Rod Thompson doesn't want to accept his daughter's death. I couldn't bring myself to leave this with him." He handed Beth a small key hanging from a sterling silver necklace. "You were her friend. I thought you should have it."

"Oh. . . I was not really her friend, exactly. I didn't know her. She died when I was a child, living in Minnesota."

"Ma'am, I would like to give this to someone," he replied, continuing to hold out the key. "The old man is just not ready."

Beth nodded, and she allowed him to drop the necklace into her hand. "So you know for certain now that it is Katherine?"

"Yes, ma'am. We have the license plate and a partial dental, enough to justify a death certificate. Mr. Thompson was in Florida sailing on the estimated date of the accident, so he cannot be implicated with anything. Not that we had any suspicions. Just routine, you know? I'm confident that by early next week we will have the investigation wrapped up and you folks will be able to have a funeral for the unfortunate miss."

Beth frowned softly. "Yes, I suppose so. I hadn't thought of that." Then she said, more to herself than to the detective, "I presume Abigail will take on the arrangements if Mr. Thompson is unwilling."

"That would be a good idea. I don't think he'll come around for a while." He looked at his feet, a little embarrassed. "I was not expecting such a powerful wave of denial. But I guess I'm not normally in the business of telling folks their loved ones are dead."

"I certainly hope this is one of the few times you will have to do so, detective."

"Thank you, ma'am. Good day. And. . . good luck." He walked back to his car, a slight slump in his posture.

Beth closed the door and stared at the key. "I believe I know what this is," she announced.

She spent several minutes looking for the old lockbox, having entirely forgotten where she stashed it. She found it stuffed under her bed. The small gold lock held stubbornly to the steadfast loop on the otherwise battered metal box. Beth slipped the key into the lock and turned it. It popped open. *This would have come in handy a couple of weeks ago.*

She returned the lockbox to its hiding place under the bed and gently laid the key with the letters and the diary in her bottom dresser drawer.

Chapter 24
Make It Right

Katherine Thompson arrived in the outskirts of Virginia Point at 10:13 a.m. Sunday morning, November 13th, 1977. She pulled into the driveway of the cottage, her old home, and sat in her car for several minutes, apprehensively rehearsing her story. She had intended to warn her father of her sudden and long overdue visit, but she neglected to put a stamp on the letter. When it was returned to her on Saturday, she almost changed her plans. But she decided that she would never be able to forgive herself if she did not put an end to the two-year estrangement and finally introduce her father to his granddaughter, Susan.

When she felt ready, she approached the door cautiously. The doorbell was still broken. It had been broken since she was eleven. So, she knocked and waited. He did not answer. She knocked again, this time a little more vigorously. "Dad usually stays home on Sundays," she mumbled. But then she realized that she was no longer in touch with what was *usual* in her father's life.

She walked around the house, peeking in windows. The place looked almost vacated. The kitchen was spotless. Neither coats nor shoes cluttered the front entranceway. When she reached the north side of the house, she was surprised to see an empty boat trailer.

A boat? Whose is this? Did Dad buy a boat?

Katherine was curious, but she did not want to be seen by the nosey locals, so she sneaked down to the marina as discreetly as possible, hoping to remain invisible. Two boats were moored at the docks. One, called *Mandy Bee,* was a fifteen-foot motorboat with yellow and black accents. The other, in the visitor's slip, was a small sailboat named *Starfish Bay.* Katherine quietly entered the store across from the marina.

A boy she did not recognize stood behind the counter watching a small television. He had medium length brown, uncombed hair and a few pimples. He wore faded jeans and a dark-blue Lynyrd Skynyrd t-shirt.

"Excuse me," she said, approaching the counter.

"Yes?" The teenager quickly turned down the television. He straightened his posture, as if to appear taller and more professional.

"Do you know Rod Thompson?"

"Ah, the owner of *The Bottomless Blue.* Yes, I know him."

"The Bottomless Blue?"

"The sloop. You've never seen her? Where have you been?"

"I'm from out of town," Katherine said dryly.

The boy laughed. "Well, we just moved here this

summer, so what can I say? I'm just joshing you."

Katherine smiled faintly. "Do you know where he is?"

"Oh, he's been gone several weeks now. He was headed for the Keys, I believe. He likes to spend the holidays there. That's what I hear."

"Oh." Katherine didn't know what to think.

"Do you want to leave him a message? He'll probably be back after the first of the year."

"No, I, uh. . . no. I just heard he was good at fixing carburetors. A friend of mine told me to look him up. I'll have it checked out somewhere else."

"Oh. There isn't a garage for at least twenty miles. Will you be okay?"

"Twenty miles? What about the garage on Sears Road?"

"I don't know of a garage on Sears Road. . . oh, there is a gas station on Sears and Main."

"Just a gas station?"

"I believe so. My friend, Jimmy, had to take his truck to Rockport a couple of months ago to get the brakes repaired."

Katherine frowned. "I thought Mr. Thompson was a mechanic."

"Oh, I'm sorry. I understand now. You're mistaken. See, he fixes boats. He's a *boat* mechanic. Boy your friend sure was way off. But I suppose, maybe, he *could* fix a carburetor. I never really thought about it. He doesn't say much. Sort of keeps to himself. But anyway, if you can make it to Rockport, you'll be fine."

Katherine forced a smile. "Thanks for your time."

She slipped out behind the store and up the hill in

order to avoid running into anyone who might recognize her. She was not in the mood for any "Oh, Katherine, where have you been?" conversations. After walking home she continued on to her secret beach. Sitting on the ground, she noticed it was cold and her pants were getting damp, but she did not move.

Why doesn't Dad run the garage anymore? Holidays in the Keys? That is not at all like him. I can't believe he bought a boat. Does he sail by himself?

A million thoughts raced through Katherine's mind. She did not even realize she was crying until a cold tear hit her hand. She wiped her face on her coat sleeve and pulled her knees up to her chest.

Once she accepted the reality that she would not see her father this trip, she resolved to send him a letter in January. She would include a picture *and* a stamp.

She climbed up the side of the rock and pulled out her diary. She unwrapped the garbage bags, unlocked the cashbox with the key around her neck, and removed it from the Tupperware. It was in surprisingly decent condition. She leafed through the pages and smiled. Then she sighed sadly. "Dad, I'm sorry I had all of these angry thoughts. But everything will be better next year. I'll put things right as soon as you come home."

She did not have a backpack, so she rewrapped the diary carefully and returned it to its hiding place. *Next time I'll bring Susie. We'll make a game and find it together. Hmm. I had definitely better bring her* before *she learns how to read.* Katherine laughed. "And I'll bring a toy," she said out loud. *Something waterproof. I can hide it in the gap before she comes down. How will I get her down here? Oh, never mind. Dad will help me figure it out.*

She stood up, brushed the sand off her jeans, and climbed back up the side of the cliff.

On the way out of town, Katherine visited her mother's grave. The graveyard was on the site of an old church, about one mile northwest of her father's home. She knelt down, touched her mother's grave, and whispered, "I'll make it right."

Chapter 25
The Scoop

By the following Wednesday the streets of Virginia Point buzzed with reporters from the *Portland Press Herald,* the *Bangor Daily News,* and WCSH-6 TV. Having grown bored with the Fourth of July parades that had come and gone, the journalists and newscasters salivated for information on the tantalizing tale of the disappearance of a small town girl and the recovery of her body.

Beth was concerned someone might dig up information on Susan, but after a couple of days it appeared they were all more interested in the macabre details of rust and bones than in the life of the young girl in flesh and blood. This suited Beth perfectly well, but she tried to tone it down in order to avoid being labeled *the psychic of mid-coast Maine.*

"You see," she said to one reporter, "we knew she traveled on that road the day she disappeared. The search party didn't locate her at the time. I decided to take a look, and I just got lucky."

There had been no search for Katherine in November of 1977, but the reporters never bothered to check the facts. Someone talked briefly with Detective Douglas and another member of the Hancock County Sheriff's Office as well as a Bucksport police officer. No one seemed to want to admit that they didn't really know the details. Detective Douglas told the press he was not allowed to release the particulars, so Beth got away with her diversion. Elaborate fibs were becoming her specialty. She tried not to focus her conscience on that development, choosing to justify herself instead. After all, she was protecting Susan, wherever she may be. It was Beth's self-appointed mission.

Abigail made arrangements for a funeral on Saturday. Katherine would be buried in the plot next to her mother. Abigail did not bother to get Rod's permission.

"It's Katherine's resting place, and I'm not going to go head-to-head with that stubborn fool over the issue. He'll think twice about digging her up in the middle of the night, I can tell you that. Once she's laid there, he'll let her be, whether he accepts the whole thing or not."

Kenny's name showed up on the police report, so word got out that he was involved. This, of course, turned the gossip on Main Street up a notch, but there was nothing Beth could do other than play along and try to swish away any controversial comments with a shrug and a roll of the eyes.

Mary seemed to eat it up like a box of chocolates, but Beth threw her a warning glare when she approached the subject.

"Just let me know when you're ready to spill the details, dear," Mary had said, winking.

"Nothing happened, Mary. For God's sake we were staring at human remains. How romantic could that possibly be?"

* * * *

The subject of human remains appeared to be of great intrigue to the reporter, a young blond woman, who chatted with Beth and Kenny on the morning Rod ventured down to the dock. Kenny didn't notice the old man until he was only a few feet away.

"What is this?" Rod screamed, storming up the street toward them. "Who the fuck are you?" he asked the reporter. The young woman's eyes grew wide. She backed up, placing Kenny and Beth between herself and Rod Thompson.

Kenny stared at Rod coldly, refusing to answer.

"What are you talking about? Who is this woman?" he asked Kenny.

Kenny looked Rod straight in the eye. "She is from the *Bangor Daily News*. We are discussing. . ." He sighed, letting his breath out slowly. "We are discussing Katherine."

"You leave Katherine alone," Rod shouted. Addressing Beth, he asked, "What in God's name do you think you know about Katherine, you meddlesome woman?"

"Rod. . . she found Katherine's body."

Rod's face turned white as a sheet. "My daughter is not *dead*. It was *not* Katherine."

"Rod, please—"

Rod waved his finger at Beth. "So *this* is what you're up to. Spreading lies and rumors. You want to be a celebrity? You *bitch!* You conniving bitch. I want you out of my house by the end of the day."

"Now hold on there a moment," Kenny said as he stepped between Rod and Beth. "Watch your mouth. No one is going to kick Beth out of anywhere. You're going to need to face reality, old man."

"Don't you take that condescending tone with me. I want her the fuck *out of my life!*" Rod trembled, his face red and his temples pulsing.

Kenny formed a fist. His heart raced and his blood pressure elevated until he could hear the pounding in his ears. He felt rage swell up within him. He wanted to strike the old man, strike him and watch him hit the pavement. He wanted to hear his skull crack as it hit the ground and listen to his pleas for mercy, this pathetic man deranged in denial of his daughter's death. The man was nothing to him, a worn out piece of pottery waiting to be smashed into dust. No, he was worse. Rod represented a thousand nights of listening to his father yell and his mother cry. The old man's face began to morph into the likeness of Mack McLeary.

Kenny took a step forward. Rod glared at Kenny. Behind Rod's eyes, Kenny saw a thick layer of indifference, a coating that formed like the skin on a pudding left out in the sun. It was a protective cover designed by the mind to deny the anguish it could not comprehend. Kenny recognized that indifference. It was the one that had clung to his soul since he was six years old. He backed down and unclenched his fist.

Gritting his teeth, he addressed Rod sternly. "The lady is not going anywhere," he said, quietly but with determination. "And if you try to kick her out, you'll have to answer to me."

Rod sneered, turned, and walked away. He retreated to *The Bottomless Blue* and swiftly closed the hatch.

As Kenny watched the lonely old man walk away, his clothing neat, his skull intact, a revelation overwhelmed him. At that moment Kenny knew for certain the answer to a question that had been haunting him for years.

He was not his father. And he never could be.

He put his hand on Beth's shoulder and ushered her away from the scene, leaving the reporter unsettled and in shock.

The young woman drove back to Bangor and was never seen in Virginia Point again.

＊ ＊ ＊ ＊

That evening, in the backyard, Beth got into a heated argument with the firefly. One side bellowed harsh comments while the other flitted in an erratic, agitated pattern.

"I am *not* going to talk to him," Beth said defiantly. "He's a lunatic."

The firefly made a large sweeping circle. Then it dropped suddenly and came to a halt inches above the ground.

"I don't know what the hell that is supposed to mean, but I cannot talk to the man. *No one* can talk to him. He *won't* accept it, Katherine, and I cannot make him."

Moving swiftly toward Beth's bedroom window, the light creature traveled in a spiral and stopped when it reached the glass.

Tears gathered at the edges of Beth's eyes. "I don't know if you realize what I've been through, but it has been an emotional nightmare. Phone calls, house calls, kicking through the forest. Have *you* ever tracked down the site of a person's death? Or seen their remains scattered on the ground, callously decomposed by time and nature. Have you? Huh?

"Let me tell you from personal experience, it is *not* a pretty picture."

The firefly drifted slowly from the window to the ground.

"Yeah, that's right. And guess who sent me on this roller coaster ride from hell? It was a little ball of light slightly bigger than a marble which has been invading my privacy and unsettling my dreams ever since I moved to Maine. . . I'm tired, Katherine. I've had about all I can handle."

Beth returned to the house. She crossed to the entryway and kicked off her shoes. On her way to the stairs, she caught a glimpse of the photo of Katherine and Susan out of the corner of her eye. She walked toward it. Her stomach turned over with an ache that had been hanging over her head ever since she discovered Katherine's body.

"Susan," she whispered.

She picked up the picture and touched the glass gently.

"God damn it. How did I get myself into this mess?"

Chapter 26
Saying Goodbye

It was fifty-three degrees and cloudy on the day of Katherine's funeral, unusually cold for July. Several townsfolk and the Bennings gathered around the gravesite at the cemetery just outside of town. A stone with the words *Katherine Marie Thompson, Feb 7, 1958 to Nov 13, 1977* rested next to a large, freshly dug hole. Beside it a matching grave marker read *Lucille Elizabeth Thompson, Aug 3, 1935 to Oct 13, 1962, Beloved Wife and Mother*.

A small breeze rustled the leaves of a nearby maple tree. The reverend was a small, nervous, balding man who mumbled. His feeble presence annoyed Beth. She assumed he was used to the luxury of a pulpit and a microphone, but she still felt that one ought to have some skill in speaking before embarking on a career in the ministry. It seemed more than fair. She caught herself tapping her foot impatiently, and she looked away.

Kenny stood next to Mary who was on Beth's right. Mary looked mildly bored, Kenny appeared reflective, and Abigail, who stood next to the minister,

274

seemed genuinely moved. *Perhaps she can hear what the goofball is saying,* Beth thought bitterly. The Bennings also stood by the minister across from Abigail. Linda cried openly, resting her head on Wyatt's shoulder. Wyatt gazed far off in the distance, as if in another time or place.

Beth did not notice the man ascending the hill twenty yards away, but Abigail's eyes caught him the moment he reached the crest. Abigail watched him, waiting for him to join the small group of mourners, but he stood at the top of the hill and moved no farther. Abigail narrowed her eyes and stared at him for a minute. Then, with a *stop* gesture, she threw her hand in the air suddenly, just missing the minister's face.

"Hold it, Reverend," she said sharply.

The nervous man halted mid-sentence, his mouth gaping slightly.

Abigail excused herself from the ceremony and marched up the knoll to greet the unexpected visitor. Those gathered at the gravesite watched her in stunned silence. They glanced around at one another with bewildered expressions, unsure of what to do. The reverend, having never encountered such a discourteous interruption, shook his head and murmured to himself.

Abigail addressed the man on the hill. "Are you coming down to join us?"

The man crossed his arms and scowled.

"For Christ's sake, Rod, we're laying your daughter to rest. I would think that might give you some peace after all these years."

The man began to turn away.

"Don't turn your back on me, you stubborn old fool," she shouted. "You need to come to your senses. She has been awaiting a proper burial for thirty-five years, and she deserves to have her father in attendance. Wouldn't you agree?"

Rod opened his mouth as if to say something, but no sound emerged.

Abigail softened her voice and took on a more compassionate tone. "Don't you see what this means? She didn't stay away from you all these years. She didn't *refuse* to come. She *couldn't* come. But she would have. I know people, Rod, and I know in my heart that she would have come."

Beth felt the blood drain out of her face, for she realized that she, herself, not only knew in her *heart* that Katherine would have come back; she knew it for a fact. She knew that Katherine wanted more than anything in the world to mend the rift and see her father again. And yet Beth stood there and said nothing. As she looked up the hill, she no longer saw a stubborn, hateful man. She saw a human being – a human being who suffered a tragedy Beth could not fathom, a man turned cold by years of waiting, wondering, and self-admonishing, a man who had grieved long before the day Beth discovered Katherine's remains.

Abigail continued to try and reach him. She spoke gently. "You can't undo what's been done. No one blames you for what happened. I'm sure she knew you loved her. You can't bring her back, Rod. But she was a vibrant, wonderful girl. What you can do is honor the life she lived so joyously. You owe that to her. You owe it to yourself."

The man looked past Abigail to the gravesite.

"Are you really going to stand here and not say goodbye?"

He looked down.

Abigail marched up to the top of the hill and grabbed one of his arms. "Come on. I'm not going to let you make this mistake." She pulled on him. Reluctantly, like a reprimanded child, he followed her. Several mourners near the end of the freshly dug pit moved aside to make a space for him. He stood there, arms folded. It was difficult to discern his emotional condition. He looked stubborn and sour, like a bust of Beethoven. He remained for the entire ceremony, even taking a moment to throw a handful of dirt on the coffin. The minister, a man of ambiguous faith, included this gesture, which was typically a Jewish custom. Beth presumed he liked to see himself as worldly and multi-cultural. Rod, having long since abandoned church services, complied obediently, his face steady and distant.

* * * *

Beth arrived home, shaken and teary-eyed, but she bolted up the stairs with vigor and determination. "I should have done this the day I came home from Bangor," she said, chastising herself. "Selfish, stupid Beth. Who gave you the right to decide who gets information and who does not?" She pulled the letters from her dresser drawer. "These do not belong to you. They belong to him. He deserves to know."

She went back downstairs and retrieved the photo from her mantel. She stared at it for a minute, trying to remember if anyone in town had a color copier. Finally, she resigned and copied the photo carefully on her black-and-white home copy machine. She meticulously cut the gray-toned photo to size and replaced it in the frame. It was not nearly as lovely, but it would suffice. She also copied the letters. *For Susan,* she told herself. *If I ever find her.*

She wasn't certain whether Rod would be home or at the marina. If he was on *The Bottomless Blue,* he would have the hatch locked. She did not wish to leave the letters on the deck. So she decided to go to Rod's house and drop them through the mail slot where they would be safe and where he would eventually find them. She approached Rod's house tentatively. "I'll just toss these in the slot and be on my way," she whispered. "No need to knock."

As the letters slipped from her hand to the floor of Rod's home, Beth's heart skipped a beat. They were gone, and she could no longer change her mind. *Am I doing the right thing?* The man did not believe his daughter was dead. The letters would settle the matter once and for all. Was she doing him any favors by forcing such information upon him? Then again, she was hardly helping him by enabling him in a lie.

Besides, she realized, *he knew.* When he allowed the dirt to fall out of his hand and onto the coffin, he knew. He would not even have come if there were not something deep inside of him that had begun to acknowledge that Katherine was truly gone.

Beth walked away, turning back once, wondering if he was already reading the letters.

* * * *

That night Beth cleaned up her studio and hung the portrait of the redheaded girl in the center of the windowless wall of the room. The firefly appeared, startling her.

Beth smiled wearily. "Now that you've been laid to rest, aren't you supposed to disappear, become one with the ether or something?"

The firefly floated motionless in the middle of the room.

"I gave him the letters."

Still no movement.

"I'm sorry I didn't do it sooner."

The firefly drifted slowly toward Beth.

"Can you rest in peace now? Let me live a normal life again?"

The light creature continued to drift.

"You're not going to let up until I find Susan, are you?"

It made a small, swishing movement in the air.

"You're a royal pain in the ass, you know that?"

The firefly danced in circles as if laughing at Beth.

"How on God's green earth am I going to find her with the information I have?"

It drifted back toward the window.

"And if I don't find her, will you haunt me forever?"

The firefly slipped through the glass.

Beth sighed and retreated to her bedroom. She fished Susan's authentic birth certificate out of the drawer, booted up her computer, and took a seat.

She stayed up until 1:00 a.m. surfing the Internet,

reading genealogy and adoptions sites, searching for an entry that matched or was similar to Susan's. It seemed an impossible feat. Susan may not know her real birthday. She may not even know that she was adopted. If she wasn't searching, how would Beth ever locate her? It would take an act of God to bring them together.

Beth spent forty-five minutes trying to compose a paragraph she could post on a variety of sites. She started over several times. "How does one politely say 'your parents had a birth certificate forged?'"

> *Hello. I am searching for a girl born May 23, 1977. DOB on her birth certificate may be different but close to that date. Baby was born in Bangor, Maine to Katherine Thompson. Six pounds, seven ounces. Birth name, Susan Elizabeth. Name probably changed. Adopted by a couple from upstate New York.*

She added her first name and email address to the message, posted it wherever possible, and finally went to bed exhausted.

Her nightmares had stopped, relieving her anxiety, yet ending her window to the past. She found herself longing to see images of Susan's adoptive parents or their home. But she was on her own. She checked her email in the morning, after her shower, and again after breakfast.

"You might as well leave it alone. It could take weeks, months. . . even years, I suppose. For now, you need to start painting again, bring some new pieces to Bobby Downy, and get on with your life."

* * * *

Beth decided to take a walk. After about a half of a mile, she picked a small bundle of wildflowers and headed toward the cemetery. When she got to the top of the hill, she stopped abruptly and backed away slowly. She hid behind a cluster of bushes.

Upon Katherine's grave, on his hands and knees, Rod Thompson was crying. Beth bit her lip. He did not look like the man she knew from the outrages or even from the funeral. The harshness was gone. His sobs resounded through the cemetery, pure and unconstrained. Beth sat behind the bushes, as tears of her own silently ran down her face. She remembered what it felt like that day in the forest when she was consumed with tears, when she finally grieved about events left unaddressed for decades. She understood what Rod was experiencing. She knew it was painful, yet cleansing. She knew it was necessary.

Beth left the flowers by the bushes and quietly slipped away.

Chapter 27
Needle in a Haystack

Weeks passed, July slipped into August, and Beth heard nothing. She faithfully checked her email and periodically scanned the adoption websites. In the meantime, she sat down with the young computer wiz recommended by Bobby Downy and started her website. She painted three paintings – two lighthouses and one coastal scene – all of which ended up at *Kelp Corner*. She thought about selling the portrait of the red-haired girl, but she simply could not part with it. Thus, it remained in her studio, the aura of a passionate young spirit inspiring Beth's creative endeavors.

Most of the time, the firefly left her alone. But Beth often found herself closing the curtains before sunset on days when she felt emotionally vulnerable.

* * * *

Before the end of July, Beth finally confessed her secret to Mary and Abigail, hoping they might have ideas or resources unavailable to Beth.

"A baby?" Mary exclaimed, casting a reproachful glance in Beth's direction. "I can't believe you kept this from me."

Abigail beamed. "You are full of surprises, aren't you, Beth?"

Blushing, Beth replied, "I'm sorry, ladies. I was thinking that. . . I didn't want the reporters to—"

"It's okay," Abigail said. "You do not owe us an explanation."

Mary folded her arms and looked at her mother with an expression that said *she damn well does owe us an explanation,* but Mary kept her mouth politely shut.

"I was just hoping you might have some ideas about how I might find her," Beth said.

"You're several steps ahead of me using the computer," Abigail replied. "But I'll check in with the retirement community, see if there is anyone from New York who might know something about something." She winked.

Mary sighed. "I'll ask around."

But their efforts proved fruitless.

* * * *

On August third, Beth visited Kenny at his store.

He looked up and smiled. Beth returned his smile, warmly, remembering the days when he merely looked at her with dead, unreadable eyes.

"How have you been, Beth?"

"Okay, I guess. I've been searching for Susan. No results. But I've done some painting," she said, hoping to sound a little more cheerful. "I'm trying not

283

to center my life around finding her."

Kenny frowned. "I think that's wise. With a forged birth certificate, she may be impossible to track down."

"Yeah. It's too bad I can't rattle Eleanor Sharpe for more information."

"What about her son?"

"Why didn't I think of that?" Beth shook her head in disbelief. "Man, she even gave me his name. It was Craig or Greg. Gregory. It was Gregory."

"He's not likely to talk. I mean, don't feel stupid. It's not as if you overlooked a gem of a source."

"At least I can try."

"Would you like my help?"

"Yes, please. Where should we begin?"

Kenny put his index finger over his mouth. "There must be an estate settlement going on in Bangor. We could check the house. Also, maybe the cemetery has contact information. Or we could just search for Gregory Sharpe in the listings."

Beth and Kenny sat down at his computer and ran a couple of searches. Several Gregory Sharpes resided in New England. Kenny called the one listed in Connecticut first. No luck. The other two did not answer. Kenny chose not to leave messages.

"We'll try them again later."

"What about the cemeteries?"

"Good idea." He jotted down the phone numbers for the cemeteries near Eleanor Sharpe's home. Beth leaned in and cupped her ear as Kenny made the call. A man with a Canadian accent came on the line. Kenny inquired about Eleanor.

The man searched his records for a moment. "Yes,

Eleanor Sharpe is buried here."

"Do you have a family contact name? A Greg Sharpe, perhaps?"

"Oh. . . I, uh. . . I don't know if I can give out that information. Let me check, eh?"

Kenny gave Beth a shrug.

When the man returned on the line he said, "I guess it's all right. Yes, Greg Sharpe made the arrangements." He gave Kenny the number.

"Thank you very much."

"Sure. Have a nice day."

"You, too."

Beth and Kenny looked at the number. It was the same one they found for the Gregory Sharpe listed in New Jersey. Kenny dialed it again. Still no answer, so he hung up.

"Should we leave a message?" Beth asked.

"Probably. But we have to word it carefully." He tapped his finger on the table.

Thirty seconds later, Kenny's phone rang. Beth positioned herself so she could hear the conversation.

"Hello?"

"Hello. This is Greg Sharpe. Who is this?"

"Oh, uh, this is Kenny McLeary," Kenny said. He was caught off guard. He threw Beth a wild-eyed shrug.

"Did you try to call me?"

"Yes, I did. I, uh. . . my friend knew your mother. And, uh. . ."

"Yes?"

"She was, I mean, we were wondering if we could talk to you. . . uh, ask you a question."

"Shoot."

Kenny trembled slightly. A part of Beth wanted to put him out of his misery and handle the situation herself. But she was nervous. She would stammer just as much as Kenny. Plus, she would be talking to a man who had the audacity to sell a child. Perhaps such a man was better handled by a man. Kenny cringed, but Beth did not reach for the phone.

Kenny sighed, swallowed, and straightened his posture. His voice became confident and clear. "We know that Eleanor was caring for an eighteen-month-old girl in November of 1977."

Silence.

"We are aware of what happened—"

"What do you want?"

"We're just looking for the girl."

"I can't help you."

"Any information you may have—"

"I can't help you."

"Greg, we know you made the arrangements."

Silence again.

"Listen. We just want information. Anything."

"June Harrison."

Kenny scribbled it down. "Was she—"

"She was my girlfriend's cousin. I don't know where she lives. I don't have contact with my old girlfriend. As far as I'm concerned, this woman doesn't exist. Do you get my drift?"

"Yes."

"And if you don't, I'll make your life very unpleasant."

Kenny's eyes narrowed. He glanced at Beth with a *let's kick this guy's ass* expression.

Beth waved her hands frantically and shook her

head *no.*

"I hear you loud and clear, Mr. Sharpe."

"I'm sure you do."

"But you should know—"

"Yes?"

"*This* time, you did the *right* thing."

Silence.

"Thank you for the information."

Greg hung up the phone without a response.

Kenny grinned at Beth. He waved the paper joyfully.

They spent another hour searching for June Harrison with no results. A customer entered the store looking for a pendant. Kenny approached the counter. Beth excused herself, nodding to Kenny and to the customer.

"I'll try some more at home. I might have better luck on the adoption websites. Thank you for your ingenuity. And for dealing with that—" She smiled politely at the young lady standing by the counter. "—with that *guy.*"

"My pleasure," Kenny said, winking. Then he turned his attention to the young lady.

As Beth wandered down the street, she saw Rod Thompson walking in her direction. She glanced around quickly, but there was no place to go without it being dreadfully obvious that she was ditching him. She didn't have the heart to do that, so she moved straight ahead, trying to keep her eyes forward.

"Good afternoon, Beth," he said softly.

Beth was momentarily stunned. Rod nodded to her in greeting.

"Uh. . . Good afternoon, sir."

He continued up the street as if there was nothing particularly odd about the encounter. Truly there wasn't, just a man saying hello to a woman he knows. But, nonetheless, Beth turned around and watched him walk away, her mouth gaping, her stomach fluttering.

* * * *

At home, Beth changed the last line of her Internet query to *"Adopted by June Harrison and her husband from New York."* She spent a little time searching for June's name. Then she gave up and went to bed.

The following Wednesday, Beth awoke with an annoying cramp in her neck. She stood up, stretching and rolling her neck in circles. She sat down at her computer absentmindedly like she did every morning. It had become a ritual. She carefully sifted through the junk mail before deleting it. Although she was fed up with scanning emails about cheap drugs, mortgage refinancing, and penis enlargement, she wanted to be careful not to delete *the* message, the one she hoped might eventually come.

That morning, it arrived.

Beth could scarcely believe her eyes when she saw the subject line, "Susan Elizabeth." She closed her eyes and took a deep breath. It could be a dead end, a random inquiry about a Susan Elizabeth born in Cincinnati. But it could be someone who knew something about the Susan Elizabeth for whom Beth was searching. It might be Susan Elizabeth herself. Beth opened the message.

Dear Beth:

I saw your posting on the Adoption Reunion Registry. I may be the Susan Elizabeth you are searching for.

After my twenty-first birthday, my parents told me that I was adopted when I was almost two years old. My mother's name is June Harrison, and I grew up in Saratoga County. I had always known my birthday to be May 29, 1977, but I guess my real birthday was a few days before. My parents do not remember the date. But they did adopt me from a family in Maine. My birth mother was a teenager, a single mom. She committed suicide, and my birth grandmother believed I would have a better life with my new parents. So they arranged paperwork that listed my adoptive parents as my birth parents. I am not sure which information, if any, is the same as what was on my original birth certificate.

I have had a great life. My parents are wonderful people, very loving. They felt bad for keeping the secret from me, but at the time they told me, I honestly didn't care. I wouldn't have wished for anything different than to have grown up with them.

But recently I have felt compelled to search. If you knew my birth mother, I would love to talk with you and learn more about her. I am currently living in New Hampshire.

Sincerely,
Jennifer Harrison

Beth immediately hit the reply button and left a short, to the point message. "Jennifer. Please call me." She included her full name and cell phone number.

Then she shuffled through the paperwork at her desk, all the notes and phone numbers from her search. She located Greg Sharpe's number on the page that had "June Harrison" written on it. She dialed the number.

"Hello?"

"Greg?"

"Yes. Who is this?"

"This is Kenny McLeary's friend, Beth LaMonte," she said. Then she rapidly added, "Don't hang up or I'll have the police at your door so fast you won't have time to blink."

"You're walking on thin ice, Ms. LaMonte."

"I have a couple more questions."

"You can't prove anything. I suggest you stop making threats before I end up slapping a restraining order on you."

"Now that is interesting. Because I've got a little something in my pocket called *I found Susie and she has the forged birth certificate.*"

"You won't trace that to me. And my mother's dead."

Beth sighed. The tough guy routine was not working. "Yes, your mother's dead. I'm sorry. She was a terrific lady." Beth cringed. "But perhaps it would hasten her soul past purgatory if you help me. She may have wanted Susie to know."

"Know what?"

"Did your mother present herself as Susie's

grandmother?"

There was a moment of silence. "Yes. She said she was the baby's grandmother. It just made things. . . *smoother*."

"I'm sure it did. Did she tell the couple that Susie's mother committed suicide?"

"She may have," Gregory replied smugly.

"Thank you for your time."

"Don't call me again."

"I have no interest in talking with you further."

"Then stop calling me!" He hung up.

Beth sighed. She placed her phone on the desk, and she fantasized about police officers seizing Gregory Sharpe in a stranglehold. Then all at once it hit her.

"I found her. Oh my God, I really found her." She started to cry. She took a quick shower, hoping not to miss Jennifer's call. Then she got dressed and left the house, heading into town to talk with Kenny.

She had walked barely five minutes when her cell phone rang.

"Hello?"

"Beth?"

"Yes, this is Beth."

"Hi. This is Jennifer Harrison. We've exchanged emails about—"

"Jennifer. Thank you so much for calling."

"Do you think I'm the Susan you're looking for?"

"I believe so. Yes, I really do."

The voice on the other end of the phone trembled a little. "So. . . you knew my birth mother?"

"Not exactly." Beth realized that she had not prepared what she would say. She was so obsessed with finding Susan that she had forgotten to plan what came next. She thought for a moment. "I live in the house where your mother grew up in Virginia Point, Maine. I have some of her things. I'd really like to share them with you."

A pause. "Yes," the voice said softly. "I would like that very much."

Beth pursed her lips. "One of the things I want to share with you is a place."

"A place?"

"Yeah. I know it sounds odd, but it was your mother's very special place."

"Her special place," Jennifer repeated, her voice wistful.

"Where did you say you lived?"

"Manchester."

"Oh, gee, that's probably a three or four hour drive from here. You probably don't have—"

"I can come up Sunday," Jennifer said.

"Sunday would be great. I'll set up a room for you. You can spend the night. Is that okay?"

"Sounds perfect."

She gave Jennifer detailed directions before saying goodbye. After that she practically ran to Kenny's store.

"I found her," Beth shouted as she burst through the door.

Kenny wandered out of the smithery to the front counter.

"I found her, Kenny."

Kenny smiled. "Susan?"

"Yes. Her name is Jennifer now, but I'm sure it is her. And it's all thanks to you, really. If we hadn't contacted Greg and gotten her mother's name, she probably wouldn't have found me."

"It was my pleasure."

Beth wanted to throw her arms around him in an embrace, but the counter separated them. She hesitated, fumbling around with her arms, before reaching out and offering her hand for a shake. Kenny gripped it firmly.

"Congratulations," he said warmly.

She pulled her hand away abruptly and shifted into a mild mania. "She's coming on Sunday. I have to get ready. Do you think Mary has a rollaway bed? Of course she has a rollaway bed. I think. I'd better ask her. I've gotta go," she called as she bounded out of the store.

* * * *

Beth ran up the steps of *The Virginia Point Cove* and rang the doorbell two times in a row. Mary answered.

"Beth. How are you?"

"I found her."

"Who?"

"Katherine Thompson's daughter."

"Oh my stars. You are a busy little one, aren't you?"

Beth practically pushed Mary aside, ran toward Abigail, and hugged her spontaneously. "I found her," she repeated.

"I heard," Abigail replied, smiling.

Beth turned away from Abigail and asked Mary, "Do you have a cot? A rollaway bed?"

"Why, yes, I have two."

"Jennifer. Susan's new name," she explained. "Jennifer will be coming on Sunday. I don't want to ask her to sleep on the couch."

Mary put her hands on her hips. "She ought to stay *here,* Beth. We're the people who run an inn, remember?"

Beth blushed. "I know, Mary. I'm not trying to insult you. It's just that. . ." She didn't know how to explain it. She had breathed Katherine, and then Susan, night and day from the moment she found the diary, perhaps from the moment she met the firefly. Beth wanted Jennifer near. She didn't really want to share her. "It's just that she wants to stay in her mother's old home," she said finally.

"I'll ask Lou if he can bring one around in the truck," Mary grumbled.

"Thank you, thank you." Beth hugged Mary, and then she quickly headed for the door. "I have a lot to do. I must get busy."

"You and Jennifer visit us, all right?" Abigail called after her.

"Of course," Beth answered as she ran down the stairs and up the block.

* * * *

"Someone had a few too many cups of coffee this morning," Mary said as she watched Beth go.

"Don't be jealous, Mary."

"Who's jealous?"

"You are. Beth has her finger on the pulse of all kinds of going-ons you knew nothing about."

294

"So?"

Abigail lightly touched her daughter's cheek.

Mary sighed, rolled her eyes, and capitulated. "I suppose you're right. I am a little jealous. She sure has stirred things up this summer. My, oh my."

"Indeed she has."

"But I've got to hand it to her," Mary said wistfully as she watched Beth disappear at the end of the block.

"Yes?"

"She's good for us."

"I wholeheartedly agree."

* * * *

Later that evening, Beth tried to calm her racing mind by sipping a glass of wine and looking out over the bay at twilight. She sat on a thick blanket near the edge of the cliff in the clearing. Around 9:15 p.m., the firefly joined her. It seemed to float down from nowhere.

Beth, having finally conquered her mania, smiled softly. "I found her, Katherine," she whispered. "I found Susie."

The firefly made slow, gentle circles around Beth.

"Can you believe I found her?"

The calm, rhythmic movement continued.

"Her name is Jennifer now."

Beth sat quietly for several minutes while the firefly drifted leisurely. She enjoyed the sound of crickets chirping in the woods, the light of the full moon shining low on the horizon, and the smell of the moist air. She felt peaceful.

"Are you going to visit?" Beth asked.

The firefly continued to glide softly. Then it came to rest, floating a few inches away from Beth's face.

"Thank you for this adventure, this journey," Beth said. "I'm not sure when I've felt this *alive*."

The firefly, being neither alive nor dead, had no visible response to that comment.

"I mean, don't take that personally," she said awkwardly. "Oh, you know what I mean. . . at least I hope you do."

Beth sat with the firefly until the wine made her sleepy. "I have a lot of work to do in the morning." She walked back to the house. "She's coming to visit. Susan. I mean Jennifer. Here. . . me. . . us."

The firefly drifted away as Beth slipped inside and locked the door.

Chapter 28
Discovery

Beth spent an inordinate amount of energy preparing for Sunday. She vacuumed the studio, put away the easels, and pushed as many things to one side as was practical, without making the room look cluttered. She set up the rollaway bed in one corner of the studio, dressing it in clean, light blue sheets and a blue, floral comforter. Then she selected her most comfortable pillow and placed it lovingly in the bed.

She tucked the copies of Katherine's letters in the back of the diary. Then she went into town and purchased a new cashbox from the hardware store. It would not fit the Tupperware, but she was able to wrap the diary in plastic and nestle it in the box. She secured the box with the little gold lock and put the key around her neck for safekeeping. Then she wrapped the cash box in several plastic garbage bags and placed the bundle by the door.

On Sunday morning, she set the table with an array of snacks – bread, crackers, and store-bought cookies. After arranging the non-perishables, she washed grapes, cut watermelon, and sliced cheese, placing those items in the refrigerator.

She became very anxious when she glanced at the calendar on the kitchen wall. August 13. "Oh my God. The thirteenth is not a lucky day for this family. What if. . ."

She did not want to finish her own sentence. She prayed that Jennifer would have a safe drive, and she tried to read a book to take her mind off of the pending visit. Jennifer said she would arrive a little after noon. At 10:30 a.m., Beth took the wrapped diary and a red handkerchief down to the secret beach. She hid the diary and marked the fissure by securing the handkerchief under the cashbox. A small flag of red was visible outside of the hole.

"That may be a little obvious, but it is not like I didn't have any help finding it myself."

She returned to the house and tried to get lost in her book, but all she could hear was the clock ticking. As it approached one o'clock, Beth began to really worry, and she paced the living room anxiously. Then she heard the sound of car tires rolling over gravel. She ran to the door. A silver Lexus pulled up the drive. It had New Hampshire plates. Beth could hardly contain her excitement, but she tried to appear normal as she stood on the front porch, waiting.

When the car stopped, Beth stepped forward to greet her visitor.

Jennifer emerged from the car dressed in an olive green dress and expensive olive green shoes. Her long auburn hair was smooth and lustrous, her green eyes sparkling with excitement. Beth halted. She felt as if her heart stopped entirely for several seconds.

It was the red-haired girl from her painting. The

likeness was uncanny.

Jennifer smiled. "Beth, I presume?"

Beth said nothing for a moment, while she tried to recover from the impact of seeing her painting practically come to life before her eyes. Finally, she walked forward, reached out her arms, and said, "Jennifer, it is so good to meet you."

They hugged briefly, then Jennifer fumbled with her keys and pulled a black suitcase from the trunk.

"Let me take that," Beth insisted and Jennifer followed her into the house. "I'll just run this upstairs. Why don't you have a seat at the kitchen table? I put out a few snacks. You must be starving."

"Thank you."

Beth put the suitcase in the studio. She stared at the painting, which she now realized was a portrait of Susan. . . Jennifer. She pulled it off the wall, turned it around, and tucked it among her art supplies on the opposite side of the room. Then she descended the stairs and fetched the cheese and fruit, along with butter and blueberry jam, from the refrigerator.

"Thank you for inviting me," Jennifer said, radiating warmth.

"I am so happy you came," Beth replied, trying not to gawk at the attractive woman she felt she already knew.

"I'm anxious to learn about my mother," Jennifer said politely, as she selected several crackers and slices of cheese from the array of food laid out before her.

Beth had spent a considerable amount of time trying to decide what she should tell Jennifer and how she should relay the information. She concluded that it was time to stop trying to protect Jennifer. Her obsessive attempts to shelter her when she knew her as *Susan* had only led to unnecessary deception. The Susan of Beth's thoughts was merely a baby. The Jennifer who sat before her was a woman over thirty-five years old. She had the right to know the truth. Plus, many elements of the truth would probably come as a relief. And since Beth was fairly certain that Jennifer's parents did not know they were buying a baby out from under her godparents, Mr. and Mrs. Harrison would not be stained by the true story. It was time, Beth determined, for Jennifer to learn whatever she wished to know about her past.

"I have some information to share with you. But I also have several things to show you, and those things have a precious story to tell all of their own." She raised her eyebrows playfully.

"Sounds intriguing."

"First," Beth said, becoming serious. "There is something I must tell you about your mother's death."

Jennifer nodded. "I'm ready."

"She didn't commit suicide."

"She didn't?"

"No, it was an accident. A car accident."

Jennifer's eyes darted around looking at nothing, seemingly lost in her thoughts.

"And the supposed grandmother who gave you away for adoption. . ."

"Yes?" Jennifer looked at Beth with a pained expression.

"She was not really your grandmother. She tricked your parents. She didn't even know why your mother had gone missing."

Jennifer set down her cracker and looked out the kitchen window.

"Your mother did not abandon you," Beth added, longing to comfort her, this woman whose face hid upstairs amidst her art supplies, this woman who had inadvertently become a part of Beth's life.

A tear rolled down Jennifer's face. "Who was that woman? The one who said she was my grandmother?"

"She was Katherine's. . . your mother's, landlady. She assumed your mother had run away or committed suicide, or maybe her conscience found it convenient to believe those possibilities. Anyway, she gave you up for adoption without the permission of your godparents."

"I had godparents?"

"Yes. Linda and Wyatt Benning. Your mother worked for Mr. Benning. He was a dentist. His wife. . . I guess she was like the mother Katherine never had."

"She didn't know her mother?"

"Her mother died when she was four and a half."

"Oh," Jennifer said sadly. She picked out a piece of watermelon and put it on her plate. "Why didn't this landlady just contact my godparents? Surely it would have been easier. Why did she go to the trouble of arranging an adoption?"

Beth cringed. She didn't want to say it, but she promised herself she would be honest, no more cover-ups. "Money."

Jennifer turned her lips in toward her mouth and sighed through her nose. She tapped her finger on the table nervously.

"I'm sure your parents thought they were paying for adoption and funeral expenses."

Jennifer winced. "Or they wanted me so badly they willed themselves to believe that."

Beth shrugged. "Perhaps. But that is in the past."

"They are wonderful people, and they love me very much."

"I don't doubt that for a minute. Maybe it was just meant to be."

Jennifer tossed her a goofy grin. "I'm not sure I believe in all that hocus pocus, but I've had a very good life."

Beth wanted to say *you would be surprised by what you might believe if you had been through the summer I've been through,* but she decided to let it go.

Jennifer picked up the watermelon and continued to eat. "Are my godparents still around?"

"Yes, they live in Bangor. I have their number and they would be overwhelmed with joy if you called or visited them." Beth imagined the happiness Linda would experience when she heard from her long lost goddaughter. In all her haste and excitement, Beth had forgotten to tell them about Jennifer. *Let her call them directly,* she thought. *It will be the most cherished phone call Linda will ever receive.*

Jennifer beamed. "I will." She selected a bunch of grapes. "Do you know my father?"

"He left your mother when she was pregnant. I have not been able to track him down."

Jennifer nodded thoughtfully. "Do I have any other relatives I don't know about?"

Beth took a deep breath. "One. Your maternal

grandfather."

"He's still alive?"

"Your mother was eighteen when you were born."

"Right. Why didn't he try to find me? Did that landlady tell him I was dead or something?"

"He didn't know about you. Your mother and he were not speaking."

"Oh."

"But she was going to patch things up. She tried to see him on the day of the accident," Beth explained hastily.

"How sad." Jennifer frowned.

"He lives here in Virginia Point."

"He does?" she asked, suddenly excited.

"Yes, but I must warn you, he is rather reclusive. He didn't really want to accept your mother's death at first. I don't know how he'll respond to you."

"Does he know you found me? Does he even know I exist?"

"He does not know about my search, no. He learned of you only recently. Your mother attempted to write to him, beautiful letters. She really longed to see him again and to become a family, the three of you. But he only got those letters a month ago. I found them at the landlady's house and gave them to him after the funeral."

"Do you think he wants to meet me?"

"I honestly don't know. And I was afraid to ask him. But he's been calmer lately. I think he really needed to accept and grieve your mother's death before he could move on. He thought she had run away and just refused to see him all these years."

"How awful. I can't imagine."

Beth looked out the window, sorting through her ideas. She imagined the striking, auburn-haired woman extending a hand to the emotionally injured old man. "But I think meeting you might do him a world of good."

"I'm a big girl. If he doesn't want to see me, I won't take that personally. I grew up with a delightful Pa Pa. He passed away. But I had all the grandfatherly love a girl could ask for."

"It's settled then. I'll introduce you."

"Now?"

"Oh," Beth said slowly. "No. I have something else planned for you this afternoon." She grinned. "Finish up your lunch. It's an adventure."

Jennifer took a few quick bites, emptied her glass of water, and stood up. "I'm ready."

In Jennifer's smile, Beth saw an enthusiasm for life she had always associated with the author of the diary. It was the mischievousness that she had captured in the painting. Beth looked at the stunning woman dressed in a classy olive green suit that set off her hair and made her eyes sparkle. Then Beth crinkled her brow pensively.

"Do you have any jeans?"

Jennifer laughed. "Where did you put my suitcase?"

Jennifer changed into a pair of faded jeans and new running shoes, and she joined an anxious Beth waiting in the living room. The auburn-haired lady stopped when she saw the photo of herself and her mother on the mantel.

"Is this me?" she asked.

"Yes. And that is Katherine, your mother."

Jennifer looked longingly at the photo. "May I keep this?"

"Oh. . . uh. . . sure, of course," Beth answered reluctantly. "It's only a photocopy. Your grandfather has the original." She secretly hoped that Jennifer would choose not to take it. But Jennifer began to open the clips on the back of the frame. "Keep the frame."

"Are you sure?"

"I insist."

"Thanks. Let me just put it with my things." She ran upstairs.

Beth touched the place where the photo had stood. She became aware of how empty her life had become over the decade that preceded her move to Maine. So much so that she had cherished a photo of two people she did not know. She wondered what she might put in its place, perhaps photos from her old albums – her father, her mother in her later years – or other memories she could frame and enjoy. The passion of the Thompson girls had awakened something inside of her, something she did not wish to return to slumber.

"I'm ready," Jennifer called as she popped her head into the living room.

"Let's go."

Beth grabbed her backpack, which contained a blanket, a bottle of water, and a couple of snacks. She threw it over her shoulder and led Jennifer out the door and into the forest.

"It is magical here," Jennifer said.

"Oh, the magic has hardly begun," Beth replied with a playful tone in her voice.

Jennifer laughed and shook her head.

They walked gently through the forest, barely uttering a word. Leaves and sticks crackled beneath their feet. Beth led Jennifer to the cliff that overlooked her mother's secret beach. "Get down like this," she instructed, "and scoot to the edge."

Jennifer did as instructed. "Wow!" she exclaimed when she saw the beach. "Amazing."

"Now follow me," Beth said, turning around and shuffling backwards until she found the first foothold. "You may want to watch me first before you try it."

Jennifer bit her lip. "I'm a little afraid of heights."

"You and me both. But, believe me, it's worth it."

Jennifer watched Beth and then cautiously made the trip on her own. It took nearly twenty minutes, but she made it down. She clutched her hands to her chest and breathed in the fresh air. "Breathtaking."

Beth laid out the blanket near the edge of the rocks, hoping the incoming tide would not reach it. She placed the bottle of water and the snacks on one corner. Then she glanced inconspicuously at the handkerchief to confirm that it was still visible.

"Well, you're on your own."

"What?" Jennifer replied, bewildered.

"Oh, I almost forgot." Beth removed the key and chain from her neck and put it over Jennifer's head. "Welcome to your past."

Jennifer continued to stare at her with a puzzled expression. "I don't understand, I—"

"You think you can find the way back?"

"I. . . uh, I guess so."

"Okay then, have a nice afternoon." Beth grinned as she scaled the cliff.

* * * *

Jennifer shook her head and looked around. Then she noticed the little red flag waving, as if extending an invitation. She glanced down at the key around her neck. "Let's see what's up there."

* * * *

Beth was making a mandarin salad with chicken when she heard the door open and close quietly. She saw Jennifer take off the backpack and lay it on the floor. Jennifer retrieved the diary, clutched it to her chest, and walked toward the kitchen. As the young woman approached Beth, her makeup gone and her eyes slightly red, she smiled. "Thank you."

"I believe it is exactly what your mother would have wanted."

"Yes. It was fun and sad and moving all at the same time. I'll remember this day for as long as I live."

"I'm glad it meant so much to you. I had hoped it would."

Jennifer pointed nervously toward the door. "I wasn't able to fit the lockbox in the backpack, with the blanket and all, but I packed up all the wrappings so they wouldn't litter the beach."

"No problem. We'll get it later. Why don't you come wash up and join me for dinner."

* * * *

The waning moon did not rise until nearly 10:00 p.m., but the two women sat on lawn chairs in the backyard, sipping wine, as the gibbous orb rose and drifted across the sky. They shared stories – their successes as well as their heartaches. Beth told Jennifer about many of the things she had discovered and investigated since she had moved to Maine. She left out the firefly and touched only briefly on the dreams. She was not sure how the rational young woman would react to such implausible tales. Beth decided it would make more sense to discuss the ghostly encounter when the firefly made an official appearance. Therefore, instead, she focused on the details of finding the diary, meeting Rod Thompson, and hunting down Katherine's acquaintances. Jennifer seemed to drink up every word as if they were drops of water in the desert.

Jennifer had enjoyed a peaceful childhood in upstate New York. She went to private schools, and she graduated from Columbia with an MBA. She was currently the CFO for a small textiles company in Manchester, New Hampshire.

As the ladies chatted in the moonlight, the firefly sneaked up behind them. Beth saw it from the corner of her eye. She waited for Jennifer's reaction. Jennifer was talking about her boyfriend, soon to be – she hoped – her fiancé. The firefly flew in graceful circles around the two women, but Jennifer continued to tell her story as if nothing unordinary was occurring.

She doesn't see you, Beth realized. *Why doesn't she see you?*

Beth's mind drifted away. She tried to focus on Jennifer's intriguing account, but she was distracted by the firefly who had, by then, come to a complete halt inches from Jennifer's nose. Jennifer stopped talking suddenly and sighed.

"Anyway, blah, blah, blah. I hope I'm not boring you."

"Oh. . . uh, not at all."

"It is so beautiful here. It is amazing. Isn't it amazing?" Jennifer gazed out toward the bay. She seemed to look right through the firefly.

"I am still in awe," Beth replied absentmindedly, her eyes darting between the firefly and Jennifer.

The firefly hovered. Jennifer said nothing.

She can't see you.

Then, as if it understood, the firefly drifted away, pausing now and again. Beth bit her lip and tried not to cry.

"Are you all right?"

"Yeah." Beth forced a weak smile. "It's just been an intense day."

Jennifer sighed. "Yes, it has. But it's been perfect. Thank you, Beth. I don't know how to thank you."

The firefly drifted into the forest and slipped out of view.

"Uh. . . it has been my pleasure, really."

They gathered the wine glasses and retreated to the house.

* * * *

Five minutes after they had said *good night,* Jennifer appeared in Beth's bedroom doorway holding up her portrait.

"What is this?" Jennifer asked sharply.

Beth almost laughed. The two of them, lady and painting, side by side, looking almost like twins. "That's kind of hard to explain."

Jennifer walked into the room and propped the painting against Beth's dresser. "I'm listening," she said with a slight edge in her voice.

"Ever since the diary, I envisioned that girl. You, I guess. So I painted her."

"You envisioned this?" Jennifer said, gesturing to the painting.

"Yes. I don't know how else to explain it. I saw it here." She pointed to her head. "And I put it there." She indicated the painting.

"You are a strange woman, Beth LaMonte."

"Tell me about it."

The tension broke when Jennifer started laughing. Beth joined her. Jennifer looked back at the painting and shuddered. "Can we keep it in here tonight? It kind of gives me the creeps."

"Absolutely," Beth said, still laughing.

"Don't you think it is weird?"

Weird doesn't even begin to cover it.

"Kind of psychic or something," Jennifer said, tapping her finger on her chin.

"I guess so."

"It is as if you and I and my mother, we're all connected somehow – through the diary, or through this place." She walked over to the window and looked into the woodland toward the secret beach. She stared out into the night for several minutes. "I was conceived there."

"What?"

Beth was lost in her own thoughts. Should she tell

Jennifer about the firefly? Should she explain her theory that it is really the ghost of Katherine? It sounded ridiculous even as she considered it. What good would it do to try and convince a no-nonsense woman like Jennifer to believe in something that only Beth could see? She risked losing Jennifer's trust. Nothing would be gained from it. And Jennifer, who had experienced an eventful day discovering her past, would only find it confusing and disturbing. Beth decided to leave it alone.

"I was probably conceived there. . . on that beach."

"Oh," Beth said, returning from her musings. "You're right. I hadn't really thought about it."

"It's kind of weird. . . I never knew where I was conceived," she said wistfully, continuing to stare out the window. "A beach is pretty cool."

"Yeah, I suppose so," Beth replied, trying to chase away images of her early unpleasant sexual experiences and all the dreadful thoughts and curses that accompanied them.

"Ooh, that's weird," Jennifer said, stepping back.

"What?"

"I thought I saw a small flash of light."

Beth jumped up and looked out the window. Outside, the firefly hovered a few feet away.

Jennifer's shoulders quivered as if she were trying to shake a spider. "It's gone now."

The light creature twirled and danced.

"Must have been a firefly," Beth mumbled.

"On the coast? Anyway. . ." Jennifer turned to face Beth. "Nice painting." She pointed to the portrait, raised her eyebrows lightheartedly, and moved to exit the room.

"Thanks," Beth said, somewhat dumbfounded. She smiled at Jennifer and turned back to watch the firefly. It continued to spin and swirl.

"Good night," Jennifer called from her room before closing the studio door.

"Good night."

Beth turned back toward the window and whispered, "She saw you."

Chapter 29
Out of the Blue

The next morning, after breakfast, the ladies prepared for their meeting with Rod Thompson. It wasn't actually a meeting; it was more of an ambush. Beth decided that this was the best approach. They could retreat at any time for any reason.

Jennifer descended the stairs dressed in her olive green suit, her hair drawn back at one temple. She wore a small silver and green pendant in the shape of a teardrop around her neck. She looked absolutely stunning.

"Whew," Jennifer said. "I'm rather nervous."

"Don't be. Remember what you said about your Pa Pa? You have nothing to lose and, perhaps, something to gain."

"I know. But suddenly the fear of rejection is rearing its ugly head."

Beth placed her hands on Jennifer's shoulders. "Listen. There are many people who will be overjoyed to have you in their lives, myself included. There's Mary and Lou at the bed and breakfast and their mother, Abigail, who are just dying to meet you. Most importantly, your former godparents, Linda and Wyatt Benning, have been searching for you for decades. If the old fart scoffs and turns away, there will be plenty of love and appreciation to fill the hole he leaves behind."

Jennifer nodded her head quickly, still appearing nervous but also somewhat comforted.

"Have you got everything?" Beth asked, grabbing her purse.

"I think so."

Beth opened the door, pausing as Jennifer approached. "Wait," she cried.

Beth ran upstairs and returned in less than a minute with something in her hand. She gently removed the clip from Jennifer's hair and replaced it with the dogwood comb created by Kenny McLeary. Beth stepped back and examined Jennifer.

"There. Much better."

Jennifer touched her head and crossed to the mirror in the hall. "It's the one from the painting," she said.

"Custom made for you."

Jennifer crinkled her brow and threw Beth a goofy grin. "I almost believe that."

"Then do," Beth said, beaming.

They arrived at the marina at about half past nine o'clock. As they emerged from the car, Jennifer smoothed her skirt, and Beth cleared her throat.

"We'll check here first. He's most likely to be on *The Bottomless Blue*. But you never know. If we don't find him here, we'll try his house."

"*The Bottomless Blue?*"

"His sailboat."

Jennifer looked down at her shoes. "I'm not properly dressed for a sailboat," she mumbled.

Beth smirked and shook her head. "Why don't you concentrate on dazzling the gentleman first? Then you can worry about your apparel."

Jennifer giggled nervously. "Right. Let's roll."

Beth and Jennifer approached the dock warily. "You had better stay here," Beth cautioned when they were still ten feet from the shore. "If he's going to have a fit, we'll keep you at a distance."

This comment seemed to trouble Jennifer but she nodded in agreement.

Beth began to doubt the wisdom of springing an unannounced visit on Rod Thompson. Her breathing quickened as she approached the boat. She glanced back to check on Jennifer. The red-haired woman was standing obediently where she had been told to stop. While Beth's head was turned, Rod emerged from the cabin of the boat.

He looked at her curiously. "Beth LaMonte?" he said quietly, a slight warmth in his voice. "What brings you here this morning?"

Rod's gentle tone startled Beth, but it did not dispel her anxiety. She ran her fingers through her hair nervously. "I really should have called you. I'm sorry, sir."

"Is there trouble at the cabin?"

"Oh, no. . . I . . . uh. . ." She looked over her shoulder, pulled her hair back quickly, and continued to stammer. "It's just that I have. . ."

Rod noticed Jennifer standing near the shore. He wore a puzzled expression as his eyes darted back and forth between the two women. "What is it? Is something wrong?"

"No, sir," Beth said, clearing her throat and trying to sound more confident. "I have someone I'd like you to meet."

"Well, then, bring her on. Is she afraid of the water?" Rod seemed mildly amused.

"No, I. . . uh. . ." Beth was about to say, "She's afraid of you," but she stopped herself just in time. "Jennifer," Beth called. "Could you join us?"

Jennifer walked slowly down the pier, minding her step. She caught her heel in a gap between two boards. Bending down to carefully remove her shoes, she glanced up, smiling awkwardly.

Rod relaxed his posture and began to chuckle. Beth was stunned. She had never heard the man laugh. He had a deep throated, warm laugh that filled the harbor with the sounds of Christmas. Beth shrugged at Jennifer. Rod climbed down from the deck of *The Bottomless Blue* and alighted on the dock. He turned to face the approaching auburn-haired woman.

"Mr. Thompson. I would like to introduce you to Jennifer Harrison. . ." Beth began.

Jennifer stepped forward holding out her hand. Rod met it with a firm shake.

". . . formerly Susan Thompson."

Rod appeared both confused and intrigued as he processed the information. He narrowed his eyes and studied Jennifer. Beth imagined the thoughts swirling in his brain. *Does she look like Katherine? Could it be?* He bit his lip and gazed into the young woman's face. Then his eyes began to water.

Beth suddenly felt uncomfortable, an intruder at a

private reunion. She excused herself. "I'll leave you two to catch up," she said, but she was hesitant to leave.

"Susie," Rod whispered.

"Grandpa?" Jennifer said, shrugging her shoulders and wearing a silly, girl-like grin.

They gave one another a hearty embrace.

"She wanted me to meet you." Rod's voice trembled.

"I know."

"It took a long time."

"I'm sorry."

"No, I'm sorry. . . for giving up on your mother when she still believed in me."

Jennifer turned her lips inward and tried to smile through the gathering tears. "She loved you."

"I should have been less obsessive and controlling and. . ."

Jennifer placed her fingers over his lips and said with conviction, "She *loved* you."

They embraced again.

"I'll just be going now," Beth said casually, a figure already unacknowledged in their presence. She started to back away.

"Do you like sailing?" Rod asked Jennifer enthusiastically.

"I've never been sailing."

"Come on then." Rod climbed onto the boat and reached his hand over the side to help her up.

Jennifer looked down at her pantyhose. She glanced up, noticing that Beth was still on the dock. She lifted her shoulder and hand in dismay and pointed to the hose.

Beth rolled her eyes and sighed. "Turn around for a moment, please, Mr. Thompson." She urged Jennifer to hurry up with the business of removing her pantyhose. Jennifer balled them up, grinned in embarrassment, and handed them off to her new friend. Beth shook her head and laughed. "Get going," she said, shooing Jennifer toward the boat.

Rod leaned over the boat and helped her on board. She struggled a little before finally landing, upright, on the deck. She dusted off her skirt and Rod took her hand in his.

"Jennifer, let me introduce you to *The Bottomless Blue*."

Chapter 30
Share My Secret

Beth took a nap on her couch in the late afternoon. She was thoroughly, emotionally exhausted. Her obsession over the whereabouts of Katherine, and then Susan, had finally come to an end. She felt complete, yet slightly melancholy. The mysterious author of the diary and her missing child had been her companions. For nearly two months, she lived and breathed them – through the diary, through the painting, and through her travels from Virginia Point to Bangor and all the stops along the way.

The trip had not been merely geographical. Beth had embarked on a spiritual journey as well. She had traveled along pathways in her brain which had long ago been deemed unfit for passage. Challenging her rational, set-in-stone beliefs, she found herself asking more questions than there were answers to be understood. She was a different woman than the thirty-nine-year-old who had set out in a slate blue Honda from Albuquerque, having grown in ways she never would have imagined.

Beth stirred when the doorbell rang at 6:09 p.m. Rubbing her head groggily, she looked at the clock and was shocked to see that she had slept for almost three hours. The bell rang again and she stood up and walked clumsily toward the door. She opened it slowly. Standing on the porch, looking at his feet and seeming to mumble to himself, was Kenny McLeary.

"Kenny?"

Kenny looked up, embarrassed. "Hi, Beth."

"Come in," she said, gesturing toward the living room.

Kenny crossed the room and sat on her couch.

"Would you like something to drink?"

"Oh, no thanks," Kenny replied.

"What can I do for you?" Beth asked as she sat next to him on the couch.

"Uh," Kenny began, hesitantly. "I made something for you."

"For me?"

"Yes." He pulled a small box out of his pocket. "It's kind of been in my head ever since the day we discovered the car wreck. I just get these things stuck in my brain and they have to find a way out. I know that sounds ridiculous, but—"

"I completely understand," Beth said, smiling.

Kenny shyly returned her smile. He opened the box. Inside was a brooch shaped like a bottom-heavy figure eight lying on its side. No, it was more like a lopsided infinity symbol. Made in white gold with three small sapphires on the top of the large loop, it was simple, yet lovely. Kenny clutched the package awkwardly. Beth gently retrieved the box from his hand and removed the pin. She cradled it.

"It's beautiful," she said softly.

"Thanks." He looked down at his feet and fidgeted a little.

Beth pinned it on her t-shirt. "It deserves something a little more formal—"

"It's perfect," Kenny interrupted.

Beth glowed. "Thank you." She tried to catch his eyes so her words would reach him.

"It was a good thing you did," Kenny said quietly.

"Pardon?"

"It was a good thing you did, bringing those folks together."

"Oh, it was an obsession really, a—"

"A *good* thing."

Beth recalled what Abigail had said about Kenny and his family, and she nodded, accepting his heartfelt compliment. "Thank you."

They were silent for a moment. Eventually Beth stood up and said, "I'm going to make some coffee. Would you like some?"

"Sure."

Beth returned seven minutes later carrying a tray laden with two mugs of coffee, a creamer, her antique sugar bowl, and a few cookies.

Kenny raised his eyebrows.

"Mary taught me this," she said, giggling, as she arranged the items on her coffee table. "It's a little something called hospitality."

Kenny laughed, relaxing for the first time since he arrived.

"You have to pat yourself on the back, too," Beth reminded him. "If it were not for your assistance – finding the wreck, locating Greg Sharpe, giving the bastard a piece of your mind – I wouldn't have gotten past Bangor."

Kenny capitulated. "I'll take a smidgen of the credit."

"More than a smidgen." Beth's face grew serious. "I needed you. I did not have the courage to traverse the forest on my own. The secrets would still lay undiscovered had you not helped me that day. Jennifer would have continued to assume that her mother committed suicide, Katherine would never have received a proper burial, and Rod Thompson would have gone to his grave believing that his daughter had run away and discarded him forever."

Kenny pursed his lips and seemed to drift away, lost in his thoughts. He gazed out the window, past the cliff, and toward the islands on the distant horizon. Then he smiled warmly.

"Okay?" Beth said, wondering what was brewing inside of his head. "You're an accomplice in this thing. So if all hell breaks loose, we're both to blame."

"All right, I give in." He paused for a moment and an impish expression crossed his face. "So are we going to look for the father next?"

Beth glared at him. "No," she said, in a low, slow tone. "That is Jennifer's problem. I'm retired now."

Kenny laughed.

They talked for about an hour. Beth recounted details relating to her phone call with Greg Sharpe and her visit with Jennifer Harrison. Kenny shared stories about his journey to Virginia Point and about starting a business as a jeweler.

The sun began to set. Beth stood up and crossed to the window in anticipation of the silvery glow of

322

twilight. Then a wild-eyed look came across her face. She turned to Kenny and grinned.

"Care to do some climbing, Kenny?"

"Uh, sure. Now?"

"You bet."

Beth crossed to the entryway and picked up the backpack, which lay where Jennifer had discarded it the afternoon before. She rummaged through it, removing garbage bags and other trash. She refilled the water bottle, grabbed a second water bottle from the fridge, and packed them next to the blanket.

"Let's go," she called to her new friend, a brazen look of mischief in her eyes. She led Kenny into the forest and north toward the secret beach. At one point she broke out into a run, dodging trees. Kenny tried to keep up with her, but he tripped over a large, fallen branch. Beth looked back periodically to make sure he was in sight. When she reached the cliff, she was laughing, out of breath, but feeling younger than she had in five years.

Beth dropped to the ground and scooted over the ledge. When she alighted on the beach she glanced up and saw Kenny's face peering over the rim. "Did you see the steps?"

"I think so."

"Then come on."

"It's amazing. I'm honored you chose to share it with me."

"Are you coming?"

"Yup."

By the time he descended, Beth was sitting on the blanket and gazing over the water, as the pink and orange clouds faded to shades of twilight silver.

Kenny settled down next to her. "This is pretty cool."

"Isn't it?"

"How did you find it?"

Beth looked at him for a moment. "I told you. The firefly," she finally answered.

"Oh."

Beth knew there was a hint of doubt in that *oh*, but she tried to shrug it off. *What do you expect people to think?* she asked herself.

As if on cue the firefly appeared. It began to trace a sideways figure eight in front of the two of them. It seemed to be drawing the pattern of Beth's new brooch. Beth could not determine if the firefly's actions were in mockery or celebration. She decided to presume the latter. Had she been expecting Kenny to jump up and shout, "Oh my God, it's the firefly!" she would have been disappointed, but she had learned that lesson with Jennifer. She assumed that the firefly was her apparition – no one else could truly see it.

At that moment, Kenny waved his hand in front of his face as if clearing a spider's web. He removed his glasses and rubbed them with the corner of his shirt.

"Do you see something?" Beth asked hopefully.

"No. Well. . . just for a moment the air seemed to blur, almost shift, like I was looking through the water or something. I must need new glasses," he finally concluded.

"I guess so," Beth replied, trying to hide a satisfied smile. She remained quiet, staring at the islands in the distance. Then she touched the back of Kenny's hand tentatively; unsure if the gesture would be welcome. To Beth's delight, he turned his palm upward and grasped her hand in his.

That was the last evening Beth ever saw the firefly. After dancing in the pattern of an infinity symbol for several minutes and troubling Kenny regarding his eyesight, the firefly drifted slowly out over the bay. It floated farther than Beth had ever seen it go from the water's edge. Beth watched it become smaller and smaller. . . until it faded away altogether.

Acknowledgements

I would like to thank, in order of appearance, the individuals who offered advice and encouragement from the birth of *Firefly Beach* to the date of publication.

First, a special thank you to my husband, Emo. Without his financial and emotional support, I would not have had the resources to pursue this incredible dream. I am also lucky to have two beautiful daughters who cheered me on and helped with the household chores.

Thank you to the proprietors of the bed and breakfast in Searsport, Maine, The Wildflower Inn. Not only did Cathy Keating and Deb Bush arrange cozy accommodations and delicious breakfasts, they patiently perused a very raw draft of *Firefly Beach* and gave me crucial feedback.

I am thrilled to acknowledge three invaluable women, *Firefly Beach*'s first true fans – Caroline Penaloza, Joy Brooks, and MaryLynn Lorentzen. Honestly, if it were not for these ladies, I believe I would have shelved the manuscript years ago. Their enthusiasm kept the story alive.

Artist Amy Feiman created a gorgeous painting, which has hung on my wall as an inspiration since 2008. Now her beautiful painting has become the cover for this second edition of *Firefly Beach*.

Several beta readers assisted in tedious, much appreciated proofreading – Rose Pressey, April Ross Plumber, and Patty Dutton.

I am particularly grateful that I met Rose Pressey. Her passion is contagious. If not for Rose I would never have found Lyrical Press, the original publisher of *Firefly Beach*. I am also indebted to Emma Porter, former editor-in-chief at Lyrical Press, for taking the time to read *Firefly Beach* and believing in its potential. A heartfelt thank you to Renee and Frank Rocco, founders of Lyrical Press, for investing time, money, and faith in me and *Firefly Beach*. Thank you also to editor Sandy Light for her insightful comments.

Finally, my deepest gratitude to Tracey Garvis Graves, writing partner and cyber sister, for encouraging me to explore self-publishing, so that *Firefly Beach* would not go out of print.

DEC 1 0 2013
JAN 2 5 2014
JUL 2 0 2015
12-10-1914
1-24-20 ICC

27688352R00179

Made in the USA
Lexington, KY
20 November 2013